ENDGAME

THE COMPLETE
ZERO LINE CHRONICLES

Endgame series

Novels:
The Calling
Sky Key

Digital Novellas:
Endgame: The Training Diaries Volume 1: Origins
Endgame: The Training Diaries Volume 2: Descendant
Endgame: The Training Diaries Volume 3: Existence
Endgame: The Zero Line Chronicles Volume 1: Incite
Endgame: The Zero Line Chronicles Volume 2: Feed
Endgame: The Zero Line Chronicles Volume 3: Reap

Novella Collections:
Endgame: The Complete Training Diaries
Endgame: The Complete Zero Line Chronicles

ENDGAME
THE COMPLETE
ZERO LINE CHRONICLES

INCITE

FEED

REAP

JAMES FREY

HARPER
An Imprint of HarperCollinsPublishers

Endgame: The Complete Zero Line Chronicles

Endgame: The Zero Line Chronicles Volume 1: Incite © 2016 by Third Floor Fun, LLC

Endgame: The Zero Line Chronicles Volume 2: Feed © 2016 by Third Floor Fun, LLC

Endgame: The Zero Line Chronicles Volume 3: Reap © 2016 by Third Floor Fun, LLC

ISBN 978-0-06-233277-6

16 17 18 19 20 PC/RRDH 10 9 8 7 6 5 4 3 2 1

❖

First Edition

Table of Contents

ENDGAME

THE COMPLETE
ZERO LINE CHRONICLES

ENDGAME

THE ZERO LINE CHRONICLES

—— VOLUME 1 ——

INCITE

PROLOGUE

"So that was your first murder?"

"No. It was my first kill," I respond. "It wasn't planned. I'm not a murderer. I killed him, but I'm not . . . it's not what you think."

He sits down across from me at the table in the corner by the hotel window. My left wrist is handcuffed to the armrest, but it's an old wooden chair, and when I lean back, the arm comes out of joint. I haven't tried to push back far enough to get my handcuff off the arm yet. I have to be ready to roll when I do that. I only have one shot at escape.

"How is that not murder?" he asks, his face a mask.

"It was self-defense." My heart is in my chest. I can't even tell if I'm bluffing anymore, or if it's the truth.

"You had just killed two other men. Was that self-defense too?"

"I didn't kill two men."

"Your friends did." The agent—I don't know if he's CIA or FBI or what—stands up from his chair and paces the room. I don't know what to say to him. All I know is that I've got to get out of here, fast. The team is counting on me. We don't have much time.

"The cop," I say, thinking fast, "had just shot my friend in the chest."

"Your *friend* was shot in the chest while you were robbing a store at gunpoint. You face charges of grand larceny, assault with a deadly weapon, and murder, and that doesn't begin to address what you're doing here in Germany."

He is the only agent here—alone and stupid. He's from the US consulate, and he clearly has no idea who he's dealing with. He thinks

I'm just a run-of-the-mill terrorist. But I'm not. I'm Zero line. What we are doing is so much bigger than one local cop's life. So much bigger than an FBI agent. So much bigger than me. He's wasting my time, and time is the one thing we need on our side.

"Listen," I say, "can I use the bathroom? You've had me handcuffed here for two hours." I've also scanned the place for anything I can use to escape. It's no prison—it's a hotel. Someone slept in the bed last night. It's probably this agent's personal room.

He stares at me through narrowed eyes. "I'll let you get up when you're finished answering my questions." He leans forward, trying to intimidate me. "Why are you in Munich? What's your plan here?"

"I want a lawyer."

"We're not in the United States," he says. "Different rules."

"Different rules?" I say, nervously laughing a little bit. "You're an American, I'm an American. The Constitution guarantees my rights."

"Here's the passenger manifest from your flight. I'm going to read through the names, and you're going to tell me who else is in your group."

"Seriously?" I say, and laugh. "You have no idea what is going on. No idea."

"I know that you are part of a terrorist group. That you're here to make a political statement at the Olympics."

"I'm not a terrorist. I didn't have any friends on the plane. I'm not here to make a political statement," I say flatly and truthfully.

"I don't believe you, kid."

While the agent talks, I lean back in my chair. The armrest isn't moving enough. The joint is loose, but the back of the chair hits the wall, and I'm not able to squeeze the handcuff out through the gap. I grip the armrest, try to guess its weight.

He's sitting again, and his chair is scooted all the way in to the table. "I know you're not here alone. Who else from the plane is working with you? I'm not going to ask again."

"You're wasting my time," I say. "I need to get out of here. I don't have time."

I grip the arm of the chair with my handcuffed left hand.

"If it's so important, why won't you tell me what it is?"

I shove the table with my right hand, tipping it into the agent's stomach. I leap to my feet, yank up the chair, and smash it into him. It loses some of its momentum as it scrapes against the wall, but I'm still able to bring it down on him hard. The chair breaks as it hits his shoulder and the table, but the armrest is still in my hand. I beat him across the face with it until he goes down. He's dazed, and I scramble out from behind the table and pieces of broken chair.

He goes for his gun, slowly pushing the broken chair away. He's bleeding from his head—a lot. I hit him again with the armrest and then give him a right hook. He's not struggling anymore, and I grab his pistol from his holster.

I pull the broken armrest out of the handcuff and kneel down next to him to find his keys. I grab them just as he tries to throw a weak punch. It catches me off guard, and I stumble back slightly. But I have his keys and gun, and I hold the pistol in my left hand while I unlock the cuffs.

He looks up at me, his eyes barely open. "Who are you?"

"I'm Zero line. This is Endgame. I'm in Munich to save the world."

CHAPTER ONE

It was a beautiful May afternoon as the bus drove into Berkeley. I was finally getting out on my own, leaving Pasadena, my job, and my parents behind. My mom had given me a halfhearted hug. We'd never been close. I wondered if my mom had ever been close to anyone. She was small and subservient and never talked.

My dad did the talking for both of them. He barked orders around the house from the minute he got home at night until long after I'd gone to my room.

He'd never wanted me to go to college. Well, to tell the truth, I was never sure what he wanted of me. After high school, I tried working at the family business for a year—Dad ran a furniture store—and I couldn't remember doing anything that he approved of. I could never meet the outrageous quotas that he gave me, and he certainly didn't make an effort to teach me anything. But when I told him I was going to college—that I'd saved up enough for tuition—he sneered at me as though I'd just said I was joining the circus.

But I'd held on to my money—everything I'd ever earned at the furniture store, and everything I'd earned the summers I'd worked for the Forest Service. My friends loved to go out to movies and dinner and spend money on girls and weed, but I knew I needed to be a penny-pinching miser if I ever planned to get out from under Dad's thumb.

After I told him that I was going to Berkeley, of all places, he stopped talking to me. It was the best two months I'd ever had at home.

I wasn't starting school until the fall, but I'd managed to get a janitorial job cleaning the empty dorms over the summer. The school let me move in early, into one of the dorms that held guys year-round, and it gave me a chance to earn a little more money and leave my parents' house.

I couldn't help smiling on the bus. This was everything I wanted. Freedom. A place where I could be in the middle of the action: the protests, the rallies, the parties, the free life and free love. I wanted a place where I could be my own man, voice my own opinions, be part of something important.

I was finally there.

After checking in at the administration building, I found my dorm and headed upstairs to room 117.

"Hey!" a guy said, jumping up when I opened the door. "Are you the new guy? I've been expecting you!"

"I'm the new guy." I had a backpack and an old duffel bag I used to store my football gear in, and dropped them both on the empty bed. "Mike Stavros." I held out my hand to him.

He shook it enthusiastically. He had medium brown skin and black hair that fell to his shoulders. "Tommy. Tommy Selestewa."

"Good to meet you."

"What are you here for? They told me you were coming, but I don't know why anyone would come this time of year. School just got out."

"Job brought me early," I said. "Why are you still here?"

"Just trying to graduate earlier. I'm a sophomore, and I don't have anything else to do—no reason to take summer off. I've loaded up on classes." Tommy sat down at his desk. "Got a major?"

"Not sure yet. I'm thinking city planning, or forestry. Or maybe political science." I sat on my bed. The mattress was thin and hard. Tommy laughed a little. "No worries, man, you've got time."

I looked at Tommy's desk and bookshelf. He had a typewriter. A book lay open beside it—Plato's *Republic*—and under it was *Nicomachean Ethics* by Aristotle. It made me feel a little small that my roommate was studying such great philosophies. This was why I'd wanted to come to college. To learn about something bigger than myself.

"I used to work for the Forest Service," I said, "during my summers in high school. I was part of a fire crew that saved a neighborhood from a forest fire. It was coming from two sides, and we were able to redirect the flames. I was really proud of that. It makes me want to do something that will make a difference. Become someone important. Or, well, just *do* something important. Not just be a furniture salesman like my old man."

"Why school, then? Why not join the fire department?"

"I thought about that, but I decided that, on the fire crew, I was just one person with a shovel and a mattock. What if I could do something bigger? Design a subdivision where fires are less likely? What if I could invent something—some kind of emergency sprinkler, or I don't know what. Something."

"I get that," he said. "So you want to fight fires on a big scale."

"Not necessarily fires. Anything, as long as it's something worth fighting for. My old man has never done shit. I just haven't figured out what I'm going to do yet." I smiled. "How about you?"

"I haven't declared yet. I've just been doing my generals. I think I'll end up in engineering. But this summer I'm taking a lot of ancient history classes."

"Whoa. Those are pretty different."

"I read a lot." He motioned to the bookshelf above his desk. It was filled with titles like *Turning Points in Ancient History* and *Inventions of the Gods*. "I'm sure I'll be boring you to death with some of my theories soon."

"Go for it. I have nothing else to do. I don't know anyone north of Santa Barbara, and I was worried it was going to be a long, lonely summer."

Tommy laughed. "You want to go out tonight? Some of my friends and I were talking about having some beers, shooting some pool. Interested?"

I was exhausted, but I didn't care. I was finally on my own, and I couldn't wait to celebrate. "Absolutely. What time?"

Tito's was a local dive, about a 20-minute walk from our dorm. It was busy, and Tommy led me through the crowd of students to a row of pool tables in the back. There was no one in the place who looked over 30, but they were all dressed better than average. Tommy had changed from jeans and a T-shirt into corduroys and a zippered sweater. I was more casual—a pair of beat-up jeans and a Rose Bowl sweatshirt.

A small group in the back called out to Tommy, and we made our way over to them.

"Guys," he said. "This is Mike, my new roomie. Mike, meet Jim, Julia, and Mary."

"Hi," I said, and stretched out my hand. Jim grabbed it. He was black, with silver-rimmed glasses and a newsboy cap.

"Jim Jefferson," he said. "Not James, definitely not JJ."

"Mike Stavros," I said back. "Good to meet you." But my eyes weren't on him. They were glued to the blonde sitting next to him, the one Tommy had called Mary.

I reached out my hand to her.

She took it in a firm grip and stood up. "This isn't a business meeting, you know."

"Is shaking hands too formal?" I asked, letting go and laughing at myself. "I've been living the life of a furniture salesman. Salesmen shake hands with people. It makes them feel at ease."

Mary laughed, a sweet, melodic tone. "I can assure you, I'm feeling very at ease." She picked up her beer and took a quick sip.

"I'm Julia," the next woman said. She was black, with short hair, and dressed in purple paisley. She reached for my hand, and I shook back. "Where you from?"

"Pasadena," I said. "You guys?"

"Northern California," Mary said. "Ever heard of Susanville?"

"Never."

"You're not missing out," she said with a quick laugh. "I grew up north of there on a ranch. Moved to Piedmont when my dad retired."

"I've never heard of Piedmont either," I said, and she laughed again.

"Touché, Mike." I beamed.

"So, how'd you all become friends?"

I noticed a look between Tommy and Mary. Mary shook her head slightly. My stomach dipped—I hoped that didn't mean they were together.

"Julia and I are locals," Jim said. "Grew up in Oakland, known each other since kindergarten. You play pool?"

"A little."

"Eight ball," Jim said. "You and Mary, me and Julia." He handed me a cue.

I was about six feet tall, and Mary had to be a foot shorter than me. But she was gorgeous. Long, blond, curly hair that flowed loose down her shoulders like a waterfall. I didn't want to say no to being on her team, but I turned to Tommy.

"That'll leave you out."

"The night is young," he said. "I'm going to get something to drink. Want anything?"

"Not now," I said.

Julia racked the balls and stood back. Mary looked at me. "You wanna break?"

"You go for it," I said. I hadn't played a lot of pool at home, and I wanted to pull off looking cool in front of this girl for as long as I could.

She broke, and the 14 ball fell into a side pocket.

"Do all of you guys go to Berkeley?" I asked.

"We do," Jim said, gesturing to himself and Julia. "Art program. She paints; I sculpt."

"Not me," Mary said, lining up her new shot. "Stanford. Prelaw."

"Really?"

"It gets better," Julia said. "She's there on scholarship. Smart kid."

"Why are you here if you're at Stanford? That's like an hour away."

"Taking a quarter off," she said. "I'm interning for a firm across the bay. Divorces and bankruptcies." She rolled her eyes and added, "Real exciting stuff." She missed her shot.

Julia took a pull from her beer and bent down, taking aim at the 3 ball.

"So, Mike," Jim asked, "why are you showing up in the summer?"

"I'm starting in the fall," I said, "but I got a job over the summer. It's no internship with a law firm, though. You're looking at Berkeley's newest janitorial staff member."

"Nice," Jim said with a laugh. "I hope you're not the poor sap who has to clean up Wurster Hall. My studio is a mess."

Julia missed, and I was up. I searched for a good shot. There was a long one, right along the bumper. I knew I couldn't make it, so I tried a closer, easier shot and missed, of course.

"No worries," I said. "Just cleaning out empty dorms."

Jim was really good. He got three balls in before missing on an awkward, reaching shot.

Tommy came back with a beer.

"So," I said as Mary leaned over to take her shot, "prelaw, huh? What kind of lawyer do you want to be?"

"It's better to ask what kind of lawyer I *wanted* to be. I'm probably going to drop out. The biggest thing I've learned about the law is that I hate it. Taking notes during back-to-back-to-back divorce settlements has made me swear off marriage too."

"John!" Tommy shouted. At once, the whole group turned. Someone was walking toward us, a huge grin on his face. Everyone smiled wide when they saw him.

"Tommy!" The guy waved as he made his way over. John was tall, wearing jeans and the coolest jacket I'd ever seen. It was denim, but embroidered intricately all over the back, shoulders, and arms. Bright splashes of color—flowers, spirals, and a peace symbol.

It was clear everyone in the place knew him. He slapped hands with the people at the bar and hugged one of the waitresses.

"What's up, man?" Jim asked, and gave him a hug, thumping him loudly on the back. John kissed Julia and Mary each on the cheek. When he got to Tommy, they did some kind of secret handshake.

"Everything is up, guys. It is a good day." He turned to the waitress and shouted, "Bring a round of—what are you guys drinking? Looks like three beers and a . . . What's that, Julia?"

"Jack."

"Three beers, a Jack, and I'll take a Scotch and water." He turned, noticing me for the first time. "You want a drink?"

"No thanks, I'm good."

"Suit yourself. I'm John, man. Good to meet you." He stretched out his hand and I took it.

"Mike," I said.

"Cool," he said, clapping me on the shoulder. "So who brought you?"

"Tommy," I said. "I'm his new roommate. Spent the day on a bus ride from Pasadena, and this is my first look at Berkeley nightlife."

"Well, we better make it a good one, then. You're not drinking anything, so we'll need a higher level of discourse."

Tommy laughed. "Higher than beer and pool?"

"Did you guys see the news today?" John asked as he sat down. I looked back at the pool table. It was my turn.

"No," Julia said, her brow crinkling. "I was in the studio all day. What's happening?"

"The bastard just said that he's mining Haiphong Harbor."

"The bastard?" I asked. I took a shot and missed the pocket by an inch.

"We don't say his name," Jim said with a laugh.

Mary laughed. "If you say Nixon three times into a mirror, he'll appear next to you."

"What's Haiphong Harbor?" I asked.

John took off his hat and twirled it in his hands. "Don't know your Vietnam geography?"

"I know Hanoi and I know Saigon," I said. "I know the Ho Chi Minh Trail and the Gulf of Tonkin."

"And what, may I ask, is your position on the war?"

It was Mary's turn, and she drilled the 5 ball into the side pocket. She held out her hand as she walked past me and I slapped it. "Good shot."

"Thank you." She lined up another one.

"My father," I said to John, "would tell you that the Vietnam War is being fought to prevent the vile spread of Red Communism and strengthen our alliance with Australia. I worked with him nine to seven almost every day of the year, selling furniture, and he said that at least four times a week."

John smiled and put his hat back on. "And what do you say?"

"I think we're sending kids over there to die just so the president can say we're doing something about the 'communist threat,' with the false belief that, as a superpower, we have the right to invade any small country we want."

Mary knocked in the 7 ball and then stood up.

John nodded his agreement, and the waitress arrived. She set the drinks on the table beside John. John paid her and, if I was seeing correctly, gave her a huge tip.

"And today," John said, "the bastard has declared that he's going to be placing mines in Haiphong Harbor, the main port of North Vietnam. There are military ships in those waters, but it'll mostly affect imports, like food and medical care. Yeah, it will hurt the army, but it's sure as hell going to hurt the civilians more."

Jim nudged me. "He was over there."

"You're a vet?" I looked at John.

He stared back at me and then pulled up his sleeve. There was a tattoo of a skull wearing a green beret.

Mary walked over next to me. "You coming? I don't want to have to win this all by myself."

"She could too," John said.

I stood up. John looked older than everyone else. He looked weathered. "John, what do you do?" I asked.

John exhaled, a deep, slow breath. "It's a long story."

Mary pulled on my arm. "Come on."

He grinned. "It's called Endgame. Now go play pool."

CHAPTER TWO

I sat on one of the couches, watching Jim and Julia play nine ball against each other. Mary had stuck with me all evening, which surprised me, but I didn't want to question it. I didn't think a girl like Mary had ever even looked at me, but here was one who was pulling me over to the couch by the hand and was in no hurry to let go. Tommy followed us and sat down in the chair next to our couch. He put his feet up on the table in the center, and I waited for John to join us.

"So, how do you know all these people?" I asked again, more to cut the silence than because I was interested.

Mary waved her hand dismissively. "Eh, I don't want to talk about them. Tell me about you. Who is Michael Stavros?"

I took a breath. "Well, I already told you the important stuff. I came to Berkeley to do something more with my life than just be a furniture salesman. But for now I'm a janitor. Classy, right?"

"Don't feel bad about that," she said. "I worked at a burger place until I got my internship. I'll probably go back there when school starts."

"I thought you were on scholarship."

"Pays for tuition, but nothing else. My dad has plenty of money, but he wants me to make my contribution, which is a buck sixty-five per hour, fifteen hours a week. But it could be worse. He originally didn't want me to go to college at all."

"You should be a janitor. We make one eighty."

"I'd rather flip burgers."

"What about your internship? That doesn't pay?"

"Nope, but that's okay, because I don't really do anything. I make coffee, I take notes in meetings, and I get ogled by men who are divorcing their wives. But I have a desk with a window on the eighteenth floor, and my mom took me on a shopping spree for business clothes. That was fun. You should see me before I change clothes after work. I look like a Republican."

"Scandalous," I said with a laugh. "I could see you as a big-name lawyer in the city."

She grimaced. "That's because you don't know me very well yet. I should get paid just for having to wear high heels every day. I'm a country girl, born and bred. I hated leaving the ranch and moving here. Give me boots and a rifle and I'm your girl."

"I liked that about Pasadena. You can be over the hills and out of the city in ten minutes. Well, scratch that. I don't like Pasadena. It's too suburban—is that the word I'm looking for? It's too bland. Nothing happens there." I laughed. "The thing I just said that I liked about it was how easy it is to get out of there."

"Never been there. Is it close to Disneyland?"

"About an hour. If you're still a country girl at heart, how did you ever get into law?"

"I like to argue," she said, and laughed.

John sat down with us and put a foot on the coffee table. He was wearing boots—looked like alligator skin.

"Mike, answer a question for me."

"Sure," I said. "Anything."

"I don't know Pasadena, but there was something in the paper about it a couple weeks ago. Made me think. There was an apartment fire. A guy had gotten out safely, but he ran back inside. They found his body in a hallway—they speculated that he'd been knocking on all the doors. Now, he wasn't the manager. Neighbors said he was quiet, and no one really knew him."

I nodded. I'd heard about the fire. "So what's the question?"

"Why did he run back in? He was safe. The fire department was there."

"Do you want details from a Pasadena native? Or just my opinion?"

"Just your opinion," John said. "Hypothetical. Let's say you're the guy."

"I think he was just a good guy. Wanted to help. Got out of his depth."

A waitress brought him a new Scotch and water, but he seemed in no hurry to drink it. "You know, the Mormon missionaries came knocking on my door once. They have a saying: 'It becometh every man who hath been warned to warn his neighbor.' You sure you don't want a drink?"

I shook my head. "No," I said, and decided to change the subject. "Tell me about that game. What's that?"

"Endgame?" John asked, and took a sip.

"It's scary shit," Tommy said.

Mary squeezed my hand.

"There's a lot to know," John said. "The history of it would take hours to tell. I'll start with a question—what do you believe about the end of the world?"

I laughed for a moment, because I didn't think he was being serious. But I was the only one laughing. "The end of the world? I don't know. My mom is the churchgoer in our family. A Baptist. I've never paid much attention. Raining fire and brimstone, and all the sinners go to hell and the good people go to heaven, I guess? Why's that important?"

"You want to know about Endgame, right? Mary, tell us what you know," John said.

"What I know? Or what I was taught in catechism?"

"First what you were taught."

She brushed some loose strands of hair out of her face. "I was raised Catholic. The Bible says that Christ will return, and that no one knows the time of his coming. The wicked will grow worse and worse and the Antichrist will come and the entire world will fall away. Finally Christ will come down to purge the wicked and sit in judgment of all people. That's what I was taught, anyway."

I smiled, first at her and then at John. "Are we really sitting in the back of a bar talking about the end of the world? Do you know what I'd be talking about if I was back home? Furniture. And if I went out with my friends—which I never had time to do—we'd talk about baseball. And I hate baseball."

"Oh, you've just never seen good baseball," John said with a laugh. "But yeah—the end of the world. It's is a crazy topic. You've got to be a little bit nuts to deal with it all. Tommy, how about you? What do you believe?"

Tommy rolled his eyes. "I'm Hopi. Everything is different for us."

"Yeah," John said, "but I like to hear it. And it will help Mike understand."

"There are, supposedly, nine signs to watch for. The first one is that white men will come. As you can see, that one's already happened." Tommy laughed. "There are prophecies about covered wagons and longhorn cattle and telescopes. But it all comes down to the ninth sign. All the others have happened already. We're currently in the Fourth World, and the ninth prophecy says we're going to hear a crash in the heavens and see a blue star. The Blue Star Kachina will be revealed and take the faithful to the Fifth World."

"So," I asked, "what happens if you're not Hopi?"

He pointed at Mary. "What happens if you're not Catholic?"

John took a sip of his drink, looked at me, and said, "What do you think the truth is?"

"Nuclear holocaust," I said. "Sooner or later."

"And you don't believe in a god or a kachina or the Rapture or anything like that?"

"I'm not saying there definitely isn't a god. I'm just saying I never really believed in one, like you."

John eyed me carefully. "I don't believe in God," he said. "I believe in Endgame."

"What?" I asked. "What religion is that?"

"It's not a religion. It's the end of the world. It could start at any moment. I don't know."

I looked at Tommy, who stared at me like he was waiting for me to say something. Mary still held my hand, her other holding her bottle of Budweiser. She looked back at me as I stared, our faces close together.

"This," I said, turning back to John and laughing, "is why I never drink. You guys are freaking me out."

"I like you, Mike." John leaned back and laughed. "Listen, when do you start work?"

Mary's hand brushed against mine, but I tried to focus on John.

"Uh . . . not till next week."

"We're having a get-together this weekend with a lot of my friends. Up at Mary's ranch. Nothing formal, just fishing and shooting and hiking. Come with us—it'll be fun."

"Thanks, man. But I don't have a car."

"That doesn't matter," John said. "We have plenty of people coming who can give you a ride. Why don't you get a lift with Mary?"

She nodded emphatically. "I have my dad's old Buick. I'll pick you up."

Tommy spoke up. "C'mon, Stavros. It's cool. You should come."

I never did anything like this. And not only that, but I never did it so spontaneously. "Well, I don't know how to shoot, and I haven't fished since I was in the Boy Scouts, but sure, sounds good."

I was happy. I'd found a group of friends who felt like they could be my people. And for a moment I forgot about all the talk of the end of the world as John bought another round of drinks.

Tommy and I walked back to our dorm. He was drunk—we'd played pool for two straight hours. For my first day of college, this had been pretty cool. I'd met a bunch of new people, including a beautiful girl who'd stayed next to me most of the night. I had no idea where that had come from—I didn't know what she meant by it.

I hoped it meant *something*.

"Tommy," I said, "how long have you known Mary?"

"Not long. I only started hanging out with that group . . . um . . . during fall semester?"

"So you're pretty new?"

"Yeah," he said, his words slightly slurred from all the beer. "I guess. She's been with the group for only a little longer than me. But I always get the feeling that she's known John forever."

"Forever?"

"For a long time. I don't know. Longer than a year anyway. Are you interested in her?"

"Well, yeah."

"Hey man, that's cool. She's not my type anyway."

We turned onto a street without any streetlights.

"A totally hot girl with deep blue eyes and blond hair isn't your type? She's on a scholarship at Stanford, so she's smart too. What *is* your type?"

"I like brunettes," he said.

"Well, your loss is my gain."

Tommy winked at me. "I assume this means you're coming on our ranch trip?"

"A whole weekend with Mary?" I said. "Are you kidding? Of course I'm in."

I really did want to go—and not just because of Mary. I'd had this picture in my head of what Berkeley was supposed to be like, and suddenly I was living it. Getting together with friends, talking about big issues—the war, the government. Even the end of the world.

Of course, at that point I had no idea what I was getting myself into.

CHAPTER THREE

We all met in the grocery store parking lot Friday at five in the morning, and I was stunned by who showed up. I thought it was going to be just our group, but it turned out to be a whole lot bigger than that. There were the people I knew—Mary, Tommy, Jim, Julia, and John—but there were also many I'd never met.

Other than a change of clothes, I hadn't brought anything with me, but most had fishing poles or shotguns or deer rifles. When we got there, Mary threw her arms around me in a huge hug. She smelled like flowers, and I let my face nuzzle in her hair. My heart sped up at what that hug could mean. But then she gave the same big hug to Tommy, and another one to John. She was a hugger, I guessed.

She looked like the youngest girl there, and I was probably the youngest guy. I introduced myself to everyone.

"We're going to have fun today," said a girl named Kat, smiling at me. She was in her twenties, super skinny, and a nurse. She gave me a hug too, and whispered in my ear, "This may seem crazy at first, but you're going to love it."

What? I thought. It seemed like such an odd thing to say. I figured she meant I'd love the group—the fishing and shooting.

"The old guy," I asked Kat. "Who's he?"

"That's Rodney. And he's only thirty-two," she said. "That's not old. It's his beard. But you should get to know him—he owns a deli in Oakland. And watch for it: he'll ask you to go fishing with him, and he'll make a bet on who will catch the first fish. Don't take him up on it. I swear, he could get a fifteen-pound bass out of a pothole."

Mary came and took my hand and led me to her car. "It's a coupe," she said, "so there's only room for the two of us."

"Great," I said. She was dressed in jeans and a T-shirt that showed her curves, and I couldn't believe Tommy wasn't interested in her. She was beautiful. Her hair was loose and long, and her skin was soft and warm in my hand. I couldn't believe how lucky I was that we had the whole car ride to ourselves.

Once everyone had arrived—there were eight cars and 21 people— Mary and I pulled out of the parking lot and headed west. Her ranch was five hours north. I'd heard Northern California was pretty, and she said there were lakes and rivers and hills on her family's property.

"Do your folks know you're going up there?" I asked.

"What makes you ask that?" she said, tilting her head.

"Just curious."

"No," she said, her expression suddenly tense. "They don't. And they can't find out, or I'm dead."

"So we have to keep the place nice and tidy?"

"Exactly." Mary glanced over at me, noticed I was smiling. Her face loosened up, and she laughed. "Really, though, my parents don't use the ranch for much anymore. So they don't care. In the spring my dad will go up and make sure the fences are okay, and in autumn he still takes us hunting. The ranch is really big—have I said that? It's fifty-five thousand acres."

"Wow," I said. I knew from my time with the Forest Service that that was enough land to get seriously lost in. It could cover whole mountain ranges.

"My oldest brother owns a feed store up in Klamath Falls, Oregon. We keep expecting him to ask for the land so he can start his cattle operation, but so far he hasn't. His wife is from there, and I think she wants to stay. For now everything works out well for the ZL, though."

"The ZL?"

"Oh," she said, glancing over at me, like maybe she'd said something she shouldn't have. "That's us. The group of us. It stands for Zero line."

"What does that mean?"

"It means . . . basically, it means that we consider each other family. You know how people talk about their bloodline? We—this group— call ourselves Zero line. We're our own kind of family."

"I like that idea," I said. "God knows I'd like to distance myself from my own family." Mary laughed. I loved her laugh: so quick and light.

"Speaking of family," I said, "where does yours think you are this weekend?"

Mary laughed. "Back at school for a workshop. There are just some things you don't want to tell your parents, you know? They're not the most open-minded people in the world. My dad—forget about sneaking onto the ranch. He wouldn't care about that too much. But if he knew I was with a boy from Berkeley, I think he'd flip."

"Too liberal?"

"My dad is a staunch Catholic, Nixon-supporting old cowboy. Just the idea that you want to study urban planning is enough to make him think you're a pot-smoking hippie with newfangled ideas and immoral goals. He thinks a man should work with his hands. He should be a self-made man with big plans for being self-reliant."

"And has that worked with the rest of the family?"

"Well, I'm the baby," she said. "And I'm going to college on scholarship, which is the only way that he'd let me go. Otherwise it would be secretarial school. I hate to say it, but my dad is a bit—well, more than a bit—sexist. My two older sisters married men my dad approved of— men like himself. One married a farmer down in Southern California. They grow avocados and artichokes. The second married a contractor who builds big modern houses in San Jose. And my two brothers: the one runs a feed store—I told you that—and the other is a doctor . . . and he got drafted. His wife, Bonnie, lives with us. She's a doctor too, and I think that drives my dad crazy, that my mom is effectively raising their baby while Bonnie works." She glanced over at me, and smiled. "I'm talking a lot. Your turn."

"I don't have much to say. I have a dad who . . . well, he's an asshole.

Not like your dad—a man of principles. You can say that your dad is sexist, but my dad is a cheat and a liar. I worked with him at his furniture store, and he cut every corner and raised prices and gouged people when they needed something. The only way he gets away with it is because he's the only shop in town, and he makes all of his profit off the old-timers who never realized there are other stores in the greater Los Angeles area. I swear, he once sold a desk, and then, when the customer was writing the check, he explained to her that the drawers were an extra five dollars each. I've tried to find some way to describe him, and the only thing I can come up with to adequately do the job is just to call him an asshole. He stays out late, and when he finally comes home, well . . ."

She was quiet, and I was beginning to wonder if she had been listening, but she finally spoke.

"That's why you don't drink."

"What?"

"You don't drink. Because your dad's a drunk . . . and an asshole."

I paused. "Well, yeah."

"Does he hit your mom?"

"What?"

"Does he hit your mom? You don't have to answer."

I didn't know what to say. I didn't like that she could see right through me. But she was right. "Yes."

"And you?"

"Sometimes."

"I'm sorry," she said, and reached over to take my hand.

"It's—" I said, and then stopped. "It's okay. I got out of there. I'm not going to be like him. I have to be different. I have to do something real."

"Well, it's a good thing that you fell in with us."

We drove in silence for most of the rest of the way. I fell asleep and dreamed of furniture until she woke me up as the caravan drove through Susanville, the town where she was born. Her ranch was still 45 miles past it, on a turnoff that was obscured from most of the houses and buildings by a small row of hills. Mary went on and on about this water pump and that orchard and I just listened and wondered what lay ahead.

We came to a turnoff with an archway made of three large logs—one standing on each side of the road and one laid across the top. The words GOLDEN PINE RANCH were carved into the crossbeam. A few of the other cars were already there.

"This is it!" Mary said excitedly. She climbed from her seat and ran over to the padlocked gate.

Beyond the gate, I couldn't see much more than tall green and yellow grass, sloping upward until the crest of the hill got obscured by forest: tall, straight white firs, short and stubby western junipers, and crooked and droopy gray pines. It reminded me of my time with the Forest Service.

Mary unlocked the gate and swung it open. I drove her Buick through after everyone else had gone in; then she closed the gate and put the lock back in place and mashed it closed with the butt of her hand.

"The house is out of sight of the road," she said, getting in the passenger seat, "or else I'd worry about bringing so many cars in here. The neighbors aren't close, but they all drive this road."

We drove over a ridge, the road taking a gentle turn around a cluster of trees.

"Those are some of the tallest gray pines I've ever seen," I said. Mary smiled wistfully.

"I don't know much about them, but they have huge pinecones. We used to collect them when I was a kid."

The ranch house was everything I was expecting: a large, gabled house with a wraparound porch. The siding was planks of red cedar, and the railings and window casements were painted white. There was plenty of space in front to park all the cars, and I was the last one to pull into a parking spot.

Everyone got out and stretched. One of the guys—Bruce, maybe 25, his muscled arms covered in tattoos and a well-trimmed goatee on his chin—called out for a beer, and people began unloading their cars. Mary led me to the front door and unlocked it.

"This is where you grew up?"

"Yep," she said. "Until I was twelve."

"Cool place."

The first floor was almost entirely open, with huge tree-trunk posts holding up the floor above. There was a kitchen to the left, and a massive dining table. It almost fit all of us—there were 18 chairs.

John came in from behind us. "Who wants to go shooting?" he asked.

I'd only fired a gun once—people as low on the totem pole as I had been in the Forest Service only carried pepper spray for dealing with rabid raccoons. Game wardens and the occasional park ranger had pistols. The only thing I'd ever shot before was a .22 rifle at Boy Scout camp. Even there, we only got five bullets. Most of that merit badge was about gun safety and maintenance.

"Come here, Mike," Mary said, and the three of us walked into a dark room. She opened the blinds, and the light revealed a large gun safe in the corner of the bedroom.

"This is my parents' room," she said, walking to the safe and bending down to turn the combination lock. She turned the dial one way, then the other, and back, and the safe opened silently to reveal eight guns.

"Can you handle a little kick?" John asked me.

"I guess." This all seemed a little off. "You guys like to shoot guns a lot?"

John laughed.

"You'll get the hang of it. Great stress reducer. Let's take the M14. And the 30.06," John said, pulling the rifles out of the safe.

Mary took one for herself that John referred to as a Winchester 94. "I got this when I turned ten," she said.

Thirty minutes later I was at the gun range. We'd gone up a canyon a short way to a spot where the winding dirt road spread out into

a wide meadow. There were six of us—John, Mary, me, and three
of the people I hadn't met before today: Molly, a tall, redheaded
Berkeley student with an English accent; Larry, a twentysomething
full-time bass player for a record studio; and Walter, an unkempt,
thick-bearded man who rarely talked, and who had been at John's side
since we'd arrived at the ranch. I couldn't guess his age—his beard
covered so much of his face. But almost everyone in this group was
pretty young in general, so I assumed he was maybe somewhere in his
thirties.

The gun range was big, with trees marked by orange spray paint that
designated the distance—50 to 500 yards.

Walter set up the targets: bottles on fence posts, paper bull's-eyes
stapled to trees, and beer cans placed on fallen logs.

"This is a good gun," John said to Mary as he inspected the M14. "This
is the civilian version of the gun I used in Vietnam. Big bullets. The
new M16s are a mess. Jam like crazy, and not as much stopping power.
I knew guys who gave up on their guns and used Soviet AK-47s that
they took from dead VC." He sounded so cool, like a badass. I bet John
had amazing stories from the war—I hoped he'd tell them at some
point this weekend.

Walter came back from the range, and John handed the M14 to me.
"You know how to shoot?"

"More or less." This gun weighed a ton, and I found it hard to sight the
targets. This was nothing like the .22 I'd shot as a kid.

"Pick an easy target, one at fifty yards," John said. "Now, get down
on one knee—sit on the side or heel of your right foot. No, don't rest
your elbow on your knee—just get the elbow as low as you can while
aiming. You still want that arm to take the full weight of the gun. It
feels a little uncomfortable at first, but it gives you better balance—
the recoil's not as bad."

I did what he said, folding my right leg under my body. It was weird to
be holding such a big gun, but part of me felt like maybe I looked as
cool as John.

"Okay, good, now bring the gun up to your face, and press your face into the stock—yeah, like that. Now put your finger on the trigger. Don't pull on it—that will pull the gun away from your target. So just press the trigger. And do it gently: press until you feel it start to resist, and when you fire, well . . . how to describe it? Surprise yourself with the shot. Don't anticipate it and tense up—if you do that, when you press the trigger, you'll flinch and miss. All right, now fire when ready."

I lined up my sights on a beer bottle and, following John's advice, I pressed down on the trigger.

The gun jumped, kicking back into my arm more than I expected. And, when I looked down the field, I could see the Budweiser still sitting there.

John grinned at me. "A little bit of a jolt, right? Try it again."

I obeyed his guidelines and finally hit it on my third shot, the glass bottle shattering. He clapped and laughed, and set down two boxes of ammunition on the rock in front of me. "Knock yourself out." With that, he walked away and began shooting with his own rifle. Mary was shooting too—her gun had a scope, and she was firing at the far targets. I stood and watched her for a minute, just taking it all in. I knew I was staring, but she was the best shot I'd ever seen. That wasn't saying much, though—this was all new to me.

Over the next hour, I got better and better at hitting the short-distance targets, and moved on to the long ones, which I missed frequently. We'd run out of cans and bottles by then, so we began aiming at whatever was left—pinecones, stumps, and the orange spray-painted markings on trees. By the time I'd spent all my ammunition, my arms and shoulder ached as if I'd been in a fight. I'd been part of a boxing league when I was a sophomore and junior—it was the one thing my dad had supported me in. Shooting through two boxes of M14 ammo made me feel like I was back in the ring. When the sun started to set, we headed back to the ranch house. We had a big dinner of steaks and potatoes that Bruce had cooked while we were shooting. Everyone talked and laughed. It felt the way big family dinners are supposed to feel—the way I'd always wanted to feel with my own family. After dinner, we all gathered around a campfire out behind the house, near the banks of a stream. There were logs in place for sitting, and I took a seat next to Tommy. I would have sat by Mary, but I was feeling like I'd been with her all day, and I didn't want to come on too strong.

"All right, guys," John said as we were all sitting. "Let's get this going. You've all been working for a month, since the last time we met here, so let's hear what you've found." He turned to me. "Mike, I know you're new to the group and don't really know much about us yet, or what we do. Just watch and listen for now, okay?" *What we do?* I nodded—what else could I do? Everyone had turned to look at me, and it was like I forgot how to talk for a second. "So," John said. "Let's hear it."

Tommy raised his hand. "I've been studying the pyramids at Giza. Found a lot of really weird things. Things that don't seem to have a ready explanation."

John pointed at him and said, "Go for it."

"First, you all know what pi is—the mathematical constant that is the ratio of a circle's circumference to its diameter? People have known about the number for a long time, but there are weird places it shows up. For example, the Great Pyramid: if you take the perimeter of the pyramid and divide it by twice its height, you get pi. Why is that?

"And another thing," he continued. "The pyramid, like most monumental architecture built in ancient times, was built perfectly north and south, east and west. But the mind-blowing thing is that it wasn't built using a compass. I mean, the first compasses didn't show up until two thousand years later anyway, but even so, the pyramid doesn't point to magnetic north, like it would if they used a compass. It points to true north. How is that even possible?"

What the hell were these guys talking about? Was this some kind of study group? With the Forest Service I'd never witnessed anyone who was camping, fishing, and target shooting who then met around the fire to talk about ancient archaeology.

Barbara, a pretty girl about the age of Kat—22 or so—with a round face and dimples, spoke. "I've been reading about the Aztecs, and they have this weird connection to the pyramids in Egypt. First, at Teotihuacan, there's the Pyramid of the Sun, and its base is almost identical to the main pyramid at Giza. I mean, within inches. It's crazy. And then there is the Temple of Quetzalcoatl and the Pyramid of the Moon. And those three line up almost perfectly with the three pyramids in Egypt. It's uncanny. How would two cultures, separated by the Atlantic Ocean and three thousand years, have any knowledge of each other?"

"Well, I've been looking into Atlantis," Larry said, "and there's—"

"Wait a minute," I interrupted. "Stop." I hadn't meant to say anything out loud, but the words just came flying out. "What are we talking about? Ancient architecture? Why do you guys care about the circumference of ancient buildings? Is this a study group or something?"

Everyone was quiet, waiting for John to answer. Mary looked at me and gave me a sympathetic, almost pitying smile.

"Mike," John finally said. "This is Endgame."

CHAPTER FOUR

"What the hell are you talking about?" The words came bursting out again. I hadn't realized how nervous and tense I'd been getting until now. I'd thought the end of the world—I'd thought *Endgame*—was just a bunch of drunk talk. A few too many beers and talk of war turns to talk of the apocalypse. But this was getting way too real for me way too fast. I felt like I had stumbled into some weird cult.

John stared at me for several seconds. I had no idea what was going through his brain.

Mary stood up. "Can I take you for a walk?"

I looked from John to her, and then one time more.

"I think that's a great idea," John said. "But, Mike, I want to make it clear that you're welcome back to the fire anytime you want so we can talk more about this."

Mary took my hand, and we left the group and headed back into the house. She led me by the hand out to the front porch, where there was a porch swing. She sat down.

"I thought we were going for a walk."

"It was a very short walk. Now we can sit here and watch the stars. You don't see skies like these anywhere near the city."

I sat down, and her fingers intertwined with mine.

"Do you like the ranch?" she asked.

I paused. "Sure. It's really nice."

"Some people like it and some people don't," she said. "Larry back there hates that we come out here for retreats. He says all that we're talking about could be done in someone's living room, but I think

Zero line is different from that."

"Mary," I said. "What is all this? I honestly don't have any idea what I'm doing here."

"You're sitting on the porch swing, talking to me."

I held up my hand, our fingers still interlaced. "I don't want to ask this, I really don't, and I hope you won't be offended."

She smiled in the moonlight. "Go ahead."

"Is this a cult?"

She laughed softly.

"No," she said. "It's not a *cult*. Not exactly."

I looked down at our hands. "I feel like there are a lot of things I should ask you next, but there's only one thing on my mind right now."

"What, Mike?"

"Are you pretending to like me so that I'll join this group?"

She laughed, loud enough that the people around the campfire probably heard it.

"No," she said, still giggling. "No. I'm not pretending. I like you."

"You latched on to me as soon as I came into the bar."

"Mike, don't you know?" she said. "You're kind of cute."

I laughed quietly and shook my head. "I'm cute?"

Her smile widened. "Yes."

"I don't understand what's going on here. I don't understand what Endgame is about. I don't know why we're talking about the end of the world. I don't know why we're talking about pyramids. When is someone going to be straight with me?"

"We are being straight with you," Mary said, letting go of my hand and standing up. She walked to the porch's guardrail and leaned out to look at the stars. "Here's the thing that you need to understand. Endgame is crazy. I mean, really, really insane. It's hard to wrap your head around. I've been involved with Zero line for about a year, and it took a lot of convincing and an open mind, because it makes you really question the way that the world works. It makes you question the history books. It makes you question church. It makes you question science. But I've seen enough that I'm convinced."

She turned around to face me. "And then, when I was convinced, I felt—I feel—the need to spread the news. It's like, if you found out that a dam was going to burst, what would you do? Would you just run away?" She paused, and I thought that she was thinking, but after a minute I realized that she was waiting for me to respond.

"No," I said. "I wouldn't run away. I'd warn everyone I could."

"Exactly," she said.

"So explain it to me."

"Let's go back to the others," Mary said. "But I want you to know this: I haven't told everyone else. I haven't told my parents. I haven't told my sisters, or Bonnie, or any of my family. They wouldn't get it. I love them, but they wouldn't get it. They are too closed-minded."

"But you told me."

"Yeah. I hope you know what that means. I haven't recruited anyone to the ZL. But there's something about you—I just wanted to tell you so bad. You have the right mind. I knew from the first moment we talked and you told me how important Berkeley was to you. I remember—and this is stupid, but just listen—Bonnie told me once about why she married my brother Hod. She said she was eating Thanksgiving dinner. They'd only started dating a few weeks before. But at dinner she had a butterflake roll. And as she was eating it, she thought, 'This is delicious. I wish Hod was here to have one.' She said that was the first time that she really knew they had a connection—because she realized how much she liked him. That's kind of how I feel about this. We're still going to tell the world that the dam is breaking—and I'm totally mixing my metaphors here—but you're the one I wanted to share the butterflake roll with." She put her hands to the sides of her face. "Am I making any sense at all?"

"No," I said. Mary looked at me, and suddenly we were both laughing. "I know I sound crazy, Mike," she said. "But will you just do one thing for me? Will you trust me? Just keep an open mind and hear what we have to say."

I looked at Mary, and I couldn't help smiling. I knew then that if I was going to do anything important in my life, she'd be the one I'd want to share my butterflake roll with too.

"What the hell," I said. "I'm in. I want to know everything."

She smiled wide. "Really?"

"Really." I took her hand. "Here goes nothing!"

And then she kissed me.

We were back at the campfire. I sat on a log, my back to the house, with Mary by my side.

John was sitting on a stump, using a stick to prod at the coals. It was after 10 o'clock now and the sky was a deep midnight blue.

"So, you're ready to learn about Endgame?" John asked.

"I guess," I said. "Ready as I'll ever be."

John nodded. "Mary has vouched for you. So has Tommy. They've only known you for a couple of days, but if they already feel this strongly about you, I trust you too."

"Yeah," I said.

Bruce, the big guy with the tattooed arms, spoke up. "How do we know you're not a narc?"

"I'm not," I said.

"We're not doing anything illegal anyway, Bruce," said Julia pointedly.

"No," John said. "We're not." He was looking at me in a way that made me feel like he was looking directly into my soul. "Where to start?"

"Start with Walter," Mary said.

"Sounds good," John said. "Walter?"

Walter leaned forward in his chair, elbows on his knees as he spoke. "I joined the army. I wasn't drafted, not like John. I wanted to be a Green Beret—the best of the best. When I got to 'Nam I was assigned to an operational detachment that was right up around the demilitarized zone, and we'd work back and forth across the line, trying to disrupt the NVA's supply runs on the Ho Chi Min Trail. We would go on missions for one or two weeks at a time, living with only what we had in our packs. And we chalked up the kills. We were brutal. We captured one soldier who told us we were known as the 'ghosts of the jungle.'"

I looked at Mary, who was listening intently to Walter, and wondered what was going on in her head. She had to be thinking of her brother Hod in Vietnam. Back at the bar, she'd said that his letters were spotty. Maybe he was out on secret raids like this.

John spoke. "I was just a drafted grunt, but I applied and made it through Green Beret training. I managed to get promoted to sergeant because everyone else outranking me kept dying. I got assigned to Walter's unit."

It was hard to think of John as a soldier, let alone a sergeant. Walter looked the part of a Green Beret vet, but I just couldn't imagine John. He was too . . . happy? No, that wasn't it. He just wasn't worn down like vets usually were.

"There's no glamorizing war," Walter said. "This is no John Wayne, World War Two movie war. It's gruesome. Inhumane. Numbing. You stop seeing people as people. They're just targets. They're just obstacles in the road. They're not even things. They're nothing. And we killed and killed until we found it funny, until one of our own men accidentally planted a claymore backward and blew himself up and we laughed and laughed because there was no other option. We were past being sad. We just couldn't feel sad anymore. We couldn't feel anything anymore. We'd seen so many Charlies blown to pieces, or cut in half by our machine guns, or hit in the head by our sniper rifles, that the only feeling we had anymore was to laugh, like we were shooting ducks at a carnival.

"And then, seven months ago, some son of a bitch at some airfield decided to bomb our position. Not their fault, of course—no one knew where we were. But they wiped us out. The only three left were me, John, and the captain, and the captain had lost both his feet and his right arm. We patched him up as best we could, and then we promised him we'd sit with him until he died. It didn't take long."

35

John spoke. "Walter made an offer to me. He said that if I followed him, obeyed his orders, we could get out of this damned war. You see, he wasn't just an average, ordinary Green Beret. He's had special training. He's Cahokian. It's his line—an ancient tribe that a huge percent of North America's population sprang from. Some of the people around this fire are probably Cahokian."

"It's hard to tell for sure," Walter said, "but Cahokians are an ancient people here in America. The Mound Builders. We come from the center of the US, around Missouri."

John stepped in, barely able to contain his excitement. You could tell this was something he loved talking about. "I want you to imagine all the way back to the beginnings of civilization on Earth. There were these twelve tribes."

Walter recited the names. "Cahokian, Minoan, Mu, Koori, La Tène, Donghu, Olmec, Shang, Harappan, Sumerian, Nabataean, Aksumite."

John continued. "It's the whole world. Cahokians are the ancestors of the Native Americans—Tommy is Hopi, so he's of Cahokian descent. Harappan are India, central Asia. The Sumerians and Nabataeans are the Middle Easterners: Egyptians, Palestinians, Persians, Arabs— Bakr is Sumerian."

Bakr—a black-haired man who was whittling with a short, curved blade—nodded his head.

"Minoans are the Greeks, Romans. Anyone with Italian blood probably descends from the Minoan line. Mike Stavros, maybe you? Aksumite is African—Phyllis, Tyson, Jim, and Julia descend from the Aksumites. Donghu is Mongolian. Shang is Chinese—Lee and Lin are both descendants of the Shang line. Mu is Japanese. La Tène accounts for a large part of Europe, Switzerland, France, Spain, Germany, England, Ireland, Scotland, Wales. Mary, Molly, and Bruce are all from the La Tène line. Olmecs are from Central America, the ancestors of the Mayans, the Aztecs. And lastly, Koori are the ancestors of most modern Australians."

John turned to me. "Mike, does all of this make sense so far?"

What they were saying made sense. But why they cared didn't. "Sure," I said. "I didn't know that this was a genealogy club. But the idea that we all came from twelve groups of common ancestors—I can see that."

Walter spoke. His voice was hard and curt. "The point is, we all fall somewhere on one of these bloodlines. It isn't as clean as we just described, but that gives the necessary background. Make no mistake, though: Zero line is not a genealogy club. When Endgame comes, there will be a war between the twelve lines. Whoever wins, wins the right to survive and have their line carry on. Everyone else perishes in the end of the world. All of us here today in the Zero line want to stop Endgame from happening. So we've turned our backs on our own lines and formed a new one.

"There is a secret council of the Cahokians that survives. I used to be their trainer, teaching the best and brightest young Cahokians to be Players and win Endgame. I joined the Green Berets with one purpose: to hone my skills in wilderness survival, to be a master of the art."

"And he's damn good," John said. "When we were bombed and our unit was almost wiped out, we were on the North Vietnamese side of the border, with no communications and few provisions. So instead of going south to the American side, we went north to the Chinese side. Walter led me through the wilderness of Vietnam and China. We eventually caught a boat to Hong Kong, and he used his contacts to get us home.

"Mike." John looked right at me. "Walter was only one of dozens of trainers to the Cahokian Player. He was the master of wilderness survival, but there was someone for hand-to-hand combat, for marksmanship, for knife fighting, for acrobatics, for lock picking, for bomb making—it just goes on and on. This Player is supposed to be the best of the best. The best on earth. One Player from each of the twelve lines is chosen to compete in Endgame."

I stared back at John, and then at the fire. They were quiet—everyone was.

"But how do they play?" I asked.

"There are three keys, hidden across the globe. The first Player to obtain all three keys—and be the last Player standing—wins."

"What do you mean, keys? And who organizes all of this? Who is hiding the keys?" I asked.

"That's a big question—" John started to say, but was cut off by Walter. "Aliens. The Sky Gods. The Makers. The Annunaki. They have many names."

I laughed uncomfortably. Walter couldn't be serious. This was all a ghost story around the campfire. "Bullshit. This whole story is shit from start to finish. You had me there for a bit. But really, what are we going to do now? Go snipe hunting? Search for Bigfoot?"

But no one else in the circle was laughing. Just me.

"Aliens," I said. "Come on. That's insane. How? *Why?*"

"Their own entertainment," Walter said. "It started with early man, with the aliens hunting us for sport. When things grew dull, they made us smarter, better competitors. And on and on until here we are. Killing us is their ultimate game. But we still have to try to win."

I still laughed, but no one else made a sound.

I turned to Mary. "Come on. Tell me. What is this really all about?"

She shook her head and then looked into my eyes. "They're telling the truth. Remember, Mike—trust me. Listen and keep an open mind."

"There are three ways this can go," Walter said. "The first is that we, Zero line, do nothing. The Players aren't called to Play the game, and we all live out our lives just fine until we die of old age or heart attacks or car accidents.

"The second is that the Calling does happen, and we don't do anything. One of the Players kills all the others and solves the puzzle, and everyone on Earth—everyone not of their bloodline—dies. I don't know how it will happen: disease, earthquake, alien invasion. But it will be something big and something bad.

"The third way is the whole reason we're meeting: If the Players can't Play, then no one will win Endgame. If no one wins Endgame, there's no end of the world. So if we can stop the Players from Playing, then the game will end. And we'll save humanity."

The group was quiet, watching my face, waiting to see how I would react.

"So do you have . . . um . . . proof?" I asked.

Mary answered. "We have Walter. He knows this inside out."

"No offense," I said, looking at Walter. "But what if I don't believe you?"

"You don't have to believe me," Walter said. "I don't care if you do. I know it's true. I've lived it since I was born, part of my Cahokian line. If you want something tangible, I have ancient texts that I found by tracing leads across the country. They lay out the truths of Endgame."

"Let me see those."

"In a moment. First, I will prove to you that I am a Cahokian."

He unbuttoned his shirt. I glanced at Mary. She nodded at me and smiled reassuringly.

He pulled off his shirt and turned his back to us. There was a tattoo that twisted back and forth on his back until it reached his neck, where a snakelike mouth stretched to swallow a large oval. In that oval there was a large scar—an *X*.

"It's the Serpent Mound in Ohio," he said. "It represents my culture and my line."

"That's a cattle brand," Mary said. "The *X*."

"That's my punishment for questioning Endgame. I returned from the war, searched for the papers, and when I found them and tried to discuss them with the line's leaders, I was branded a traitor and kicked out. Excommunicated from my family, my line."

He pulled the shirt back on, only buttoning a few of the buttons before pulling two folded pieces of paper from his pocket. They looked tattered and worn. He read from the first.

This is the lie, the one that has fueled your life and the lives of all who have come [unreadable] before you. I have risked everything to remove the veil of mystery that shrouds the

Annunaki, to show [unreadable] It will all be for nothing
[unreadable] understand.
The Mu had a choice. You have a choice.
To Play the game is to lose the game; success, survival, freedom
can only come . . .
Prove to the Annunaki that you are not mindless animals, that
you can think [unreadable] we, all of us, deserve a chance to
live.
Choose to question what you have been taught.
Choose to be free, that we might all be free.
Choose not to Play.

Everyone was quiet. Some nodded. Some looked up at the sky. Some turned toward me, as if my reaction was important to them. I just shrugged. Phyllis broke the silence. "I've researched the Annunaki. They were the gods in Mesopotamia. Kinda like the Titans in Greek legends—they were there before the gods. They even *made* the other gods. I found them in the Epic of Gilgamesh. They created something called Esagila—this crazy temple to the protector god. Standard kinds of stuff from old legends. But if we accept that they were the Makers, aliens—not myths, not real gods—then it's easy to cast them as aliens who helped start the human race."

I looked at her for a moment and then stared into the depths of the fire, where the coals were glowing white and flaking apart like little bits of paper in the wind. "So is that what you're saying?" I asked no one in particular. "You're saying that aliens started the human race?"

"Look," Mary said, turning to face me. She touched her finger to my chin and made me look back at her. "We've all been brought into this. Every one of us has had the same doubts that you do, because—I mean, aliens, right? That's crazy stuff. But is it really crazy?"

I nodded. "Yes."

John laughed, but Mary reached out and grabbed my shoulders. "We know the universe is unimaginably huge. Our galaxy has a hundred billion stars. And there are a hundred billion galaxies in the universe. Isn't it the height of arrogance to say that we're the only planet with people on it? I don't care if you're religious or not. It doesn't matter. I was raised Catholic and still go to mass every week. But we're talking about science here, not religion, not myth. I doubted like you. But I find it easier now to say that aliens are out there than to say they're not. With that many solar systems, there's got to be something out there—"

I cut her off. "I'm honestly not stumbling over the existence of aliens. Sure. They exist somewhere. That's logical. What I'm fighting against is the idea that the entirety of human experience is one big game."

John stood up, looking at me but speaking loud enough for everyone to hear. He grinned. "Would you like to meet someone else caught up in this spider web?"

There was an audible gasp around the campfire. Mary swung around to face him. "Who?" Then she looked at Walter. "Another Cahokian?"

John answered. "Not Cahokian. La Tène. She actually found Walter. Well, they found each other. She doesn't want to be a part of that world anymore. She was a Player until a couple years ago—" He looked at me. "All players have to be twenty or younger."

"How did she find you?" Bruce asked, worry on his face.

"That, I don't know," John said.

Walter shook his head and looked at Bruce. "You have to understand, these people are experts at everything. I was one of dozens of trainers. The Players are constantly being tutored: practicing martial arts, boxing, swimming, rock climbing. They know how to tail someone— on the street or in a car. They know how to disappear. And they can find anyone. It's one of the biggest things we stressed during training, because they have to kill all the other Players, and that means they have to hunt them down. Our contact lived that life."

"So, when do we meet her?" asked Bruce.

John smiled. "What are you doing next weekend?"

CHAPTER FIVE

"This is huge," I said to Tommy as we made our way through the crowd on Sproul Plaza, back in Berkeley.

He looked back at me with a grin. "You need to come to more protests. This is small, maybe five or six hundred."

"Five hundred is small?"

We'd been back from the ranch for five days. It was Thursday, and we knew that we'd be meeting the La Tène Player tomorrow. Zero line was electric—like a kid counting down the days until Christmas morning. But all we could do was wait.

"I finished that book this morning," I said. "The one by the German guy."

"That book is something like eight hundred pages," he said with a laugh.

"I take it to work with me. I figure, if one of the other janitors can spend all day in the stairwell smoking grass, I can sit in a room and read."

"You're going to get fired."

"Come on, it doesn't take long to mop some floors. Have you read that book, cover to cover?"

"No," Tommy said, peering over heads, looking for the rest of the group. "I've barely cracked the spine."

"Have you heard of the Piri Reis map?"

"No."

"Okay, get this. There's a map that was drawn in, like, 1500 AD. So, not long after Columbus. It shows the Atlantic Ocean, and everything that touches it: Europe, Africa, North America, South America, and, the crazy one, Antarctica. The map makes some mistakes, but it shows the exact coastline of Antarctica. The Air Force was shown the map and they confirmed the accuracy of the map's representation of the coast."

"So what?" he said, and looked at me with a grin.

"Back then, big maps were compiled from older maps, so this exploration of the Antarctic must have been done before 1500—or whatever that date was. 1515, maybe. But the first known exploration of Antarctica was in the seventeen hundreds."

"And why do we care about Antarctica?" He was still smiling, as if he suspected the answer.

"Because that shoreline has been under a mile of ice for six thousand years."

"And what does that tell us?" Tommy said.

"I have no idea," I said, laughing.

"What it means is that you're joining Zero line. I was having my doubts about you, Mike. Didn't know if you could open your mind to it. But you're coming along, bud. You've found evidence of some kind of ancient knowledge that must have been delivered by advanced technology. It's just another sign. Let's get up closer to the front. I don't even know what we're protesting."

I nodded and followed him through the crowd until he spotted Jim over on the far side.

I still had reservations. Big reservations. At this point, a lot of arguments had been made, but all of it hinged on whether I could trust Walter. And he wasn't the easiest person to get to know. He was terse and angry, and he'd spent the entire time at the ranch with a bottle in his hand.

I didn't trust people who drank like that.

That said, I liked Mary, and I felt like I could trust her. She was so smart, so down-to-earth. And it really did seem like *she* trusted Walter. Maybe I couldn't dig up enough belief to trust Walter, but maybe I could put that trust in Mary.

The girl with the megaphone was yelling the same antiwar rhetoric that I'd heard for as long as I'd been paying attention. I was 19, and the Vietnam War had been going on since I was a kid. I hardly remembered a world without it. It was on the news every night, as much a standard as the weather report or the baseball scores.

And so were the protests. I'd been hearing about them forever, it seemed. At times I wondered if America was going to survive this whole thing. There was a war going on far away, and a war going on at home too.

Mary found us at the side of the plaza, against the wall of a building. "This is amazing," she said, slipping her arm through mine. Her lips almost touched my ear so I could hear her over the noise.

I glanced over my shoulder and saw that the lower part of Sproul Plaza was filling up.

"What makes you trust Walter?" I shouted. I hadn't gotten to see Mary at all this week, and I still felt like we had so much to talk about from the previous weekend.

Mary looked thoughtful. She leaned in and spoke into my ear. "I believe what he has to say. I believe his story, and his mission."

"But do you trust him?" Right now, my trust in the group rested firmly on the shoulders of Mary and Tommy. If they could trust, I could trust.

"With my life." She pulled back, and looked at me. "He's going to officially ask you to join Zero line, Mike."

I took a deep breath. "Whoa. Okay. So, was last weekend some kind of test? Was it like a tryout to see if I should join your group?"

Mary smiled, sheepish. "Kind of. Look, we have to cover our bases. There have been people who we've invited in who have refused. They think we're crazy. One of them called the police on us—they accused us of being another Manson Family. You're different. You've been to the ranch; the others never came. You met everybody. I'll be honest: there were a handful of people who thought that you shouldn't have come up there. But John and I both trusted you."

"So," I asked jokingly, "will they kill me if I say no? Do I know too much?"

But Mary wasn't smiling anymore. "Don't even kid about that. Of course that won't happen, but this is serious. I mean, you know—it's the end of the *world*. We're not joking about this, and I would really appreciate it if you didn't either."

I glanced around the crowd and saw dozens of police officers standing around the protestors, watching everything. I didn't know why, but I felt uncomfortable. We weren't doing anything but listening. We weren't going to get into trouble. Still, just by talking about Zero line, I felt like we were involved in something wrong. I felt like they were watching me. "Are you angry?" the woman said into the bullhorn. The crowd shouted back "Yes!"

Mary shouted too, but I could tell she was unhappy for a different reason. *She's upset because I still don't believe her,* I realized.

"Well, I'll tell you one thing," the woman with the megaphone shouted. "We're not alone. Today, fifteen thousand people marched on Washington to protest the mining of Vietnam's waters. That's what we have to remember. We are not alone. And in the coming months and years, we'll need to remember it even more: we are one people, one civilization, one humanity. It's not us versus Charlie. It's not West versus East. It's not United States versus USSR. It's one Earth, and we're fighting for a good cause."

The crowd cheered. I saw John get up onstage and start making his way toward the speakers. Mary saw him too.

"Damn it, John. Let's get up there," Mary said. "We need to get him off the stage. We're going to meet the La Tène girl tomorrow. We can't screw this up. He can't get arrested. He's AWOL."

I looked over at Mary, wondering what I was getting myself into. But I followed. I couldn't resist the pull she had on me. She held my hand and dragged me through the crowd, up to the stairs.

From there we could see an entirely new column of protestors, off to the north of the stage—another thousand between Sproul Hall and the Student Center.

Someone else took the megaphone, but the police were starting to move in toward us.

The new guy with the megaphone saw the police and immediately changed the subject. "You know what? There's nothing we can do about Haiphong right now. But I think we can tear down a fence. How many times do we have to mourn our compatriots? How many times do we need to tear down those fences? Everybody to People's Park!"

Mary and I dashed up the steps. John was about to take the microphone, but we pulled him away just in time. "John, what the hell are you doing? You can't get on that mic! We've got to get out of here. We can't screw up before tomorrow. What about the La Tène girl? Zero line is on the verge of something big. Things are happening. You're jeopardizing everything we've worked for." One of the cops was coming up toward us, his nightstick out. There were six of us on the upper plaza—John, Mary and me, and the three protest leaders who'd been speaking before we got there.

John shook his head. "This time will be different. There aren't many cops. This won't affect tomorrow." He pointed around. Everyone was moving toward us.

"John," Mary said. "Mike and I can get arrested and spend the night in jail. But if you get caught, you're going to be in real trouble. Without you, Zero line won't have a leader. You're going to blow our whole mission for nothing!"

John started walking—we were at the head of the crowd, the leaders in front of the mass of people. "You're right, Mary. You're right. Let's get out of here."

I could hear the sirens before we got to the park, but that didn't matter. There were a thousand of us, at least, and there was nowhere for us to go. There were police to our left and right, and behind us was the wave of people. Where the campus sidewalk ended and turned into Bancroft Way, there were only six police cars with flashing lights. People poured into the street to join us.

Mary and I held hands as we went, trying to push back into the crowd, but there was no stopping it: the people behind us were being pushed by the people behind them, and so on all the way back. John tried to weave his way through to get out of the front lines, but it wasn't working. People kept trying to join arms in a line across the front of the crowd. We were at the tip of the spear, the very front of a massive tidal wave of hundreds of people.

This reminded me of all the protests I'd seen on TV, from draft-card burnings in Boston to the Days of Rage riots to the Kent State shootings. People were killed—students, police, bystanders. But here there were only a couple dozen cops against a thousand of us; they had to retreat.

And I realized for the first time that this was real life, and that Mary was standing next to me, holding my hand. What would I do if this turned violent? And if I was this nervous about a protest, how would I be able to handle something like Endgame?

We wanted to move back through the crowd, away from the cops, but the mass of people was as reasonable as an avalanche.

It won't turn violent, I told myself. There were too few cops. They'd retreat.

And if they had shotguns again? I'd defend Mary. I'd defend John. I could hold my own in a fight, if it came to that.

"We're not here for a fight!" John shouted at the cops, but his voice was drowned out in a sea of voices. He took off his hat and turned in a circle. "We're unarmed. This is a peaceful protest!"

The mob pushed, and Mary and I stumbled a step forward. The whole front line did. Everyone was trying to stop as we faced the roadblock of cop cars, but there were too many people pushing from behind.

One of the officers spoke into a handset on a long cord that stretched into his car window. "We—" *EEEEEEE!* There was an enormous squawk from the speaker, and the crowd erupted in shouts and laughter. "We order you to disperse! Return to your homes."

Mary and I got pushed forward again. We were no more than 15 feet from the officers.

"Shit," she said, starting to panic. "Push back, Mike. We can't get pushed to the front. Hang on!"

John gestured with one hand to get the cops' attention. "Just let us pass. There's no stopping these guys."

Another shove forward, but I grabbed Mary's hand tighter and held my ground. I looked behind us and all I could see was an endless sea of people—most of them still marching toward us—packing harder into the mob.

John didn't have much room now between the crowd and the police.

"Get back," the officer's loudspeaker blared.

Another push. There was nowhere to go. John was almost face-to-face with the cop. He had his hands up. "I can't get back! We don't want to fight!"

But there was another surge forward—I almost fell to my knees, and Mary had to grab my arm to keep me on my feet.

"No!" Mary yelled. "This is so bad!"

The cop in front of us was getting scared. I could see it in his eyes. His hand went to his gun, but he didn't draw.

Another officer shouted into his loudspeaker. "Disperse. We order you to disperse." But nothing was stopping the wave. John was next to me, on my left, Mary was on my right, and all of us were pleading with the cop.

The frightened officer moved his hand to his nightstick and swung. John ducked his head, but he wasn't fast enough, and the stick cracked loudly across John's scalp.

The cop raised the stick again to bring another blow down, but as the nightstick sliced through the air, instinct kicked into gear. I let go of Mary's hand and dove into the fray.

The nightstick crashed into the back of John's shoulder, and I tackled the cop, slamming him into his squad car. I didn't wait to see how he would respond—I suddenly saw myself in all those Friday-night fights Dad and I used to watch. A punch to the stomach and then an uppercut to the chin.

He swung at me with the nightstick, but it was wild, blind, and I avoided it easily and threw a right hook. The cop dropped to the asphalt.

And, just as I looked up, I saw a reporter on the other side of the car pointing a camera at us. I stared at him as the flash popped.

"Damn it," I said. The mob was splitting around us, some climbing over the car. I could chase the man down, steal his camera, break it, expose the film. But we were being passed by the mob now, as we crouched beside the cop car, and the photographer was lost in a sea of people. The cop in front of us was dazed, and John reached down to take the officer's gun.

"John!" Mary whisper-yelled. "Put it back! Are you crazy?"

"I don't want to be shot in the back," John hissed, blood dripping down his face. He popped out the six rounds from the revolver and broke down the pistol, dropping the pieces to the ground.

"Damn it, damn it, damn it. Shit shit shit." I dropped back down by the car.

"It's nothing," John said, a hand on his scalp. Blood trickled on his hand, face, and jacket.

"No," I said. "I think a reporter just got pictures of the whole thing, me punching the cop."

John pulled off his jacket and pressed it against his head. "Let's go."

It took the mob nearly 10 minutes to thin out enough for us to head back, swimming against the current.

"Mary, are you okay?" I shouted to be heard as the people poured past us toward the park. John started leading us down an alley, away from the park and the university.

Mary nodded at me. "If the photographer got you, he got me too."

"Where's your car?" I asked.

"A couple blocks from here. We've got to get you to a hospital—"

John interrupted. "You guys go ahead. I've got a place I can go." While he talked, he kept his eyes on the street, back and forth. "You two have really proven yourselves today, you know? See you at the meeting tomorrow. We may need to move up our schedule, especially if that photo surfaces." He took a few steps back, then stopped and smiled at me. "Mike," he said. "There's no way you can't join us after this! You're a part of it now! We all are!"

He whooped and threw his fist into the air, then jogged across the busy road and disappeared into the shadows of another alley. Mary laughed, watching him go.

"You can't tell me this isn't all exciting, Mike," she said. "You wanted to be a part of something bigger. Well, this is it."

I turned to her. Her cheeks were flushed with excitement; her eyes sparkled. So why did I feel dread creeping into my stomach? "What did he mean, we may need to move the schedule up?" I asked.

CHAPTER SIX

"Don't worry about the schedule," Mary said to me, and let out a long breath. "Everything will depend on the meeting with the La Tène Player."

"Fine," I said. "Let's worry about that photo. If that's in the paper, that's it for me. I'll be arrested. Assaulting a cop. That's gotta be— what? Five years? Ten?"

"It'd be battery," she said. "Not assault."

"Why are you being so calm about this?" I said, almost shouting. "This is my life we're talking about! I'm finally out of my dad's house and out on my own! I can't go to prison!"

"I'm not exactly happy about it," she said. "But panicking isn't going to help anything. I'm just trying to think. I may have been in that picture too, you know."

"But you weren't punching a cop."

"We don't know what that picture will be. Maybe it's a picture of you hitting a cop, but maybe it was taken just before or just after. We don't need to freak out yet. Who knows? Maybe the shot will be of the policeman attacking John."

"So what am I supposed to do? Just go back to my dorm and wait?"

She exhaled and folded her arms. "Yes. And if police come to see you, demand to see a lawyer."

"I can't afford a lawyer."

"The court will appoint one for you. But it won't come to that. You're overreacting, Mike. Do you know how many marches and protests there have been in this city? About Nixon, Vietnam, freedom of speech, equal rights? People get arrested at every one, and they get a misdemeanor slap on the wrist and they have to pay five hundred dollars, or something like that, and they move on with their lives. No one's sending you to jail."

"Unless that picture comes out."

"Unless that picture comes out," she agreed. "But let's cross that bridge when we get there. Listen: I work in a law office. On Monday I'll ask them what we should do."

"I don't want you to get involved in this."

She laughed. "Mike," she said, "I'm more involved in this than you even know." She ran her fingers through her long hair and leaned back against the brick wall of the alley. "Let's go get ice cream."

I snorted. "What?"

"Yeah," she said. "Let's go get ice cream. There's a place right down the road."

"Shouldn't we be trying to get out of here?"

"Think about it. If that photo is blurry—and it might very well be, because everyone was jostling around—they may not know who exactly it was. So let's go make an alibi. Act totally normal, like we've never been to a protest. We'll act like it's a date. Then when the police come looking for you, you can say, 'No, I wasn't there. I was at the Creamy Freeze with Mary Nesmith.' And the employees there will back us up."

I smiled, my first real smile since we'd gotten into the mob of people. I didn't know how Mary was so calm under pressure—I wasn't, that's for sure.

"A date, huh?" I nudged her with my elbow.

She rolled her eyes. "I said we'll *act* like it's a date."

"For now," I said, grinning. "Okay, let's do it."

She reached out her hand, and I took it. Her fingers were cold as I interlaced mine with hers, and my heart began to race. As much as I wasn't entirely sure of Zero line, I liked that I was doing stuff with her, that when we left the protest, she was going with me. We started walking—quickly so that we could be at the ice cream shop before anyone else from the march could get there.

"So you never answered me. What did John mean by moving the schedule up?" I asked.

"That is a question that is better answered by John," she said.

"That's evasive."

"Not trying to be evasive," she said. "You ever go to church?"

"What does that have to do with it?"

"Did you ever study the Bible?"

"I've listened to a lot of preachers. My mom is Baptist."

"You know I still go to church," she said. "Isaiah says that you learn 'precept upon precept, line upon line, here a little and there a little.' That's the way that John teaches people. I've seen him bring several people into Zero line that way. He talks about one part of Endgame, then another, deeper part, and so on until . . ."

She didn't finish, but she didn't have to. *By that point they're already too deep in it to leave.*

Part of me knew I should get out now. But there was a part of me too that had to see what would happen next.

"So," I said, "he was talking about me? He's moving up the schedule for how fast I'm going to learn." Mary nodded. "How much more is there? I mean, what else could possibly be left to tell me? He's already talked about how all of human existence is a big game run by aliens, and how twelve Players are supposedly competing to outsmart them and save their lines from the end of the world. There's *more*?"

"A little more. But you're learning fast; it's great. I think tomorrow, when we meet with the La Tène Player, we're going to hear most of what there is to know—probably a lot of stuff even *I* don't know."

Darkness was settling in as we crossed the street. A police car flipped its lights on and sped off in the direction of People's Park.

"So, here's a question," I said. "If you believe those alien guys, why do you still go to church?"

"You really are Mr. Inquisitor, aren't you?"

53

"I just punched a cop to protect John, who could be a cult leader for all I know."

Mary's faced turned serious. "Zero line isn't a cult."

"It's definitely not a book club."

"Are those the only choices? Book club or cult? I believe that's what's called a false dichotomy."

I smiled to relieve some of the tension that was building. "You Stanford kids with your big words."

"Look. We're not the Manson Family, but we're not exactly the PTA either. And as long as we're laying our cards on the table, John isn't sleeping with any of us, and I haven't seen anyone use anything stronger than marijuana."

"Walter drinks a lot. I mean, a lot. I don't like that."

"I know," she said. Walter drank even more than my dad, but he didn't seem to have the angry streak in him. "I bet you would too, if you'd seen the kinds of things he has. It surprises me more that John doesn't drink with him. They were there together. They both saw and did the same things. And about church, I go because I like it. I was raised going to church, and I feel like it's a part of who I am. Is that good enough?"

"Sure."

We turned a corner and could see the big sign of the Creamy Freeze. This was definitely the weirdest first-date conversation I'd ever had.

"Hey," I said, taking her hand and swinging it. "How did you become a member of Zero line?"

"Kind of a boring story, really. Kat—you remember her? The nurse?"

I nodded. She was cute, but nowhere near as pretty as Mary. She was also older than me by three or four years.

"She works at a clinic near my dorm." Mary raised her right arm and showed me a jagged scar on her arm, just below the elbow. I'd never noticed it before. "My second day at Stanford I fell down the stairs and caught it on a carpet nail. Not my proudest moment. Kat treated me, and we became friends. She's the one who introduced me to John."

I opened the door of the Creamy Freeze for her and then followed her in.

"I like to joke that they use me for my ranch. And the funny part is that it's totally true. While Kat and I were talking, I found out she was camping a lot on land up by Susanville, and I told her my family had the ranch. Four days later, John and Kat showed up at my Stanford apartment and laid out the sales pitch. Nothing about the Zero line then, of course. They just wanted to do some fishing and shooting. I found out more and more as we went—like I told you, precept upon precept, line upon line. I've been with them ever since."

We stepped up to the counter in an otherwise empty shop and ordered. She got a vanilla ice cream cone, which I told her was the most boring thing in the place. I got a banana split with a scoop each of Rocky Road and strawberry. We made sure to stand at the counter and talk happily with the teenaged scooper, trying to make a clear impression on her so that she could pick us out of a lineup.

It had been at least 25 minutes since we'd gotten away from the mob and police. Probably more. But we acted as though we didn't have a care in the world.

As we headed for a booth, I didn't know what to think. I liked Mary, and she seemed to like me. But part of my brain kept telling me that this Zero line stuff was crazy and this Endgame story was bullshit. Yet each time I saw Mary, I couldn't wait until the next time I could see her. I'd never felt this way after knowing someone for only a couple of days. It felt like much longer.

I'd never had a girlfriend before. I'd been to prom, but that was just a group of guys asking out a group of girls. I went out a few times with Camille Edwards because my friends goaded me into it more than because I liked her. We made out a bit, but that was it. And I mean, that was it. I, Michael Stavros, was a virgin. It was one of those things that I hoped Berkeley would solve for me. College would be a fresh start—no one from my high school was there. I was a new man; this was a new life. One that now included Mary. And Endgame.

CHAPTER SEVEN

It was on the front page.

When I woke up, the first thing I did was go to the mail room to check the copy of the *San Francisco Chronicle* we got delivered each day. It was clean. I felt light-headed with relief. There was a story on page three about the march (they called it a riot), but no picture and no mention of me. One man, Officer Scott Hoover, had suffered a dislocated jaw. But that was it, and I felt like I was walking three feet off the ground. There was no picture, no names, no ongoing investigation.

It wasn't until I got to the dorm cafeteria, got my breakfast, and sat down at the table that I saw a discarded copy of the *Daily Californian*, Berkeley's student paper. I came crashing back to Earth. My face was three inches tall, completely clear and in focus. My fist looked like it had just connected with the cop's chin. It was a perfect picture. It looked as professional as if it had been taken at a prizefight. My face, the cop's face, and the top of John's head—he was looking down, and his face couldn't be seen.

I surprised myself by not freaking out. I picked up the newspaper, took my full tray of food to the dishwashers, and quietly left the building. By the time I got to the bottom step I was sprinting, running as fast as I could from the other students and desperately trying to avoid anyone. I had to get to my dorm, to the phone. I had to talk to John. He could make this go away. I was stepping in to save him—couldn't he step in to save me? He knew the leaders of the protest. Something could be done. Someone could save me.

I got to my dorm and ran up the stairs, hoping Tommy would be in the room, but he wasn't. I darted into the bathroom and called his name. No answer. I jogged down to the common room, but he wasn't there either.

"Damn it," I said, digging in my pocket for coins. I tried to compose myself as I went down the hall to use the pay phone. Except I didn't have any phone numbers. I had no way to reach Tommy, and no idea how to get in touch with John. I realized I didn't even know his last name. There was no one to call. I walked back to my room, but before I went in, a thought struck me: if the campus police—or the city police—were looking for me, of course they would check my room. But I'd only been in Berkeley for a little over a week, and I'd spent a whole weekend of that at Mary's ranch. My boss never paid any attention to me when he was assigning tasks. But he did always have a copy of the newspaper open on the table in the supply room. He'd recognize me, sooner or later.

I looked down at the paper and began reading the story. My heart sank, and I thought I was going to be sick. I'd only just gotten to Berkeley and my time here was already over. What was I going to do? There was no caption under the photo, but now my face was all over campus.

I had money in my room. I had brought it all in cash, everything I'd saved for tuition. Yes, it was stupid of me, but I'd planned to open an account at a local bank once I got to Berkeley. I just hadn't done it yet. The cops could be watching my room, but I had 3,000 dollars in there—everything that I'd saved from working for my dad and two summers with the Forest Service. I could go get it and some clothes, hide out in a hotel for a couple weeks, and grow a beard.

Shit. I needed help.

I cautiously walked back to my room, quietly inserted the key, and turned the lock. The door swung open.

It was still empty. I let out a long, slow breath.

I rushed to my desk and unlocked the drawers. In the back of one, behind a divider, was all my money—a thick stack, wrapped in two rubber bands. Eventually someone would search my room once they figured out who I was. I pulled my wallet from my back pocket and tried to fit in as many bills as I could. In between the folds of the wallet I found what I needed: a business card for the law firm of Goodman and Odenkirk. Mary's job. It listed a phone number, even though it didn't have her name—it just said *Legal Assistant.* She could help me. She worked in a law firm, after all. At the very least, she'd be able to point to someone for me to talk to.

My wallet was bulging as I crammed it into my back pocket, and I put the remainder of the cash into my front right pocket. There were neighborhoods in Los Angeles where I would never dare carry a wallet that was so obviously big, but Berkeley seemed safer. Or maybe I was just clueless.

My hands were shaking, and I didn't want to use the pay phone on this floor. I wanted to get out, away from here, away from any place where there was a copy of that newspaper.

The police would have seen the photo by now. They'd be investigating the assault on the cop, and nothing that I did could change that, could throw them off the scent. The only thing I could wish for was that no one at the school would be able to identify me. But there were so many people that I'd interacted with: the admissions office, the cafeteria and dorm staff, my boss and the other janitors, local shop owners, and all the students who were hanging around campus over summer session.

I left the dorm and headed off campus. It was too warm for a jacket and scarf to hide me, but I had a ball cap, which I pulled low over my eyes. I stopped at the closest phone booth—it was on the corner next to a gas station.

I held the business card in front of me as I dialed the number.

On the third ring, someone answered.

"Mary Nesmith, please," I said.

"One moment."

I waited for what seemed like an eternity, but which was probably only 30 seconds.

"This is Mary." I recognized her voice.

"Hey," I said. "This is Mike."

There was a pause, and then her voice was much softer. "You can't call me here. I'm not supposed to take any personal calls."

"You gave me your business card."

"I didn't think you'd call."

"They got a picture of me, Mary. It's all over campus, in every newspaper rack in every lobby."

"Oh my God. What are you going to do?"

"I don't know," I said. "That's why I called you. Yours was the only phone number I had."

There was a pause. "Am I in it too?"

"No. Neither is John's face."

"Can you talk to Tommy?"

"I don't know where he is. Police are going to see this, Mary. They're going to search my room."

"Is there anything they'll find?"

I thought of my meager belongings. Books, bedding, some clothes. No photos that might connect me to the one in the paper. "Nothing important."

"Good."

"Do you think Tommy will lie? Will he say that it's a picture of me? I know they'll question him."

"Tommy's . . . I don't know what he'll do. Do you have a lawyer?"

"Of course not, unless your firm wants to represent me."

"We do divorces and bankruptcies. We're not defense attorneys."

"Then what am I supposed to do?"

"Can you make it to the meeting today?"

"I don't know where the Berkeley Rose Garden is," I said.

"It's less than a mile from campus," she said. "Take Euclid and just walk north. You'll find it."

"Is there a pavilion or somewhere we'll meet?"

"There's a room. I'll show you."

"Okay."

"You can call me again if you need to."

"Thanks."

I was about to end the call, but she said, "Mike?"

"Yeah?"

"Be careful."

"I'll do my best."

I hung up. I couldn't go to work. I couldn't hang around campus, or stay in my room. And I had almost seven hours before the meeting. I was going to need to find something to do all day. Instead of heading north, I walked west to the public library. It was close to campus, but there wouldn't be any university newspapers in the foyer.

I went to the card catalog, looking for law books. I wanted to see what I was in for if I got caught. But after an hour and five books, I couldn't find anything about sentencing recommendations for assaulting a policeman. One book, though, made it clear that there was a big difference between assaulting a regular person and assaulting a police officer. Assault was usually a misdemeanor, but if the injured party was injured—and a dislocated jaw definitely counted—then it would be a felony charge. Worse, another book, which talked about the marches and protests of the sixties, said that riots were a whole other ball game. I could be charged with rioting, disorderly conduct, and criminal mischief. And the law said that it didn't matter whether the rioters' cause was just: attacking police was always assault, even if the protest was against something horrible.

I was screwed.

As the day wore on, I ran out of things to research, at least in regard to the law. But I didn't have anywhere else to go. I found myself looking for other books. Books related to Endgame. There was nothing in the card catalog with that name except for a play by Samuel Beckett. I looked at it, and it had nothing to do with what John and Walter were talking about.

Then I remembered what Phyllis had said about the Annunaki, the aliens in Walter's papers. There were a handful of results in the history section. The Annunaki were a group of gods in Mesopotamia, the cradle of civilization. Sumerian, Assyrian, Babylonian. According to legend, they were the seven judges of hell. Was it possible that they were really aliens?

I looked at the time. The meeting was going to start in an hour.

I didn't know what secrets were waiting for me. I was in a new city, at a new school, and I didn't have many people I could really trust. I was in trouble, and I was alone. I needed to lie low, and maybe the Zero line could help me with that. At this point, I didn't have anyone else.

CHAPTER EIGHT

Mary was waiting for me in her car when I got to the rose garden. She got out. She was wearing a printed black-and-white dress—she probably had just come from work—and she ran to me. She wasn't smiling.

"I passed by an electronics store on my way here that was playing the evening news on the TVs in the window. I stopped to watch." She threw her arms around me in a hug. "They talked about the march, and they showed the picture. They said the cop was still in the hospital—they're saying you broke his jaw."

"Shit." I held her tightly.

She pulled back. "They're going to come after you, Mike. Hard. That's what one of the lawyers in my office said—and no, I didn't tell him I was there or that I knew you."

"What am I supposed to do?" I asked, my heart pounding. "I can't go back home. I won't."

"John might know what to do. In the meantime, quit shaving. Maybe we can dye your hair."

"I can't go back to my dorm."

"Definitely not. Let's talk to John. He'll know what to do."

She hooked her arm with mine and started leading me into the rose garden. It looked like a Roman amphitheater: a large half circle, terraced several steps down to an epicenter, which led to a tunnel under the street. I would have found it beautiful if my world hadn't been falling apart around me. I had been on the news. Everyone would have seen it. Now it wasn't just a matter of hiding from the

Berkeley campus. I had to hide from everyone in the city.

"It's going to be okay," Mary said. She probably could hear my heartbeat—it felt like it was thudding in my chest, pounding in my ears.

"How is this going to be okay? You just said your lawyer thinks I'm sunk."

"That's only if they can find you."

"Where else can I go? Back to Pasadena? I've spent my whole life trying to get out of there."

"You could get a job and an apartment."

"Not anywhere around here. Besides, what about school? I've wanted to go to Berkeley forever. I've been saving money for years."

"Well, there's your answer. Lie low, get a place out of town, and wait for all of this to blow over. They'll be looking for you now, but soon they'll move on to something else. One cop's broken jaw is not going to warrant an all-points bulletin."

"Thanks, Mary, but that doesn't change the fact that my time at Berkeley is over. There's no way I can return to school. I can't believe this is happening."

"We don't know if anyone has your name. Just stop going to work, lay low, and then go back in the fall when the new semester starts and you have a beard. You haven't even started classes yet, no one will remember you. You'll be fine."

I nodded. It made sense. But it required that no one connect my face with my name, which still scared me.

We both went quiet as we reached the tunnel entrance. It was narrow and dim, a low, curved ceiling closing in on us. There was the silhouette of someone standing in the center holding a push broom. We approached him and he stopped sweeping.

"Is there a secret word?" I whispered to her.

"No. We just give him a ten."

I dug into my pocket, but she was faster than me, and in a moment she slipped him the money. He opened a door and let us into a small, dimly lit room.

The room smelled of motor oil and grass clippings. It was an equipment room for the care of the rose garden and the park on the other side. There were two desks, each with a chair, and a beat-up sofa. About 20 people were already there. I recognized most from last weekend. Jim stood up from one of the desk chairs and offered the seat to Mary. She protested, but he insisted.

Tommy rushed over when he saw me. "Mike! I've been worried, man. I saw the paper this morning but I haven't been to the room all day. I was hoping I'd see you here."

John came over too. He shook my hand and then clapped me on the back. He had a ball cap on, but I could see a gauze bandage peeking out under the brim. "First things first," he said. "We know about the picture. And I want you to know that you have our complete loyalty. You're one of us now, Mike. A part of Zero line, if you want to be."

I shrugged, angry. "I don't know what good I'll be to you after this. I've got to get out of town. I'm screwed if they find me."

"I know, Mike. It's a bad spot. But you'll be a lot of good to a lot of us. A lot of people in this room have stuff. You know that I'm AWOL, don't you? Walter too."

Eugene, a scrawny guy with a wispy beard, spoke up. "I was right there with you at the march yesterday. I saw—you were trying to help John. I'd have done the same thing if I'd been closer. And I've got a record."

Mary leaned over and whispered to me. "Eugene robbed a couple banks."

One of the older guys, Henry—maybe 30 years old—waved his hand. "I've got warrants. Three of them. Battery and possession."

Bruce nodded. "I served sixty days for failure to appear."

"See, Mike?" John said. "We get it. And we're going to be watching out for you."

I nodded. "Thanks, guys. Seriously—I don't know what else I would do. I mean, I don't know anybody else. You guys are my lifeline right now."

"And we'll protect you. Keep a roof over your head," John said. "That's a promise."

He nodded at me, but then pointed at a girl I didn't know. "We'll come back to this," John said. "But first, let me introduce you to our guest of honor. Agatha, a former Player from the La Tène line. She's seen all of this lifestyle up close and personal."

A pale-faced woman with reddish-blond hair stood up. I couldn't believe it—she was so young! I was expecting a grizzled warrior, not a girl just a few years older than me. Watching her now, I was disturbed by her age. She, and others like her, would be deciding our world's destiny.

"Agatha," John said, "you've already been introduced to everyone else. Mary here has been part of our group for a year. And Mike is our newest recruit."

"What do they bring to the table?" she asked.

John seemed surprised by the question, and paused for a moment.

"Mary is smart as a whip, an aspiring lawyer, and a passionate supporter of the cause. And you should see the ranch she's got up in Northern California. Lots of land, secluded, private. A great place to train. We've been going up there for about a year now."

"What about him?" Agatha said. "What's he good for? Sounds like he's a wanted man." She tapped a cigarette out of a pack from her pocket and lit it. She took a long, deep drag, and then blew the smoke into the air above her.

"He's got a famous right hook," John said with a smile, giving me a little wink. "It was on the front page of the paper."

I didn't smile back. It may have been a clever thing to say, but I was still wanted by the police. I was still wondering where I was going to sleep that night.

Agatha looked at Mary, then at me. "So is everybody here, then?"

"Yes," John said. "We can get started."

"All right," she said, tapping ash onto the cement floor. "Well, where to begin? I know all of you, though you don't know me."

"Well," John said. "I've told you their names, but—"

Agatha held up her hand. "I've been to the Bay Area several times, watching. Ever since you reached out to me, John. I know all about you."

John stared at her for a moment and finally smiled.

"Told you," said Walter.

John laughed uncomfortably. It was strange to see him shaken up. Even at the rally, he'd seemed to have everything under control.

"Well, Agatha," John said. "We have Walter, from the Cahokian line. He has told us as much as he knows, but there are holes."

"Before we get started," Agatha said, "I want to make sure of what we're all talking about. The Zero line's goal is to stop the Players, stop Endgame before it happens for real, right?"

"Absolutely," Walter answered. "We're in one hundred percent. It's all or nothing."

"Good," she said. Despite her freckles and cigarette, she came across as an expert, like a warrior, like a sage. "Because that's the only way that you can make this work. Everybody has to agree; all the Players need to be stopped. We need to make them all see Endgame for what it is. If even one goes behind the other Players' backs and seeks the keys, they can still 'win' this goddamned thing." She spoke like someone a lot older than she looked. I had to admit, she was intimidating.

"Several years ago, I discovered documents about the origins of Endgame. I stole them from the archive at the La Tène compound," she continued, handing an unbound sheaf of paper over to John, who looked at it and then passed it to Walter. "Only a few people know about these papers. Stealing them led to my excommunication from my line. Worse, the day I started asking questions about this, they killed my sister. They told me to keep my mouth shut, and that if I ever spoke out against Endgame—that if I ever did something like speaking to you—I'd be killed. But I learned the truth. It cost me my family and the only life I've ever known, but I learned the truth. I've been on the run, in hiding ever since, but I swore to myself that I would find a way to stop Endgame. If you want to know the true story of Endgame, read this."

Walter flipped through the pages. He looked like he'd seen a ghost. He reached into his shirt pocket for the paper he had read to us, and then looked at the last page of Agatha's papers again.

"It's the same," Walter said, startled.

"The same as what?" Agatha said.

Walter handed his paper to her. "I stole this one from the Cahokian vault."

Agatha read through the paper, and Walter handed the unbound pages back to John.

"We don't know where it comes from," Agatha said. "It was written by a member of the Brotherhood of the Snake. I translated it from Latin. Annunaki is a Sumerian word, but it can mean lots of things: Sky People, Gods, Makers, aliens." She stepped over to John, turned a couple pages. "Read that. Out loud."

John cleared his throat.

The Annunaki's presence in the pages of human history becomes obvious, if you know where to look. Their fingerprints are everywhere. We find the Annunaki in the enormous stone heads of Central America's Olmec civilization, whose depictions of ancient Olmec rulers include elaborately carved stone headdresses—headdresses that are actually Annunaki helmets that protect against the harsh light of the sun, marking these rulers as aliens in disguise. Though a volcanic eruption in the 1st millennium BCE spelled the end of the Olmec, enough survived to pass their culture down to the civilizations that followed. And so even in the Maya and Aztec traditions, we can see shadows of the Sky People.

We have forgotten what we are; we have forgotten where and who we came from. And our creators will not take kindly to the oversight. The Annunaki are, as I have said, a proud race. They crave the worship and dread of their human servants.

They do not appreciate being forgotten.

The Annunaki have not been kind to us, but they have, in their way, been generous. Our success as a species is due only to their repeated and continual intervention. We have forgotten this too. We believe we owe nothing to any being other than ourselves. We believe we are the highest power in the universe. We have become proud, as proud as our old masters.

I fear the Annunaki will not abide it for much longer.

Endgame is their corrective, their reminder to us, the human race, that we are nothing but tools. Endgame is their way of putting us in our place. They defeated us once—they taught us humility, and obedience, and fear. We may have forgotten this, but the Annunaki have not.

They have great patience, these beings from the stars. But their patience is not infinite, and time grows short.

Heed me now: They are coming.

It is coming.

Endgame is coming.

We cannot prevent it. I, certainly, cannot prevent it. But I will do what I can—I have always done that.

I have inscribed what I know in these pages, and I will do everything in my power to circulate them among the lines, so that they and their Players can know the truth.

So that you can know the truth.

The room was silent.

It seemed so real, so rooted in history. If this document told the truth, Endgame sounded terrifying. I was starting to understand why the Zero line would do anything they could to prevent it from happening. But the more I thought about it, the more it seemed like a bigger task than even we could take on. If Endgame was real, was stopping it even possible?

"You can keep that copy," Agatha said. "Read it, every one of you."

"Has it stopped the La Tène line?" John asked as he stared at one of the pages.

"It was part of what convinced me to change my mind. But few agree with me, and of those few, none would dare risk their lives to speak up about it. Especially after I was cast out. Not many have seen this document or even know of its existence. I asked the wrong people about it—the power brokers within the line didn't want everyone to know that I was questioning Endgame. They're on the wrong side of this. I'm happy I'm out. So, of the twelve lines, you don't need to worry about La Tène. I'll take care of the La Tène Player."

"Tell us about the Players," Julia said. "Are there any like you?"

"What do you mean?" Agatha said. "Do you mean 'are they as well-trained' or 'are they thinking of quitting?'"

"Both, I guess."

"All are highly trained. One thing to remember, though, is that some of the Players are pretty young. Players have to be older than thirteen and younger than twenty. I'm twenty-two, and I'm sure I could easily take care of any tough guy. Face-to-face with someone my age—who's had as much training and experience as I've had—it would be a toss-up. But none of you, with the possible exception of Walter, should ever let yourself go one-on-one against a Player. They'll eat you alive. Even the thirteen-year-olds."

Tommy said, "So tell us what we're supposed to do. We've got eleven people we need to track down and talk into giving it all up, like you. And there's only twenty-one of us. First, how do we find them, and next, how do we stop them?"

Agatha stretched. "I can help you find them. La Tène have spies. All the lines do, don't they, Walter?"

Walter nodded.

"We know where everyone else is living," she said, taking Walter's bottle of whiskey and taking a healthy swig. "I still have enough friends in my line to get the latest intel. We can get to their compounds."

John spoke up. "But, Tommy, you're right. If we split up into smaller units, we wouldn't want to face them with just two or three of us. Agatha, Walter, and I have been talking, and we have a plan worked up. We'll vote on it, of course."

Henry folded his arms and audibly scowled. Henry was a Vietnam vet himself, and I got the impression that he didn't like looking up to someone who had gone AWOL—or the idea that a kid could take him out.

"First," John said, "Agatha, tell us more about the Calling."

She took another drag on her cigarette. "The Calling is a big event that will be seen by all the Players on a global scale. So we're not talking about an earthquake in Istanbul. It would be an earthquake in Istanbul *and* New York *and* Ulaanbaatar and every other place the Players are. When the Calling happens, each Player is sent a message about where to go and meet."

"How do you know?" I asked.

"I don't *know*," Agatha said. "That's what the council tells us. A real Calling has never happened. Legend and ancient documents are all we can go on."

"But that's a good thing, right?" John asked. "That means it's unlikely to happen anytime soon?"

"Yes, but we'll come back to that. For now, just think of the Calling as a disaster meant to get our attention. Natural disasters: earthquakes, fires, hurricanes, tornadoes. We would literally get a tornado in every city where a Player is living."

"So," Kat began, "tell me if I'm understanding this correctly. What we're going to do is have you, Agatha, direct us to the other eleven compounds and try to get all the Players to sign some kind of peace treaty?"

"No," Agatha said. "You can't get into a compound. If you went to my house and asked to see me, my line members would kill you on the spot and make it look like you disappeared. No one would ever see or hear from you again."

"Then what?" I asked. "There has to be something we can do. How did we find you?"

"You didn't. I found you. I found Walter originally. I've been looking for a way out for a long time now. There are a few other groups like yours—people who have stumbled onto Endgame. But no one as organized as you, no one who knows as much. You're our best shot." John opened a notebook. There were dozens of papers. He looked at us. "We've been communicating through letters for some time now."

"The thing is," Agatha said, "all of us Players are constantly under threat of death if things don't work out well. I've been keeping my eye on you. It took me months to believe you guys were real—and serious about stopping Endgame."

Kat spoke up again. The sarcasm dripped from her voice. "So is that *really* what we're going to do? Write letters to all of the Players?"

"No," John replied firmly. "We're going to fake a Calling."

CHAPTER NINE

"How the hell do we fake a Calling?" I asked. Agatha's story was convincing—she at least seemed sincere—but how could we fake an earthquake? Let alone do it simultaneously around the world?

"Here's the plan," John said. "I'll go through it and explain exactly what we need to do, and then we can discuss the details."

Mary looked at me. Her eyes were wide with excitement and determination. I could see it on her face: the talk was over. This was it—when Zero line finally met its purpose.

"We're going to use explosives," John said, "and we'll hit all twelve compounds at the same time, all over the world. With the explosives, we'll leave a signature—the symbol of the Munich Olympics. They'll take it as a message from the Makers that that's where they need to go. We'll be one step ahead of them, go there first, wait for them to arrive. And then, well, we'll stop the game."

Henry laughed sardonically. "That sure makes it sound easy."

"Well, let's take all the pieces individually," John said. "First, we use explosives that Lee and Lin have been smuggling to various warehouses all over the world."

I looked at Lee and Lin. They were not much older than me, but they were smugglers?

"We set the bomb, and Lee has made some thermite artwork."

Walter stepped up, holding a large roll of black fabric. As he opened it across the desk, I saw it was a symbol I'd seen in the papers—a spiral of rectangles. "This will burn into walls, floors, asphalt, lawns—wherever we put the bomb in each location."

"So they see this burning," Tommy said, "and they'll go to Munich?"

"Exactly," John said. "There's a replica of this symbol built into the Olympic plaza—big cement thing. I've seen pictures on the news and in the papers. Exactly the kind of place you'd see a group gathering."

Walter added, "Agatha is coming to help identify who is who so we can make sure we don't miss anyone."

"And we'll just walk up to these trained killers and kindly explain to them why they should not play the game?" I asked, getting suspicious.

"We'll use Agatha as an example. We'll convince them to go rogue, like her, when the *real* Calling finally occurs. We'll get them to join Zero line with us, abandon their lines and their lives as Players. Or else . . ."

"Or else what?" I asked.

Walter's eyes blazed. "Or we stop them permanently. Kill them. Send a powerful message back to their lines that people in this world won't stand for Endgame."

"*Kill* them?" Mary's hand gripped my leg tightly, and I turned to look her right in the eyes.

"Only if they won't listen, Mike," she said. "We'll all be there to explain. And Agatha's giving us more—she stole a lot of documents."

"You have to understand," Agatha said. "These people are trained in death. They can kill you with a bullet, a knife, or the side of their hand. And they're desensitized to pain and fear. Yes, I think we can reason with some of them. But not all of them. The most important thing is to stop them. And you can't hesitate, because they certainly won't. That's all there is to it." She leaned in. "Look, we can't stop the Makers. But we can stop the Players. We can convince them to end this multimillennium bloodline feud."

I took a deep breath and held it. If the Players didn't agree, we'd *stop* them. We'd kill them. Dead players couldn't win the game. And if no one won, no other lines would be wiped off the face of the planet. Killing 12—11—teenagers was going to save the world. I exhaled, looking Mary in the eyes. She believed this. And I wanted so badly to believe her, to *be* with her. I had a feeling that if I opted out of Zero line, a future with Mary was unlikely.

I exhaled.

"Won't this just be seen as a fake?" Bruce said. "Explosions from regular explosives?"

Agatha shook her head. "Not at their compounds. Coordinated explosions at those sensitive locations—and there's more to it. We don't have a long time to get ready for this. In addition to trainers, La Tène's best and brightest have been doing research. And in the course of their studies, they talked to some NASA scientists who said a meteor is headed our way—it may collide with Earth, or it just may fly through the atmosphere like a fireball. But this is the kind of thing that could be a sign of the Calling. I spoke with a friend about it last week and the asteroid should either impact or pass through the atmosphere around August 10th. No one can fake that."

She was right. No one could fake that. But that wasn't what made up my mind for me. It was staring at Mary that did it. We weren't from the same line. They'd said I was probably Minoan and she was probably La Tène. I didn't have anything else. I couldn't go back to Berkeley, couldn't go back to my parents. I needed to grow a beard just to stay free in town, and even then it was a crapshoot. So I could find an apartment, get a crappy job, and say good-bye to Mary, or I could go with her and do something that saved lives.

If it was true.

It had to be true.

Agatha disappeared after the meeting. The only evidence that she left was the book and a handful of loose papers, and John wanted to keep that to read it first—he said he'd pass it along soon enough. I wondered if anyone had followed her—was there a Walter-type person from the La Tène line who had watched Agatha come to our meeting and was going to kill us off if we got involved?

I wasn't the only one who wondered if it was all a ruse: an ex–La

Tène Player's plan to have us stop the other Players and clear the way for her line. Tommy and I talked about it, and he voiced the same concerns, when he brought me some clothes from our room. Mary had more confidence, but Mary always seemed to have confidence.

I spent the next five days in a motel on the edge of town. The plans were set and everyone was getting their affairs in order. All of Zero line was going to spend the several months between now and August at Mary's ranch, hiding on a back road somewhere, preparing and training, getting ready for the meteor to signal a Calling.

It was only a five-hour drive. Mary could go home on the weekends, not giving her parents any reason to think she wasn't continuing on with her internship.

She came to the motel every day. And on the last day, she spent the night.

CHAPTER TEN

In Reno—it was the closest city—we bought a few of the supplies that we didn't think we could get in Susanville: three pairs of walkie-talkies, four large canvas tents, an ax, a few cast-iron skillets and Dutch ovens, and canvas tarps. Walter was watching us buy everything, directing us.

Afterward we stopped at an army-surplus store, and Walter filled our carts with three huge rolls of camouflage netting, camo clothing for all of us (although Lin and Mary couldn't find sizes small enough for them, and Rodney couldn't find a size large enough for his beer gut). Most of the gear was Korean War– or World War II–era equipment. Walter found two ghillie suits and immediately bought them, even though they were in strange sizes—one very small and one very large. Our final stop in Reno was at the grocery store, where we stocked up on cases of canned goods: beans and corn and chili and peaches. We cleaned out their shelves of dehydrated potatoes and instant noodles.

We drove in silence for most of the rest of the way. Mary's ranch was still 45 miles past Susanville, on a turnoff that was obscured from most of the houses and buildings by a small row of hills.

We soon came to the familiar turnoff. We all stopped.

"We're going to be here for a while," I said. "What's the chance that your family comes up?"

"My parents normally wouldn't come up until fall for the hunting season. But if they find out that I'm not at Stanford, they might come up here to look for me."

John came to her window. "We're leaving Bruce, Jim, and Walter to watch the road. Eventually we'll all rotate through security detail, and the rest of us will head up—" He handed the map to Mary. "Pick the place they're least likely to check."

"Sheep Creek Canyon," she said, without even looking. "There's nothing up there—it's just rocky, and the creek is always dry. My brother and I used to go up on horseback, but Dad never had a reason to go there. Plus, it's got a good place we can set up a shooting range, and there's a small lake that's good for fishing."

"Can cars get up there?"

"It's rocky, but it's our best bet. At least for now."

He nodded and smiled. "I'm just being overcautious. I think we're going to be okay."

"I'm right there with you," she said.

"I'm excited for this," he said, patting the roof of Mary's car. "We're going to do good things. Can I fit in your car?"

"Sure," I said. "It'll be tight."

"Well, we're all good friends," he said with a laugh.

Henry took John's place in the van. Mary drove at the head of the caravan, the van right behind us. Henry stopped three times to drop off the security team—Walter first, by a group of trees, then Jim at the crest of a hill, and finally Bruce at the house. Each of them had a walkie-talkie, and John kept one for himself.

"Other than the M14, we have deer rifles and shotguns in there," Mary reminded John as we watched Bruce. "And not enough for everyone."

"I've thought about that," John said. "We're going to need to be training. Seriously, real training. Training until August is going to chew through a lot of ammunition."

I nodded and took a deep breath. I knew that what we were preparing for was going to be intense. It was going to be hard—the hardest thing I'd ever done, by a mile. I had nothing to compare it to.

I took another deep breath and exhaled slowly. I told myself that it was going to be okay. And I thought about the viciousness that Agatha had talked about: the cold-blooded murderers we were going to have to stop. I knew it had to be done—for the preservation of humanity. I was committed. But that didn't chase all my fears away.

John handed the walkie-talkie to me and turned the knob to increase the volume.

Walter's voice: "Okay, I'm about thirty-five feet up the fir. I've got a good look in every direction. I see two cars coming from the south. Wait—let me look through my scope."

"They have rifles?" Mary asked.

"Just as telescopic sights," John said.

"Okay," Walter said. "A Ford Galaxie and a station wagon. I think it's a Chevy Brookwood. Galaxie's blue and Brookwood's tan. Neither of them is slowing down."

Mary's eyes never left the road as she spoke. "What will they do if they see my dad's car? They won't shoot him, will they?"

"No," John said. "No way. The whole point is to watch him come and do what he came to do, and then let him leave. Hey—this is a big mud puddle. Is there a road around it so we don't leave tracks?"

"Yeah," Mary said. She followed side road by side road. We passed several outbuildings: two barns, a toolshed, a birthing pen, multiple corrals, water tanks, and a utility shed. And Mary said there were more in the fields and woods.

Near the canyon road, John got on the walkie-talkie and told Eugene and Kat, who were driving in a Jeep—definitely the most rugged vehicle with us—to go up the other three canyons and see if anyone was out there.

The Sheep Creek road was worse than Mary had described it. It was narrow—frighteningly narrow, with a 50-foot drop on one side. And the roadbed was nothing but rocks the size of baseballs. The wide van probably had the worst time of all, sliding in the scree, perilously close to the edge.

After half an hour the road we were on widened, and Mary pulled to the side. The other cars behind us did too.

"Here we are," Mary said. "Just right up this embankment there's a meadow. I used to bring my horse out here."

Mary went to the trunk of her car and found a saw while we were all climbing out. She handed it to me. "We need to cover the cars with pine boughs—a lot of these ranchers have airstrips and little Cessnas." John turned to Henry and Phyllis. "Get these tents up. Follow Mary—she'll show you where."

Mary was listening to the walkie-talkie.

I nearly stripped a couple of pines, sawing the low boughs and putting one after another onto the car. Before I could finish, the tents were all erected, and they'd spread the camo netting across the top of them and the cars.

Every five or 10 minutes Eugene reported that they had cleared a building and were moving on to another. The worst wait was when they took a drive up Christmas Tree Canyon to check on a small hunting cabin. It was 45 minutes up and 45 minutes back. Henry and Tyson spent the time splitting wood for a campfire. Douglas lit one cigarette with the end of the last one. Rodney surprised us all with sandwiches, and I could see why his deli had been so lucrative.

Finally Jim gave the word that Eugene and Kat were back from the hunting cabin, the last outbuilding where we might find Mary's extended family, and all was clear. He was stopping at the house again.

Mary and I sat in the grass and talked, and I wished, not for the last time, that we were alone and had never heard of Endgame or Zero line.

CHAPTER ELEVEN

The next morning I woke early. Tommy was next to me on one side and Larry and Bruce were on the other. I was the only one up, and I carefully got dressed, trying not to disturb anyone else. I stepped out of the tent and checked my shoes for bugs, a lesson I'd learned in the Forest Service: it wouldn't be unusual to find beetles and ants in there, and once, I found a scorpion.

There was no sunlight in the meadow, and the sky was still gray. I walked over a large fallen tree to where Walter, John, Jim, and Julia were looking at a map. Barbara and Kat had made a small fire and were warming themselves by it.

"What are you guys doing up so early?" I asked.

"Trying to put together a training regimen," Walter said without taking his eyes off the map. He shook his head. "I'm telling you, John. There's nothing we can do in time to get these people ready for direct combat with a Player."

"I don't think they can beat one," John said. "But training results in discipline. And even if they can survive a minute longer in a fight with a Player, that's an extra minute that someone with a gun can help."

"It can give them complacency. Let's worry about guns first, and then I'll see what I can put together."

"Bruce knows karate," Julia said. "He said it in the car on the way up. We could put him in charge."

Walter didn't answer, but John nodded. "Good idea. So what do we need for the gun range? A pistol for everyone, and a rifle too?"

"How are we going to get our guns over to Germany?" I asked.

"Lee and Lin," John replied. "Three weeks before we go, we'll ship them, and they'll work their smuggling magic."

"There are twenty-one of us," I said. "Where are we going to get that many guns?"

"Excellent question," John said, smiling and clapping me on the shoulder. "We're picking a team to do just that, and we thought you were a good candidate."

"A good candidate for what?"

"I have rifles," Mary said, as if she wasn't sure of what John meant. "We can use them like we always do."

"We need more close-quarters guns, I'm thinking. A deer rifle might get you one sniping shot at a Player, but if you miss and they run, then it's all over. We need to have people on the ground with pistols, submachine guns, assault weapons. Anything semi- or fully automatic. We need to train with them, and we'll need to get them to the Calling."

"I can teach gun safety," Julia said. "Proper grip too, I guess. But even that's going to change since we don't know what kind of guns everyone will be using."

"So," Walter said, looking much more sober than I was used to seeing him, "we're going to rob a gun store."

"What?" Bruce said, wandering up behind us. "Maybe you don't understand gun people. But they don't get scared and hand you their wallet and tell you everything is okay and please don't shoot them. Gun-store owners have a sawed-off shotgun behind the counter, and they eagerly wait for the day they get to use it."

Walter seemed unmoved. "If you did it, Bruce, how would you do it?"

"Well, I wouldn't do it."

"If you had to."

He sighed. "Send someone in first to scout the place, but they can't look like a scout. They have to know about guns, and they just go in and out. Just go in to buy some ammo. Count how many customers are in there. If there're customers in the store, they're just as bad as the guy at the counter—they could be carrying. You need to look and see if there're any employees in the back, but without looking like you're checking the back."

He rubbed the sleep from his eyes and continued. "Then, if there aren't customers, and if there isn't someone in the back, you hit the place fast and hard—rush it, guns up, everybody ready to shoot the guy behind the counter—before he can get his shotgun. And time it perfectly with your scout customer: he cuts the telephone as soon as you go in."

Walter scratched at his beard and then lit a cigarette. "That's about how I figured it too." He took a long pull on the cigarette and blew the smoke out his nostrils. "Julia will be our scout. She knows plenty about guns. Our assault team will be me, Bruce, Mike, and Tommy."

"No," John said to Walter. "If shit hits the fan, we can't afford to lose you."

"And we're expendable?" Bruce asked.

"I want you to be the squad leader," John said, lowering his voice. "I need you to clean out that store—rifles, handguns, and ammo, lots and lots of ammo. We don't need deer rifles. Guys are coming home from 'Nam and need money, and they're selling their souvenirs. I'm talking anything full auto, or something they're selling out of the back: AK-47s, MAC-10s, AR-15s, grenades, grenade launchers, mortars. You'll know it when you see it. The good stuff. But clear out everything. Take the van."

"I want at least one more guy," Bruce said. "I've got Julia as scout, and she can cut the phone lines, but that just leaves me with Mike and Tommy. I want at least one more with real combat experience."

"I've only shot at targets with a rifle," I said, feeling my heart begin to race. "Nothing close. Never a person."

John clapped me on the shoulder and said, "Mike's got one mean punch. I think he's going to teach us all a little bit of hand-to-hand combat in the next couple of months."

I scoffed. "I've heard you're not supposed to bring a knife to a gunfight. But just bringing fists? I think the gun would win."

"Right," John said. "I mean, we'll give you a gun, but you have instincts. That's the key."

"Give me Eugene too," Bruce said. "He knocked over a couple banks. This is a little similar."

"Okay." Walter nodded. "Eugene is out front watching the entrance. Take Lee with you and switch him out."

Bruce agreed, and went to his tent to get his gun.

I found Mary sitting on a large rock by the fire pit, holding her hands out to warm them. "What's up?" she asked as I sat down next to her, and she put a hand on my knee.

"We're going to rob a gun store," I said, trying to sound as unconcerned as possible, but inside I was filled with fear. A month ago, I had never committed any crime worse than a parking ticket. Now I'd punched a cop and was about to commit armed robbery. I was only at 51 percent agreeing with this plan. We needed the guns, sure, but what if the shop owner got to his weapon and shot us all? I'd thought getting arrested was the worst thing that could happen to me. Now I couldn't believe what I'd gotten myself into.

I could still walk away from this. I could take Mary's car and just head out on the open road—go to Canada and live off my 3,000 dollars, get a job, get an apartment. Hide.

"Mike," Mary said, leaning against me. "Don't let anything stupid happen. I don't know what I'd do without you."

"Mary. I'll be fine."

"That's what everyone says. Just promise me you'll be smart, stay out of the line of fire."

"I will," I said. "That's what John told me. I swear, they said they want me because I can throw a punch, but I'm sure they just need an extra hand loading the van with all the boxes of ammo."

She turned to look at me. "Mike, I really care about you."

I stared back at her, our faces inches apart. I touched her face with my cold hands. "I care about you too. More than I ever have about anyone."

We kissed, silent and slow. Her face was cold, but her lips were warm, and she put her arms around me. I promised her I'd take every precaution.

She could have talked me out of it. I half expected her to. But she didn't. She wanted me to go. I think that was the moment when everything changed for me—when I fully embraced Zero line. When I knew I'd follow Mary wherever she took me.

I looked across the fire. Lee and Lin were grinning at us.

I pointed across the fire. "Lee, you're moving up to a guard post."

"Cool," he said with a nod.

"Be careful," Mary said, looking at me. There were a thousand words in her eyes. A hundred emotions. But all that came out was "Be careful."

"I don't want to do this," I whispered.

"It's okay to be scared," she said. "But that's courage, right? It's being afraid and doing it anyway."

She held me by my shoulders and looked me in the eye. "Be careful."

"We will."

CHAPTER TWELVE

Bruce, John, and Walter decided that we'd go all the way to Redding instead of just Susanville. It was a bigger town, and one that we'd—hopefully—never have to go back to. It added two hours to the drive each way, which gave the highway patrol two extra hours to catch us if they caught wind of what we'd done. But we needed good guns, and this was our best bet.

We woke Eugene and filled him in on the plan.

"I don't suppose this place will have any night-vision devices?" Eugene asked. "Porky Pig coulda come over that rise last night when I was on watch and I never woulda seen him."

"It's a gun store, not an army-surplus store," Bruce said as we climbed into the van. "Besides, those things have got to be so expensive that no one would ever let one wind up in a gun shop in Redding."

"Who knows?" Julia said. "Like John said, vets coming home might have anything with them."

"What's the deal with you?" Bruce asked. "You're an artist. I would expect you to be one of those hippie antigun types. Why are you hanging out with us?"

"Why are any of us doing this?" Julia asked. "We're trying to save the world."

"There's got to be more than that to this."

"Well," she said, "I was too young to take part in the civil rights protests. Now I finally have the chance to do my part for a cause that's important to me. I can't just sit back and let Endgame happen."

We drove on through the farms and forests of Northern California, and every time I saw a cabin or cottage, I imagined Mary and me living there, getting old together there.

I dozed off, and Tommy woke me up just as we came into Redding. We drove around for a little while, just looking at businesses, before Bruce finally stopped at a gas station and tore the map from the phone book while I topped off the tank.

Aside from pawnshops, which Bruce said would be more trouble than they were worth, there was only one gun shop listed: Dead Zone Guns 'n' Ammo. Once Bruce figured out the maps, it was a short five-minute drive.

"You know what you're going to do, Julia?" Bruce asked.

"Relax," she said, "or you're going to get people killed. I know what I'm doing. Pull the van right there, right under the phone line."

The store was a freestanding building, not part of a strip mall or anything like that. It was cinder block, painted white, with one door in the front and no door anywhere else that we could see. We parked in the back, out of sight from the street and the front door.

Julia had to climb through the back of the van to get out—Bruce had pulled in so tightly against the wall and under the phone line that she couldn't open her door. She was dressed in a pair of very tight-fitting bell-bottom jeans, a plaid shirt (strategically unbuttoned to show just enough), and a pair of worn boots.

As soon as she was gone, Bruce climbed in the back and handed a submachine gun to Eugene and another to Tommy. "These are simple. S&W M76. Okay, this tab switches from single shot to full auto. Let's leave it on full. Now hit the magazine release button here to put in a fresh mag. Easy. Take an extra each. Always best to have extra. Now pull back on the charging handle to chamber a round. Okay. You're ready."

"What about me?" I asked.

"Mike," Bruce said, "I only have so many guns, and none of the deer rifles from Mary's gun safe are going to be useful in there. You're going to be watching the door, making sure nobody comes in behind us.

But if something happens, here's this: M1911. Simplest pistol there is. Safety is up here. Just use your thumb. It's already loaded. Just pull the slide back and it's ready to rock and roll."

I looked at the pistol, hefted its weight in my hand. It weighed more than I expected. "How many bullets are in here?"

"Thirteen," Bruce said.

I pointed the gun at the floor and pulled back the slide.

Bruce nodded. "Now you just point and pull the trigger. Just try not to. Okay, guys. Masks. Eugene, you cover the door Julia saw."

We all pulled our ski masks on—we'd picked them up in Reno too. There was a knock on the van door, and then it opened. Julia stood there with two boxes of shotgun shells. "Only the owner. There's a door to a back room, but it was closed, so I don't know if anyone's in there. No customers."

Julia pulled a pair of bolt cutters from the van and moved to the front to climb up to the phone line.

"Okay, guys," Bruce said. "We hit it hard and fast, before the owner has a chance to get his gun. Eugene and I go in first, then Tommy, then Mike. Let's go!"

Bruce and Eugene jumped from the van.

They ran to the front door and threw it open. Tommy and I were right behind them.

"Don't touch it," Bruce barked at the man behind the counter, who was just ducking down as Bruce burst through the door. "Stand up real easy, you son of a bitch. Show me your hands."

Very slowly, the man stood.

Eugene hopped over the counter and trained his gun on the store owner too.

The shop was dark, compared to the midday light outside, and wood paneling gave everything a golden hue. There was a glass counter that ran the length of the shop, turning at the end to make an L shape, and behind it the walls were lined with long guns: shotguns at our end, deer rifles next, and then combat weapons—submachine guns, assault weapons, and antiques. I didn't know guns well enough to put names to any of them, except to say that the assault weapons looked like the guns I saw every night on the news, being carried by soldiers in Vietnam. Some of the submachine guns looked vaguely like ours, but others looked tiny—I'd seen them in movies, being carried by bodyguards. The glass counter was filled with pistols, revolvers— every type of handgun. The only thing on our side of the counter was a floor-to-ceiling rack of ammunition.

The steel door was at the far end of the L. We guessed there was no back door to the building, so it was likely an office or storeroom. Maybe a bathroom.

I tried to aim my gun at the shopkeeper and found that my hand was trembling far too much to keep the sight on him. I used both hands, and that barely helped. Sweat poured down my back. I turned back to watch the door.

"You've got three guns trained on you," Bruce said. "Are you right-handed or left?"

"Right," the man answered.

"Use your left, just two fingers. Pick up your gun and place it on the counter."

We all watched as he reached for the gun. I kept glancing back and forth between the owner and the door.

"Put your other hand on your bald old head," Bruce said.

He obeyed, and then continued to reach for the gun. And then he shouted, "Morris!"

The steel door flew open, and an elderly man fired blindly at us. The shopkeeper raised the barrel of his sawed-off shotgun, but Eugene and Bruce blasted him in a cacophony of gunfire. I fired at Morris, once, twice, and then Bruce turned his gun on the old man.

In less than five seconds it was all over.

"Nice work," Bruce said to me. "Next time just aim a little higher and . . ."

We both saw Tommy at the same time. He was slumped against the back wall, behind all of us. His green shirt was black with blood. I dropped to my knees beside him, immediately checking for a pulse, knowing that of course there wouldn't be one. He'd taken Morris's shotgun blast full in the chest.

This was nothing like the movies. No eyes open to tell me a last request, to tell me it was okay, to make an ironic joke. He was just dead.

"We need to get the hell out of here," Eugene said.

"This was your fault, jackass!" I yelled at Eugene. "You were supposed to cover that back door."

"I did! As soon as I saw the guy, I dropped him."

I felt hot tears on my cheeks. "I don't give a shit, man. Tommy is fucking dead because of you."

"Come on," Bruce said, and then pointed at my arm. "It looks like you're hit, Mike."

For the first time, I noticed that I was bleeding down my right arm. I pulled up my T-shirt sleeve and saw two entry wounds in my shoulder. I didn't feel any pain, but knew I would soon.

"I can patch that," Eugene said, taking hold of my arm.

"The hell with you," I snapped, shrugging him off me.

I should have been watching, I thought. I was supposed to be with this group because of my instincts, but what good had they done me? What good had they done Tommy? I shouldn't have been there. It should have been John the Green Beret, or Henry, or Jim, or anyone else who actually knew what they were doing. I was there, I was supposed to be protecting everyone, and now Tommy was dead.

Bruce had already found the keys locking the chains on the long guns. "Guys, I said come on."

Julia came in and saw Tommy's body. "What the fuck happened? Oh my God."

"Yeah," Bruce said. "Help us with these."

We weren't picky. We scrambled to collect every assault rifle and shotgun in the shop and carried them, one in each hand, to the van.

When we had a full layer across the floor of the van, Bruce and I laid a tarp over the top of them, and Bruce started bringing out pistols. He ordered Eugene to start packing ammunition into boxes he found in the storeroom.

Bruce stopped me from carrying and had Julia bandage my arm—I was bleeding everywhere. After she patched me up, I went back into the store to help with the last load.

Bruce had two assault rifles in his hands, and Eugene was carrying a box of ammo, when we heard a voice: "Morris, I've been trying to get you on the horn for ten minutes. What's with this call I got about gunfire . . ."

A sheriff walked into the shop. He froze, eyes going from Tommy to Eugene to Bruce to me.

He started for his gun, but mine was in my hand—I didn't have a holster. I fired, just like Bruce had told me, but aiming a little higher: sternum, throat, chin, face.

CHAPTER THIRTEEN

I sat and stared at the sheriff while the others flew through the store, filling boxes with ammo and searching for anything else of value. Time seemed to stop for me. I saw the sheriff's face, saw the cop's face back at the protest, saw the hole in Tommy's chest.

Bruce found all the Vietnam contraband in the back room: dozens of grenades, three claymores, five flak vests, two portable radios, and a mortar with four rounds. I had no idea what we'd even do with half the stuff. Bruce drove very slowly back toward Mary's ranch. As my head began to clear, I could see that he was driving five miles under the speed limit, giving the highway patrol no reason to pull him over—and avoiding the risk of a bump in the road setting our whole van ablaze.

We'd had to leave Tommy there, after putting all the bodies in a pile to make them harder to identify. The building was cinder block, but the gun mounts were wood, and the rest of the walls had wood paneling. The incendiary grenade we threw onto the pile would cause havoc for a small town's law investigation. With any luck, they wouldn't even realize that there were four bodies there. One of them was my roommate. My friend.

But we needed the guns, didn't we? We were trying to save the world. We'd agreed to be full participants of this group. If we hadn't done this, then we wouldn't be prepared for the mission ahead. And we had to stop the Players. We had to. I had to fight even harder now, so that Tommy's death wouldn't have been in vain. I'd make it up to him.

Then something occurred to me. What would Mary think when I told her I'd killed someone? This was so much worse than just punching a cop in the middle of a protest. I'd ended another person's life. The whole reason I'd gotten involved in Zero line was for Mary. The whole reason I'd gone on this robbery was because she'd told me she couldn't do this without me. But would she still want me when she found out what I'd done?

Mary had told me to come. She'd known what could happen. It wasn't her innocence I should worry about—it was mine. I was a murderer.

I felt filthy, covered in other people's blood and my own. My arm stung and ached at the same time. I had buckshot in me—the buckshot from the same blast that had killed Tommy.

Julia sat in the front seat while Bruce drove. Eugene was in the back, silently staring out the window.

I moved a box of ammo and reached down to pick up an assault rifle with a scope. I rooted through the box of ammo until I found one that said 7.62X51.

"Julia? Do these match this gun?"

"Yes," she said. "Why do you want to know?"

Bruce looked back at me through the rearview mirror.

"I want to be a scout. I want you to leave me at the front when we get back to the ranch." I couldn't see anyone at the ranch. Not like this. If I did, I'd crack. My doubts about Endgame would come flooding out, and I couldn't voice them. They couldn't be true. If they were, all would be lost.

"Can't do that," they both said, almost in unison.

"You've never shot that gun before," Bruce said. "I'm not going to put you in charge of guarding the camp."

"And your arm's going to need attention. You've got buckshot in there," Julia said. "If you don't get that out, it'll get infected."

"I can't go back to camp," I said.

"Why not?" Bruce asked. "And it better not have anything to do with you shooting that sheriff. You saved all of our lives."

"Four people are dead right now who woke up this morning feeling fine. Lives are destroyed."

"Lives get destroyed every day, damn it," Bruce said, "by car accidents or house fires or getting a knock on the door from the Department of Defense. You need to suck it up and realize that we're not on a Boy Scout camping trip. This is war. War to save humanity. Unfortunately, there will be casualties."

I looked down at the floor beneath me, guns stacked six inches deep. At the blood covering my arm and shirt. At the gun I'd used to kill the sheriff. *I don't know if I can do this,* I thought.

Bruce turned off the road. I hadn't realized we were back at the Golden Pines Ranch. Even though I knew where our scouts were, I couldn't see them.

"Kat bought medical supplies in Reno," Julia said, not looking back at me. "She's not an ER nurse, but I think she should know how to suture a wound."

We got to the camp to see that they'd been busy. Tables had been built around a real fire pit, and it looked like someone had shot a deer, which they were cooking over the fire.

I took the automatic rifle with me and two boxes of ammunition. I still had the pistol Bruce had given me, and I tucked it in the back of my pants.

The camp rushed toward the van.

Mary ran over to throw her arms around me, but I waved her off, and she saw the pained look on my face.

"Mike, what happened? Kat! Kat! Get over here with your kit."

I sat on a log away from the group. I dropped the two flak jackets that I'd taken for Mary and me, and on top I set the pistol and then the rifle. Walter had given me a look when I took the jackets, but he didn't say anything. I was going to make sure Mary and I were safe. They could argue with me later.

"Mike," Mary said, kneeling next to me, "talk to me. What happened? You're shot."

My chin began to quiver. "Tommy . . . he's dead." And then I fell apart into tears.

Training would start in earnest now. We had a stockpile of ammo, and more than enough guns.

John approached me, and I stared up at him with wet cheeks.

"Mike, I'm sorry about Tommy, but you did the right thing by taking out the sheriff," he said. "Your first kill is always the hardest. Remember, you saved the mission and protected Zero line. We're one step closer to saving the world from Endgame."

He started to walk away and then stopped, turning back around.

"Let's have a memorial for Tommy tonight."

"We'll be there," Mary said.

Kat knelt down in the dirt and pulled back my blood-soaked sleeve.

"That looks worse than it is, Mike. You're going to be fine. Just fine."

It was a lie. Total bullshit. I would never be fine again.

ENDGAME

THE ZERO LINE CHRONICLES

— VOLUME 2 —

FEED

CHAPTER ONE

I knelt in the rocks, sharp stones digging into my knees and shins, and placed the bomb. It was small, about the size of two bricks, and was contained inside a cardboard box. There wasn't much to it: a chunk of C4—a plastic explosive with the consistency of soft clay—a few components of an alarm clock, and four D-size batteries. I took the two wires from the clock, twisted them onto the leads of the detonators— short metal cylinders. I pushed the detonators into the C4.

C4 was supposed to be extremely stable—you could drop it or shoot it or rip it in half, and it wouldn't explode. It needed an electric current to detonate. And I'd just given it that electric current. It was ready to blow, and sweat dripped down my forehead onto my nose and into my eyes.

This wasn't the first time that I'd done this: I'd prepped a dozen practice bombs, where the C4 was replaced with Play-Doh. This was the first time I'd done it for real, though: real batteries, real detonators, real explosive. My fingers trembled with every step.

I looked over at Kat. She was older than me by five years: 24. She was tall and pretty, with brown hair that shone like copper in the evening sun. Eugene was with her, the two of them unrolling a tarp that had been painted with a thick and heavy coat of thermite. The design was a spiraling series of rectangles—the logo for the Munich Olympics. At the bottom was painted "9-5-1972."

This was how we would "invite" the Players to meet with us. John and Walter didn't know for certain how a real Calling worked. Walter had said that the Cahokians believed that there would be a sign from heaven—possibly something violent. The only thing they knew for sure was that it would be unmistakable, and the Players would know where they were to gather. So we'd use bombs to get their attention, and use the thermite to burn the Olympic logo into the ground.

When they had the tarp unrolled, Eugene unrolled the fuse and pulled out a lighter.

I hit the timer on the clock, and it started to count down.

I stood up and walked to them. Eugene touched the unlit lighter to the fuse, and we all headed for the trees. As we walked, Bakr, the man who'd made the bombs, walked past me, heading toward the bomb to check it.

Eugene held his hand out to me, and I slapped it, reluctantly.

"Nice job, man," he said.

"Let's see what Bakr says," Kat said, stopping at the tree line and turning around.

I looked back at him, 30 yards away in a natural low spot in the forest. It was muddy in the middle, which we'd worked around, but he had boots on and walked right through the mud, just as he'd done for the other groups who had practiced this exercise. We were now the eighth group to practice with the real equipment. Four more to go. All the Zero line members were getting their chance, because practicing with Play-Doh was one thing but sticking detonators into real C4 was something completely different. I hadn't expected to be so intimidated by the bomb.

Bakr turned around and gave a thumbs-up sign. I'd done it right.

"Nice job, Mike," Kat said, and squeezed my arm.

"We've rehearsed this enough," I said. "I should be able to do it in my sleep."

Walter spoke without looking at me. "Don't get cocky. Forget a single step in there and you could blow yourself to hell."

"I know," I said. "That's not what I meant. I'm just saying we've practiced enough. We're ready. As ready as we can be."

"You and your team need to be a well-oiled machine," John said.

Then why is Eugene with me? I thought. The whole group blamed Eugene for Tommy's death—at least I assumed they did. It was obvious in the way they talked to him, talked about him, and spoke about Tommy. Eugene screwed up and Tommy had died. And now I was in a squad with him and Kat.

I sat down on the hillside next to Mary. Why we'd gotten split up, I couldn't explain. We had grown so close throughout the summer spent on her family's ranch. We each knew how the other thought, how we'd respond in any given situation. But she was leaving with Bruce—just the two of them—going after the Olmec.

"Nice job," she said as I sat.

"It's easy," I replied. "Like I said, we've done it so much."

"But this time the bomb is real. Come on, I had my turn, and it wasn't the same thing at all. I kept freaking out that there was going to be a spark—from the clock wires, or even the static electricity in my clothes. Nerves, you know?"

"Yeah," I said. "Nerves. I think we've all had our final turns. No more until the real deal. How's the weather in Veracruz this time of year?"

"Shut up," she said, and laughed a little. "It's not like this is a vacation."

"You get to go to the beaches of Mexico, and I get to go to Istanbul and Baghdad."

"It's going to be hot."

"You think Baghdad isn't?"

"It's probably more humid in Mexico."

Kat squatted down next to us and laughed. "You can wear a bikini in Veracruz. I have to wear a hijab in Baghdad's heat."

Bakr took the disassembled bomb to the west side of the depression, and Bruce and Eugene rolled the tarp up again and then hauled it back to the bomb. Bakr had grown up in Baghdad—one of the cities Eugene, Kat, and I were going to, but he wasn't part of our team. He said he didn't want to be accidently recognized.

"Rodney, Jim, Julia," John said. "You're up."

Jim was right behind me, and he stood up.

"Last time," John said to him. "We're off to Reno tomorrow, so make it count."

Reno tomorrow. That gave us a week before the meteor would come and we'd have to go off to plant the bombs—to send the invitations to the Calling. It would only be a few more weeks before we were all reunited in Munich at the Olympics.

Weeks that I would be away from Mary. Weeks that Bruce would spend pretending to be her boyfriend, on a vacation on the sapphire shores of Mexico, drinking margaritas and tequila, and—

"What are you thinking about?" Mary asked.

Fifty yards away from us, Julia had picked up the bomb and Rodney and Jim were carrying the tarp into position.

I kept my voice low. "I think you should ask John to swap you out for Kat. Or Eugene—even better."

She didn't immediately answer. She leaned back on her elbows, watching the bomb being moved into place.

I knew what she'd say by this point. We'd been over it a dozen times.

"Mike," she said, a sigh in her voice.

Walter reached over and smacked me lightly in the head. He wasn't quiet when he spoke. "Get over it already. We've been practicing in these groups for six weeks. I'm not going to change it at the last minute. You have the streets of Istanbul memorized. You learned conversational Turkish. You need to worry about the plan now, and about your love life later."

"I don't speak Turkish. I've learned how to count to ten and how to ask directions to the hotel."

John looked at me. "We'll all be back together soon."

"I just think that Mary and I work well together. Look," I said, pointing at the group planting the bomb and tarp. "Jim and Julia are staying together."

"Because they know how to work together," Walter said, his tone cold as ice. "You don't. You think you do, but in every combat exercise we did, you'd ignore mission objectives to defend Mary."

"So you're putting her in a different unit so I'll be less worried about her?" I said rhetorically. I knew his answers.

"We're saving the world. We have to make sacrifices. You've never seemed to understand that."

"I don't understand that?" I said, standing up. "Are you fucking kidding me? I've given up all my life's goals. I gave up my admission to Berkeley. I gave up my life savings. I killed a man for Christ's sake. I've given it all up, and you can't cut me a little slack."

"Quiet," John said, watching Julia kneeling next to the bomb.

"I asked to be on a different team," Mary said. "You know that."

"I know. And I'm asking for you to change your mind."

"It's too late to change," John said. "Even if she wanted it. She knows Spanish. Four years in school. Bruce does too. Not to mention all of the intel she's memorized—and the intel you've memorized. Tell me, where in Veracruz is the best place to find black-market guns? The best place to hide if the police come after you?"

"I don't need to know it. Mary already does."

"What if she gets shot?"

Then what's the point? I thought. I believed in Zero line's goals, but I had my priorities, and Mary was placed above the mission.

Walter spoke. "Where do you get the bomb and tarp in Turkey?"

I ignored him.

"I'm asking you a question, Mike. Where do you get the bomb in Turkey?"

I glared at him. "The Fethiye fish market, from an anchovy dealer named Salomao."

"And what's it going to be packaged in?"

"A case of fish with a false bottom. Look, I know what you're getting at."

"Then shut up," Walter said.

Mary looked at me and took my hand.

Something inside me wondered if I was losing her. Yes, I did defend her. Of course I would. I wasn't an unfeeling bastard like Walter. If chasing down Players meant leaving Mary on her own, of course I would stay with her.

I knew the Players were tough—Walter and Agatha had drilled that into us—but we would operate as a team. In every practice—the daily runs and obstacle courses, the shooting drills, the bomb practice, the sales dialogues—we were a team, and we stuck together. The only times where I changed the plan and defended Mary were when there was an error: when we were attacked from behind, or when we lost radio communication. That wasn't a reason to tear Mary and me apart. It was adapting to the changing conditions.

Julia stood up from the bomb, and Rodney touched the fuse with his unlit lighter.

Bakr once again trotted out to disassemble the bomb, readying it for squad nine, which was just John by himself. John and Walter were taking on their jobs alone. We had so few of us that this was the only option. Groups of three—like me, Eugene, and Kat—had two targets to hit. Others had just one.

I squeezed Mary's hand. I wanted all of this to be over.

John stood up. "We're leaving for Reno tomorrow afternoon. We have more practice ahead of us before our flights next week. And we've scouted out a good place to watch for the meteor."

CHAPTER TWO

"We still have more training we need to do," Walter said. All of us were back in camp, except for Tyson, who was staying out front guarding the gate. "We've started surveillance training, but we need to do it in a city environment. We need to teach you how to follow people, both in a car and on foot. So we're going to hit it hard this week—we'll need this to track down the Players when they get to Germany."

Rodney spoke. "I know we've been over this already, but are we really sure about this? Does that meteor affect our plans? My squad is supposed to go to the Aksumite compound first. Ethiopia. That's on the other side of the world. They wouldn't have seen any meteor."

"It's a trigger event," Walter said with a hint of anger. "It would make the news, and this is what the Cahokian line believed would be the signal. A big natural event. It could have been an earthquake in Rome or a tsunami in Japan. Some big event that sets everything into motion. Nature is sending us a big break, but now it's our turn to use it and send out these invitations to the Players."

"But why bombs?" Lee asked. He was smiling—obviously not concerned about the morality of bombing anyone. After all, he'd been the one to design the thermite and smuggle all the bombs out to our destinations. "We want to call them, not kill them, right?"

"It's what Walter knows and Agatha described," John said. "She said that the invitation would be violent. It sends a message."

"Speaking of which," Henry said, "why does the La Tène get a free pass? Why aren't we stopping him?"

"We've been over this before," John said. "Agatha said she'd handle it.

We have to trust her. She has no reason to betray us since she's been excommunicated by her line."

"And remember," John said, "our goal is not to kill these people. We're stopping them. We're going to, hopefully, enlighten them."

"And more importantly," Walter said tiredly, "as I've said a hundred times: this is not a real Calling. It takes more to win Endgame than just killing the other competitors. You have to follow clues and solve a puzzle. Even if Agatha is lying to us about the La Tène Player, he couldn't win anything."

Henry stood up and started to pace. "Do we know that? This meteor is a big deal. Too big, I think. How do we know it won't set off a real Calling and game?"

"All the more reason to hurry," John said.

"Right," Walter said, "let's just worry about the task at hand. We have a lot to do, every one of us, and it's going to be dangerous and deadly serious. We can't lose sight of what we're about to do. We need to get to Reno, train there, and then get moving."

Henry waved his hand dismissively.

"Don't be discouraged," John said. "We know that there will be problems. We just need to remember that there's twenty of us and eleven of them. We're luring them onto our turf. They'll all be on their guard, but they'll be waiting for the other Players at that sunburst plaza. They won't be ready when we knock on their doors, wanting to talk. Yes, we'll have guns, bombs, anything we need, but that's the backup plan. The ideal is that we convince them all, and they walk away."

"And if someone turns on us?" Henry asked. "You've made them out to be killing machines."

"They're also very savvy. Smart, tactically and strategically. A good argument, well made, could do wonders," said John. "Yes, there are some vicious sons of bitches in the group. For them, a bullet might be the only solution. But most of them should listen to reason."

I walked to the supply tent—it wasn't so much a tent as it was a waterproof shelter built of tarps—and got a couple of boxes of 7.62 ammo. Ever since the gun-store robbery, I hadn't been able to sit still. I needed to be doing something, and sitting around camp wasn't one of those things.

Shooting helped, sometimes. I practiced almost entirely to fire at long range; the precision and concentration that it required helped drive thoughts of the sheriff out of my mind. I could hear someone coming up behind me.

"Hey, Mike."

"Mary," I said, and smiled for the first time all day.

"I caught the tail end of Henry's rant. Can't take these bullets on the plane. Well, not as carry-on, at least," she said, with a quick smile. She set down a box of 9 mm hollow points and pulled her Beretta from her hip.

I pulled the ear protection down into place. I picked a target at 200 yards, and took the straight-forward stance that Walter had recommended to me months ago. I made sure Mary had earplugs in before I let off my first round. The target was a one-inch sheet of steel. I'd hit it hundreds of times by now. It took me about five minutes to go through each shot: gauge the wind, adjust for the falling bullet. Mary, on the other hand, emptied her magazine into a target at 30 yards. When we were out of ammo, she pulled her earplugs off and draped them around her neck like a necklace. She put her arm in mine, interrupting my reloading of the magazine. I set the M14 onto the hastily constructed plywood table.

"I'm still not happy we're not going to the same place for these invitations," I said. "I don't care what Walter and John say."

"I know, Mike. I know," Mary said, exasperated.

"Do you think the thermite will work?" I asked.

She shook her head. "Barbara told me about it. Supposed to light up like fireworks. So I guess we're going to the Olympics, huh?"

"I don't think we'll have much time to watch anything."

"We might," she said. "Once the Players are stopped, we'll have won.

We can do whatever we want."

Mary took the binoculars from the table and spotted for me while I shot at the 300- and 400-yard targets. I was getting so much better with the rifle—I was one of the best in the group, beating everyone except the recent war vets: John, Walter, Bruce, and Henry. In all honesty, I was better than Bruce, but I had decided not to talk about it, as cranky as he was. He'd learned to shoot during Vietnam, but he'd served in the Navy, in the engine room of a destroyer, and never had the need to use his shooting skills after basic training.

I took aim at the 300-yard target through my scope, exhaled slowly, and squeezed the trigger.

"Hit," Mary said. "Upper left shoulder."

The target was just a chalk outline drawn on the trunk of a thick pine tree. I adjusted my aim and fired again.

In the instant I pulled the trigger, my mind was back in Redding, in the gun store where Tommy had been killed. The chalk outline on the tree was no longer a chalk outline but the image of the sheriff, his blood spouting forth from his chest, neck, and head. I closed my eyes to get rid of the image, but it was still there—it was always there. I hadn't told anyone about it, but Mary had to know, right?

"Hit," she said. "Center of the chest. Kill shot."

My heart was pounding, and I began to sweat as I sighted the target once more. I could feel my hands trembling, and the crosshairs on the sight were dancing around the tree. I blinked and the sheriff was back.

Morris, I've been trying to get you on the horn for ten minutes. What's with this call I got about gunfire . . .

Tommy was lying on the floor. The huge blast of buckshot that had come from Morris's sawed-off shotgun had killed him immediately—no time to suffer, or move, or speak. I had been hit in the shoulder, and I could still feel the dribble of blood.

I fired the gun again.

"Whoa," Mary said with a smile in her voice. "Way off to the left."

I tried to hold my hands steady. I didn't know how Bruce and Eugene were able to shrug it off. Bruce had killed Morris, and the guy who shot Tommy.

I fired again, and a chip of bark blew away two feet above the outline's head.

"I can't do it, Mary," I said, dropping the gun onto the ground and standing up.

"Now you'll have to resight the scope," she said, picking up the rifle.

"Didn't you hear me? I can't do this!"

"Just practice," she said. "You can do it. You've been beating everyone in camp for weeks. You're beating me, and I grew up with guns. I had my first twenty-two when I was ten, and my dad had been teaching me to shoot his guns since I was seven. And as of our last competition, you came in third place out of twenty."

"That was a fluke. So what if I shoot like this when we're in Munich? What if I'm shaking so hard I can't even look through the scope? I'm supposed to be a sniper. At this rate I'll kill our own people who are down on the ground."

"Two bad shots don't make you a bad sniper. You probably just need water and something in your stomach."

"I see him every time I shoot," I said.

Mary was quiet. She was looking down at the rifle in her hands, checking the scope to see if it was damaged.

Without looking at me, she said, "I know you do."

"How am I supposed to live with that? And don't tell me that it's better to kill one person than lose billions, because I'm so sick of John saying that. The Players are legitimate targets—we need to stop them. Even kill them if they don't listen to us. That sheriff was one of the good guys. He didn't need to die. He shouldn't have even been there. Damn Eugene."

"I agree," she said simply. "It was Eugene's fault. I worry every day about you and Kat. Kat's smart, but Eugene is a screw-up. He'll get you killed if something doesn't change."

"Well, we're out of time for things to change. The meteor can't be postponed, and that means that we have to send the invitations."

"We have time. The Olympics don't start for another two weeks."

I took the rifle back from her and aimed at the closest target—a white fir with a big red dot spray-painted on the trunk. It was only 25 yards away. I fired.

"Wide right," Mary said.

I fired again, aiming to the left of the tree trunk.

"Hit," she said.

I fired again. And again. And again until the magazine was empty.

CHAPTER THREE

It didn't take long to break camp and load our equipment. We left the tents and the rest of our camping gear—our Coleman stoves, sleeping bags, coolers—and just took what we thought we would need. One day Mary was going to come back and return to her old life, maybe. But for now the camp was secluded in a place where no one should stumble across it until hunting season. And if they did, they wouldn't necessarily know it was us. The only thing she insisted we clean up was the thousands of brass shells at the gun range. She wasn't worried about her family finding a shooting range—they were all shooters, and there was another range somewhere else on the ranch—but the sheer quantity of spent shells made it obvious that this range was not for casual use.

It was nearly three in the afternoon when we started driving to Reno. Mary and I rode in the Suburban, the second vehicle in our little convoy. We wanted to leave the van behind—it was what we used to rob the gun store, and it might have been seen by someone—but we just had too many people and too much gear. We planned to ditch it as soon as we found something else.

We had pooled our money together as soon as we got to the ranch. We didn't have enough, though; it had cost Lee and Lin quite a bit to secretly obtain enough C4 and thermite for our invitations. We'd have to find another business to rob to get the kind of cash we'd need for plane tickets: traveling to Munich was expensive in itself, but first we had to fly people to all kinds of unusual places. My squad was going to Istanbul for the Minoan Player and then Baghdad for the Sumerian.

Lee and Lin had to get into China, which was almost impossible. We had to get to Syria and Ethiopia and India, and all those flights would be pricey, not to mention the hotels we'd need, and food, bribes, and tickets to Munich.

No one had made plans for anything after Munich. No one had even brought it up. I think we were all too nervous.

Our caravan of vehicles—the Jeep, the Suburban, the van, and the Skylark—stopped at a grocery store in Susanville. Douglas and Barbara, who had spent much more time out of camp than the rest of us, went inside to buy dinner.

"Everybody else stay in your vehicle," Walter said over the walkie-talkie. "Molly, can you find a new license plate for the van?"

She was in the Jeep, ahead of us, and jumped out. She walked confidently into the back of the parking lot.

"How long is it to Reno?" Bruce asked from the driver's seat.

"Ninety minutes," Mary said. "And I don't care what anyone else says: I'm taking the first shower."

"Tired of washing in the stream?" Kat asked. "I may fight you for that shower."

"How many rooms are we getting for the twenty of us?" Jim asked. "I vote we splurge. I want a bed."

"A bed," I said, relishing the thought. "I haven't gotten a single good night's sleep in forever."

"I'm with you guys," Bruce said. "But I'm not the one holding the money. I'm just driving the car."

"I donated my life savings to this," I said. "And I'm getting a bed."

Mary squeezed my hand. We had shared a tent, along with Bruce and Larry. I had gotten used to nuzzling up next to her, wrapping my arms around her as we slept.

Mary had become a part of me, more than I had ever thought possible. We spent every waking minute together. We knew how to press each other's buttons. When we ran the hills at camp, I could tell when she was just tired or when she needed real help—and she did the same for me. When she was fussing with the camping gear, making dinner or stoking the fire or sweeping dirt out of the floor of the tent, I knew what must be troubling her. I knew her thoughts, and she knew mine. And she helped me as I struggled to get over killing the sheriff. When I woke in the middle of the night, screaming and fighting against the claustrophobic confines of my sleeping bag, she could whisper me back to sleep.

When this Calling was over, I would have nothing left—no home to go back to, no money to live on, no friends I could turn to. Except Mary. But could I truly turn to Mary? Now that she was going off with Bruce, I . . . Well, I didn't know. What if something happened to her?

I had to get that out of my head. I shouldn't be paranoid. This had been the plan for two months, almost. I should have come to terms with it.

Ahead of us I saw Molly climb back into the Jeep, the old license plate in her hand. She worked fast.

It took 20 more minutes for Douglas and Barbara to return from the grocery store, and they had a full cart. I wished that it could be a hot meal, but at least it was food. They stopped at each vehicle and handed off bread, cold cuts, mayo and mustard, and far more snacks than we'd ever need: potato chips, Hydrox cookies, Hershey bars, caramels, Ring Dings, Twinkies, and several six-packs of Fanta, 7Up, and TaB.

Mary took the bread and cold cuts and took sandwich orders from everyone in the car. It wasn't fine dining, but it tasted fresh, and it was the first meat we'd eaten in months that hadn't been cooked over a campfire.

We ate and ate. The sudden sugar rush of snack foods we hadn't had since June made us all a little sick, but I stuffed myself nonetheless. I think I ate half the Ring Dings all by myself.

Kat held the newspaper on her lap while she ate. "They're calling it the Great Daylight Fireball," she said. "And dig this—it'll fly over Nevada up to Canada."

Mary finished chewing a bite of her salami sandwich and read over Kat's shoulder. "It says it might not hit. It's close enough to pass through the atmosphere and burn. We just need it to work as the trigger."

John came up to the car and Bruce rolled down his window.
"We're going to hit the bank," John said.
"Whoa," Bruce said.
"Are you serious?" Kat asked.
"It's almost closing time," John said, looking at his watch. "We want to hit it before they lock up. Look, I know you're not happy with him, but Eugene is taking the lead. He's robbed three banks before."
Bruce laughed. "And he spent five years in jail for it."
"Because his getaway car chickened out."
"And you're asking me to go with him?" Bruce asked. "To make sure he doesn't accidentally shoot someone?"
"I'm not worried about that."
"This isn't something easy to walk away from," Bruce said. "Do we have a getaway car?"
"We'll take the Skylark. Molly will switch the plates. In the meantime, I want you and the other two vehicles to go to Reno now. Find us rooms at Harrah's. Use your fake IDs."
John looked back at me. "You're coming with us, Mikey. You too, Kat. This is your team's operation."
"What?" I asked, flabbergasted. "Why?"
"Partly because you saved everyone's asses at the gun store, but also because you have grown a hell of a distinctive beard. It's gonna be you, me, Kat, Eugene. Grab a pistol and make sure it's loaded."
As John left the window, Mary squeezed my hand. I kissed her and grabbed my M1911.
"Don't say it," I said as she stared at me. "I'll be careful."
But even as I took the pistol and tucked it in the back of my pants, hidden under my shirt, I could feel myself trembling. Still, I climbed

out of the Suburban and walked back to the Skylark, where the six
of us robbers gathered. Kat walked with me. She was in a T-shirt and
jeans.

"I didn't expect to be doing this today," Kat said to me.

I put my hands in my pockets to hide their trembling. "You'll do
great," I said. "We've practiced working as a team. And we have both
Walter and John to help us, and they know what they're doing. We just
need to make sure we keep Eugene under control."

"He's done this kind of thing before," she assured me.

"I know what he's done."

"Listen," Kat said. "I know you hate him for what happened at the gun
store. But we have to work together. This whole trip to Turkey and
Iraq is going to be for nothing if we can't work together."

"I know it," I said.

She touched my arm. "It's going to be fine."

"We're robbing a bank."

"We need to. We can't buy plane tickets if we don't. We have to live in
Turkey and Baghdad for three weeks, remember."

I stopped, and looked at her. "I trust you," I said. "I just don't know
what to do about him."

"I trust you, too," she said. "It'll work out. We'll just rely on each other.
Just you and me. We'll let Eugene take care of his jobs, but think about
this. It's just you and me. We can do this, together."

I looked into her green eyes. I didn't know what it was. But I believed
her. She hugged me and told me it was all going to be okay, and then
we walked to the car.

Molly sat in the driver's seat, her long red hair hidden under a very
convincing Afro wig.

I climbed in beside John. Eugene was next to him. Kat took the front
seat.

"This is going to be easy," Eugene said as the other three vehicles
pulled away on their way to Reno. "Walter, you stand outside and
don't let anyone in or out. We want customers in there. Anyone we can

threaten with a gun is going to be important. John, you go in first and ask to open a checking account. Mike, take two hundreds with you and ask the teller to give you change. Kat, you go with him. Act like you're filling out a form—a deposit slip or something. I'll be the last in. You're all there backing me up if something goes wrong. Make sure there are no heroes. This isn't going to be a quiet robbery—I'm going to be loud, get in their faces. Don't show your guns unless you have to. Kat and Mike, don't even get into the action unless you have to. Just act normal. Molly, how long will it take for you to steal new wheels?"

"Faster than it will take you to rob the bank."

"Okay, good." He looked at his watch. It was 20 minutes from closing time. "Let's go."

Molly drove three blocks down and turned into a parking lot that was shared by the bank, an insurance company, and a Burger King. Everyone checked their guns. John and Kat had pistols, like me, but Eugene carried the Beretta Model 12 submachine gun that he'd been practicing with all summer. All the guys had beards, and we all smelled of wood smoke. I doubted we'd really blend into the crowd very well.

Eugene put a backpack on.

John hopped out of the car and sauntered to the door. He looked so relaxed. I didn't know how he did it. Especially with Eugene calling the shots.

I got out of the car and walked into the bank. There was a line of just two people. Three tellers were at their stations, helping customers. I made a show of pulling money out of my pocket.

The pistol seemed so heavy and so bulky against my back, only hidden by my Los Angeles Rams T-shirt. I felt very exposed, like this was the dumbest thing I could be doing. I started breathing too fast, and I tried to use the meditation techniques John had taught us all at camp, forcing myself to breathe five times per minute.

The door squeaked as Kat came in behind me. She went to the table in the middle of the bank and started filling out a deposit slip.

I watched her. Her fingers were shaking as she tried to separate one slip from the others behind it.

Eugene kicked in the door; its glass cracked with a loud pop. "If anyone touches the silent alarm I'll kill every single person in this bank," he shouted, waving his gun back and forth. "If I hear a siren, you're all dead. And don't test me—I've already got two murder charges in Sacramento. I'm getting the chair whether I kill all of you or not, so don't test me."

The bank guard, an older man with a beer belly, backed away from Eugene. His voice shook as he spoke. "Don't do it, son."

"I'm only going to do it if I hear a siren, or if some idiot tries to be a hero. Now give me your gun."

The two customers in front of me had fallen to the floor and were hiding behind a narrow counter. I dropped down next to them.

The guard unholstered his revolver and very slowly laid the gun on the floor. Eugene picked it up and shoved it in the back of his pants.

Eugene pointed his gun at the first teller, a young man in a suit and tie. "Did you touch the alarm?"

"No sir."

"How about you?" He pointed to the woman at the next stall. She shook her head. The man on the end raised his hands and said, "I didn't either."

"Was I talking to you?" Eugene shouted. "Now find a bag and put all the money you have in it. Empty all the drawers. Where's the bank manager?"

The man sitting at a desk with John stood. John very calmly pulled his gun from his belt and pointed it at the manager.

"Hi," John said, smiling casually and cocking his gun.

Eugene walked to the counter and held his submachine gun up to the customer—an overweight woman with an enormous purse. "She's dead if I don't see more money coming, Mr. Manager."

"We put the money in a time-lock safe," the manager said.

"She's dead if I don't see more money coming," Eugene repeated. "Did I mention this gun fires five hundred fifty rounds per minute? But don't worry, because it only has forty in the magazine."

"We don't have any more," the manager pleaded.

John spoke. "Well, I reckon you'd better find some more. How about everybody in here empties their wallets?"

Eugene shouted again. "That's right. Everything out of your pockets. Jewelry, too."

The woman next to me on the floor touched a gold chain with a heart pendant on her neck, trying to hide it behind her hand, but I stood up and pulled my gun. "Hand it over."

I took the necklace and pocketed it. Then I reached in her purse and found sixty dollars. Eugene had the bag of money and was walking back and forth with it.

"Is everybody drained dry?" he asked, and John and I said yes. Kat was still acting like a customer. She'd given her handbag to Eugene.

Eugene tossed the bag of money over to John, who proceeded to empty it on the bank manager's desk. The manager looked stunned.

"Mr. Manager," John said, "help me search through this mess and find the dye packs." The manager slumped back into his chair. There was a lot of loose money, and John scooped all of that up to put it away in the bag. He took the wallets, emptied them, and dropped them on the floor. Meanwhile the manager dejectedly flipped through the bundles of new bills. He put one aside, and John looked at it. "Come on. I know there's more."

The manager eventually pulled five stacks of bills from the stash, and John double-checked every one.

He turned to Eugene and said, "I think we're done here."

Eugene looked back at the people and took off his backpack. "A couple more things. Inside this backpack is a bomb. It's extremely sensitive. Once I set it, I don't recommend that you try to move it. Nod if you agree." Everybody nodded.

Kat stood up and joined us.

John, Kat, and I walked past Eugene out the door. He followed us, turning around once the glass double doors shut. He looped the backpack straps over the door handles.

"Let's get the hell out of here," John said, and, fighting the urge to run, we walked away, giving no indication that we were in a hurry.

Kat never even had to draw her gun.

Molly, still sporting her Afro, met us in the parking lot in a tan-and-brown Monte Carlo.

Once we were inside, everyone patted Eugene on the back. Even I had to admit he knew what he was doing.

There was a paper sack on the front seat, and Molly reached in as she drove. "Gentlemen, it's time to be civilized." Out of the bag came four razors, four towels, and a can of shaving cream. "Let's go to Reno."

I only nicked myself twice.

CHAPTER FOUR

I stood in front of the window of a department store, facing the
TVs on the other side of the glass. *All in the Family* was on, but I
wasn't paying attention to it; I was watching a man in a three-piece
suit walking down Second Street. He'd left Harrah's, and John had
declared him "the mark."

It had been four days since the bank robbery, and we were a
completely different-looking team. The guys were all clean shaven,
with the exception of a few well-trimmed mustaches, and the women
all wore makeup and had styled hair. All the clothes that we had worn
camping for months had been thrown in a Dumpster behind the Bank
Club casino.

We had a lot of cash from the bank robbery, but we hadn't tried
to pawn the jewelry: we were too close to Susanville, and Eugene
insisted that the cops had probably reported the thefts to the shops
in Reno. We decided to pawn the jewelry in whatever cities our flight
layovers would be on the way to deliver the invitations to the Players.
But for now we were in Reno to train in a city setting, to hone a
different skill set from what we'd learned in camp. That was all about
fighting: shooting, throwing knives, wrestling, and stacking up to
enter a house.

We were learning how to shadow and track. I was in a position I
hadn't thought of before: I was leading the mark—walking down the
sidewalk about 50 feet ahead of him, only occasionally stopping to
make sure I could still see him. There was someone else—Eugene—
following him about 100 feet behind. And Kat, the third member

of our squad, was on the opposite side of the street about 300 feet behind. Her job was to move up and take over for Eugene if he was worried the mark had noticed him.

I could move pretty casually—it was summer and there were a lot of tourists, so one kid in a baseball cap and T-shirt didn't stand out in the crowd.

The mark wasn't in a hurry. It was probably his lunch break. He had to be getting tired, though: it was a scorching August afternoon, and he was in a wool suit.

I moved a little farther down the road to a gift shop, where there was a rack by the door full of postcards. I picked one up and glanced at the mark. He was getting close to me—walking quickly now, as if he might be late to get back to work. I tucked the postcard back and hurried down the road to stay in front of him. I didn't want to look like I was moving in any relationship to him, but I was new to this and didn't know what to do if he got in front of me.

I stopped again, this time at a restaurant. A glass case showed the menu. Chinese food—I hadn't even stopped to notice the name of the place. I had to be standing out in the crowd. Any real mark would have me pegged by now. I knew the signal for Kat to hurry forward and take over, but she'd have to sprint to get in front of this man. There wasn't anything I could do. After the Chinese restaurant was a cross street, and I had no idea which way he'd turn. I paused at the corner, looked up and down the street like I was trying to figure out which way to go. The mark was 10 feet from me.

So I did the only thing I could think of. I pretended not to notice him, and then turned quickly, timing the turn perfectly so that I collided with him.

"Excuse me," the man said, stumbling backward.

"My fault," I said. "Sorry."

"Excuse me," he said again, annoyance in his voice. He patted his pockets, checking for his wallet.

He thought I was a pickpocket!

The light turned green and he began walking away. I didn't follow. Instead I turned and headed back to Eugene. I could see Kat jogging up to us.

"What was that?" Eugene asked, obviously angry at how it went.

"Hey," Kat said, catching up. "What happened?"

"I didn't know what to do. So I stabbed him."

Kat looked past me at the man continuing down the road. "What?"

"Well, not really," I said. "But he was going to get away, so I turned and—if this were real—I stabbed him."

"What if we didn't want him stabbed?" Eugene asked.

"Sorry," I said. I didn't care about his attitude. "He was getting away."

"No," Eugene said. "You should have waited at the light and then crossed with him, whichever direction he was going. Then give the signal to me or Kat, and we would have hurried up to take your place."

Kat spoke. "Or you could have just fallen back, turned the corner. We're here to relieve you. At least that's how I understood it. It's like juggling: there's always one person up in front of the mark, but the three of us rotate position to position. Stabbing him was smart, though," she added, "if he was a Player. It was a good move."

"If he was a Player, he would have recognized me earlier, I bet. And if I stabbed a Player, he'd be fighting back for sure. It feels like we're the Mod Squad, but a stupider version. And I don't mean that as an insult. I just bet that this would work better if John and Walter gave more advice."

Kat took a deep breath. "I don't think that they know what they're doing either. I mean, they gave us instructions and all that, but I think they're making them up. My brother's a vet, just like them—and the Marines didn't teach this kind of spy stuff in basic training."

Eugene nodded his head. "Right, but they were Special Forces. The problem is we don't have anyone in our entire group who really knows how to do this or has done it before. I mean, I've robbed people, but it was stores and banks. I'm not a mugger."

"The guy—the mark—thought I was pickpocketing him when I bumped into him. We don't even have a pickpocket on our team."

"That's not true," Kat said. "I bet Molly could give us some tips."

Eugene let out a long breath. "Well, we'll have to ask her tonight. For now let's pick a new mark. Kat, you want to take the lead?"

"Sure."

"Mike, you take my spot in the middle, and I'll go to the back."

We worked for the rest of the afternoon, choosing targets of every demographic. We ended up following a real pickpocket around five thirty p.m. and watched him steal from at least three people. Finally he noticed that I was following him, and we suddenly had a real mark. He didn't run—he was too smart for that—but he went into Red's Casino and stripped off his blue shirt, revealing another, white T-shirt underneath that one. I would have missed it if I'd been 10 seconds slower. As he threw the shirt away, our eyes met for a moment. If he'd been a Player, he would have killed me right then and there, but he was just a street crook, and he headed into the chaotic maze of slot machines to ditch me. I followed closer—now that it was real—and tried to catch him while both of us tried not to get noticed by casino security. I stayed on his tail until he left the slots and made a speed-walking break for the doors. When I got outside, Eugene had the pickpocket in his hands, and Kat was playing the role of undercover cop.

"Cough it up," she said as Eugene pushed the crook against the brick-walled exterior of Red's.

"I don't know what you're talking about."

"Bullshit," Eugene said. He looked at me. "How much did he lift?"

"I saw three people."

Eugene grabbed him by the collar and turned him around, face against the wall. There were wallets in both his back pockets. Eugene grabbed one and opened it. "So, you're Daphne Shelton, age fifty-three?"

"It's my mother," the man said.

"Then who is Rachel Johnson, age forty-six? That you?"

"Your mother."

"Oh, and I was going to let you go. You lose, princess." He pulled the guy over to the casino doors. There was a very tall, very large man in a suit standing just inside.

I took the wallets from Eugene and held them out to the security guard. "This guy tried to pick my friend's pocket while he was in your casino. It looks like he's already stolen from a few people."

"No problem," the guard said, taking the wallets and looking at the IDs inside. After a moment he stepped to a phone on the wall and muttered something into it. He hung up and then came back, taking the thief's arm and slapping a handcuff onto his wrist. The guard looked at me. "I'm sorry you had a bad experience in our casino. Here, on the house."

He reached out to me and dropped a twenty-dollar chip in my hand.

Kat, Eugene, and I spent the next hour playing blackjack. I was too young to even be on the casino floor, but my fake driver's license showed that I was 22. I played conservatively, sometimes winning a few dollars and sometimes losing several dollars, while Eugene and Kat each used their own money (well, the group's money, but I wasn't going to throw a fit about it) and made big bets. Eugene lost 35 dollars before giving up. Kat quit while she was ahead, and had turned her 20 into 60. I bet and bet, trying to get back the money I was losing, until I had spent my final chip.

Kat bought drinks, a luxury they had gone without on the ranch. I just had a club soda—I still didn't drink—while Eugene did shots and Kat sipped wine.

After tracking the pickpocket and catching him, we all felt pretty good.

We toasted Istanbul. If all went according to plan, we would be on the plane in two days.

CHAPTER FIVE

"If even one of us Plays, then I lose," John said, cutting a piece of steak and dabbing it in the broken yolk of an over-easy egg. "And you know what losing means. My entire line—all my family, everyone I know—will die. Do you even comprehend that?"

"And if no one Plays, the Makers will lose," I said. "That's what we want. That's what we need to have happen."

"They don't lose. They have all the power. Don't you get that they are insanely powerful? They're talking about wiping out eleven-twelfths of the planet's population when one Player wins. What are they going to do to us if we refuse to Play?" John stabbed his steak again. It was rare—red in the middle. I'd already eaten mine.

"But," I said, searching for words. Some Zero line members in the otherwise-empty casino restaurant were listening to us, but most were practicing their own arguments. We had the place to ourselves as we waited and watched out the huge northwest-facing windows. "But think about the last time the Makers were here. We were cavemen, essentially. We were hunter-gatherers. What if we—the world—can fight them off now? The last time they came, we had rocks and spears. This time we have nukes."

"They have interstellar space travel," John said, smiling.

We'd been practicing these dialogues all summer, and now we had all the debates planned out, argument by argument. We didn't want to fight 11 Players—that was tantamount to suicide. We wanted to convince them not to Play, to follow the counsel of the ancient writings from the Brotherhood of the Snake:

To Play the game is to lose the game; success, survival, freedom can only come from refusing to Play.

Prove to the Annunaki that you are not mindless animals, that you can think for yourselves. That we, all of us, deserve the chance to live.

Choose to question what you have been taught.

Choose to be free, that we might all be free.

Choose not to Play.

"Your own book says," John said, "and I quote: 'we, the human race, are nothing but tools.' Do you think our atom bombs are going to beat them?"

"We," I said, "are going to beat them. The book says we should refuse to Play the game. And at the time this book was written, they were far more advanced, but they aren't anymore. Look, I'm not talking about you and me fighting them off. I'm talking about a spaceship coming to Earth, and the American military juggernaut goes after them. The Russians would fight too. Everyone would come together to save the human race."

"Is that the same military juggernaut that hasn't gained any ground in Vietnam in the last ten years?"

I leaned forward, elbows on the table. "We would be united against a common enemy. That's what I'm asking you to do: unite with the other Players against a common enemy."

"Has anyone else agreed yet?"

"We have people at their hotels right now. We're talking to all of you at the same time."

"So what guarantee do I have that I'll quit the game, become a pacifist, and some crazy kid from the Olmec line won't stab me in the back?" John said, and took a sip of coffee.

I stammered, not knowing what to say. "You've read the pages."

"What's the provenance of that book, anyway? You say you got it from the La Tène—but what if the La Tène gave it to you just so you could do all their dirty work? Take out some of the competition, help the La Tène win."

"An excerpt of those same pages came from the Cahokian line. Two witnesses."

"Except that, for all I know, you've made this whole thing up."

"There are some things you'll have to take on faith."

"You can't tell me where it came from, or who wrote it, or how they knew what they were talking about. That's just more faith than I've got."

"I . . ." I couldn't think of anything to say.

"Now if you will excuse me," John said. "I have a game to go win." He held up a hand, shaped like a gun, and said "B—"

"We kill them," I interrupted. "If someone won't join us in peace, then we take them out of the picture."

"So you'll kill me if I don't agree?" He snapped his thumb down on his index finger. "Bang."

"Damn it."

"Remember the ground rules," John said, stretching his arms out.

"I wrote the ground rules," I said. "I taught you guys how to do this."

I was the only one in the group who'd ever worked in sales—at my family's furniture store. I'd helped write the dialogues, and I'd taught them over the summer at the ranch.

Then again, I'd never been good at sales. I'd hated it.

"Come on," John said with a grin. "You always beat the rest of us at this. But you went for the book as evidence. Weren't you the one who told us not to use the book?"

"Yes," I said, and took a long drink of my orange juice.

"What are the keys of selling the story?"

I hated repeating it back to him. "I wrote this stuff."

"Show empathy. Build a relationship of trust. Customers care about themselves, not you," John said.

"And don't cite facts you can't back up."

"The book is out," he said.

"I know it."

"Good news," John said, pointing at my keno ticket. "I think you've just

125

hit the big time. You put five dollars on that?"

I picked up the ticket and turned to look at the big board of numbers on the restaurant wall. "Ha! Seven!" It was a 10-pick game, and I'd guessed seven correctly.

"We have a winner!" Mary said, motioning to the waitress.

I'd been putting five dollars on the keno game all day, as we'd been sitting in this restaurant for hours. I'd already blown 50 or 60 dollars. A casino employee—not the waitress—came over to our table. Light was pouring in from the north and west windows, illuminating the burgundy décor: the carpets, the booth seats, the paint on the walls. He was holding the Keno card I'd given the waitress.

"Seven correct guesses in a ten spot," he said with a gleaming smile, reviewing my card. "With a five-dollar bet, and fifty dollars per dollar, is two hundred and fifty. May I please see your identification?"

"Oh," I said. "Yeah, sure."

I reached into my back pocket. "Does my passport work?"

"That will be perfect."

The passport was forged, and this was the first time that I'd ever had to use it. Technically I wasn't old enough to be gambling. But I shouldn't have shot a sheriff, either. Lying about my age to gamble, in comparison, didn't feel like something to worry about anymore.

"Frank Finn," he read. "Congratulations." He handed me an envelope with the money and my passport.

"Nice job," Mary said. She'd been sitting next to me through my practice with John.

"Yeah, if I have one skill, it's guessing random numbers."

She held up a stack of 10 or 12 keno cards I'd lost with. "I don't think this counts as a skill," she said with a smile.

"I made back all my money and some extra," I said, handing her the envelope.

Suddenly we heard a loud rumble, and the tables shook like a plane was flying overhead.

"Damn," Jim said, standing up and running to the window. "Guys, this is it!"

All of us—all twenty of us—got up and crossed the lounge.

The windows were large, looking down on the parking lot of the Tombstone Casino and out into the desert northeast of Reno. But we weren't looking at anything on the ground. In the sky, to our east, was the meteor, a shining fireball leaving a trail of smoke. The meteor Agatha had told us about, the meteor that we were going to adopt as our own and use to convince Players about a supposed Calling at the Munich Olympics. Agatha, a former La Tène Player who had been expelled from her line, had told us it was coming—she had contacts at NASA. But I wasn't prepared for something so spectacular.

The streak of fire was moving slowly from south to north, and it must have been far away from us if it looked so slow.

"This is it, guys," John said, and looked around, then whispered, "Keep quiet."

I turned to look and saw that the casino staff were joining us at the windows, looking in amazement at the ball of light. It looked like it was actually on fire, but I didn't know much about meteors. This couldn't be the same kind of thing that gave us a shooting star—those were quick and gone in an eye blink. This one was still moving across the sky.

"It's gotta be a hundred miles away," Bruce said. "At least."

"Gonna touch down in Canada, I bet," Eugene replied.

"Could be like the Tunguska event," Rodney said. "Meteor slammed into Siberia fifty, sixty years ago."

"I've heard about that," John said, and laughed. "A lot of conspiracies about that."

"Well," Rodney said, "there's a fool born every minute."

The waitress touched the glass. "Do we know that that's not a Russian missile? I mean, is there someone we need to call?"

"Who would we call?" the hostess answered.

"The police?"

"What are our local police going to do about it?" the hostess said. "Besides, I'm sure it'll be all over the news."

A moment later, as people were turning away and getting back to what they had been doing, there was an enormous crash, and all the windows shattered.

I ducked, and shards of glass flew at me, scratching the side of my face.

"Oh!" Mary shrieked. "Is everyone okay?"

"I think I've got something in my eye," Bruce said. "Shit."

The waitress had blood on her arm, and I saw where it was coming from: a daggerlike piece of glass, maybe three inches long, stabbed into her forearm, bleeding a steady, bright red.

Bruce was calling for water to flush out the glass from his eye as Mary found Julia bleeding from her forehead. I touched the back of my scalp, and a few drops of blood came back on my hands, but nothing stung as though there was glass embedded.

Barbara was checking Kat's neck, where there was a small trickle of blood.

John grabbed me and whispered in my ear. "Get back to your room and make sure everything is packed. Spread the word."

Mary and I shared a room at the hotel, and I tried to get her to leave with me, but she wanted to stay and help Bruce.

Every one of us was trained in first aid, because we'd be traveling in such small groups. Kat was a nurse, and we'd spent four or five hours a week learning first aid from her.

Someone ran into the restaurant with a white first-aid box. Kat took it from him and yanked it open. "I'm a nurse."

She went to Bruce first. "Damn it. Why is there no saline in here?"

I moved to the waitress, but Walter was already there, using a cloth napkin to make a tourniquet. He made her sit down so she wouldn't faint. The hostess was on the phone, dialing the police.

Mary was now standing above Bruce and Kat, and I grabbed her elbow, pulling her toward me.

"John wants us to go back to the room and get ready to leave."

"I'm not going while Bruce is lying here with glass in his eye," she said.

"Okay," I said, and then moved on to the next bystanders—Julia and Jim. I told them what John had said, and they nodded and headed toward the exit. Eugene was next.

"What if this is real?" Eugene said, still staring out the window. "I mean, we've talked to John and Walter about this, but what if that meteor was a real Calling? That was pretty incredible."

"If it's a real Calling, then we need to get to the Players as soon as possible. We have to stop them from Playing or even going to the *real* Calling."

"It's still flying," Eugene said, pointing out the window. "Where did the blast come from?"

"Sonic boom," Walter said.

Sirens were going off now. I didn't know where the police were going, but at some point they'd head here to the casino. The hostess had already called them.

"We have to get out of here, Eugene."

"Not just you and me," he said. "We all do."

Through the window I saw a police car pull up in the parking lot, its red-and-blue lights flashing. The parking lot was full of broken glass— many of the cars had had their windows blown out too.

I pushed through the group, whispering to everyone to clear out, and I finally made it back to Mary.

"Cops," I said. "The bank robbery. And that photo in Berkeley can still be traced to me. Come on. Kat's taking care of Bruce."

She looked at Bruce for several seconds and then followed me out of the restaurant.

CHAPTER SIX

Mary and I lay on the king-sized bed, the TV on, and we kept rotating through the channels in search of news about the meteor.

At long last there was a knock at the door. We both jumped.

She went to the peephole, and I grabbed my M1911 pistol off the desk, standing beside Mary. I flicked the safety off.

"It's John," she said, and undid the chain.

As she opened the door, I put the safety on and slid the gun into the back of my waistband. I was comfortable with guns now. We'd trained every day all summer—not only target shooting, but tactics for raids too. A lot of it made me think we were going overboard, that it was unnecessary to our plans, but Walter said that the Players had trained to do it, so we were going to train how to do it.

John came in the room, closing the door behind him.

"How's Bruce?" Mary asked.

"He's going to be fine," John said. "Kat got the glass out, and we got out of there before the paramedics showed up."

"I saw the cop car," I said.

"We were gone from the restaurant before they even came upstairs. There was pandemonium in the casino, and the police headed that way first."

Mary ran her fingers anxiously through her hair. "Is this going to change any of our plans?"

"No. Everything is the same as before. You and Bruce to Mexico. Mike: you, Kat, and Eugene to Turkey and Iraq."

"I want to renew my objection to Eugene."

"I know how you feel about him," John said. "But you were there in the bank, and he did a great job. The gun shop was a fluke."

"A fluke?" I said, raising my voice.

"Yes," he said calmly. "A fluke. You've been holding on to that grudge all summer. It was a fluke, plain and simple."

"Tommy died."

"It could have been any one of us. We're all risking our lives, Mike. Tommy knew that going into this." John patted my shoulder. "Flights are tonight. I'll see you there. Don't let this change anything. We have work to do, so I want the two of you to smooth this out. We're a team or we're not. And if we're not, the Players will take us apart."

He turned and opened the door. "Barbara has your plane tickets and your share of the money. And don't blow the money—you'll need it for all your operations: getting from city to city, eating, getting safely out of Munich. Wait here for it. She'll come by."

I didn't speak as the door closed, leaving Mary and me alone together.

"Eugene is going to be fine," Mary said. "He'll be good to have on your team."

"You weren't there at the gun store."

"I feel like I was. You've told me about it so much. You need to get over it."

"Get over it? It was Tommy's life."

"Mike, don't do this. Not right now."

I picked up my suitcase and put it on the bed. I unzipped it to check the contents, despite the fact that I had packed it days ago. There was everything in there for a trip to Turkey and Iraq. Guidebooks, maps, translation dictionaries, and dossiers on the Minoan and Sumerian lines. Mary was standing off to my right, closer to the door. I could only see her in my peripheral vision. She wasn't moving.

"The only person I want on my team is you."

"Mike. You know that's a bad idea. For so many reasons."

"Because I'm better off without you?"

"We've talked about this, Mike. A lot. And remember two weeks ago?"
I knew what she was talking about. We'd been on a practice run—we trained constantly for every possible situation we could think of. This one had me, Bruce, Mary, Kat, and Eugene clearing an abandoned textile factory in Sacramento's industrial district. We had all gone into the building with our guns ready, just as Walter and John had trained us. Bruce was the leader, Mary next in line, then Kat, Eugene, and me in the back. After we had cleared the ground floor, Bruce had me position myself behind a fifteen-foot loom, guarding the stairs and watching the door. He and Mary had gone upstairs. They were silent. We had trained for this kind of thing for months—how to walk quietly, how to communicate with hand signals—and we were good at it. I had been focused on the door just long enough for my mind to wander. I knew that this wasn't real, and I was tired, and staring down the sights of my M14 carbine was getting old.

And then Mary had yelped and there'd been a clatter upstairs.

"That wasn't a real situation," I said now to Mary. "I wouldn't have left my position if it had been a real situation."

"I called out and you came running," she said. "It was very sweet, but then Jim, Julia, and Rodney came up the stairs and killed us."

"It wasn't real. It was an exercise. I was calling a time-out."

"What if it had been real? Would you still have come running?"

"That's what I'm saying. I only did it because I knew that it was an exercise. You gashed your leg open. It was a good thing that Kat came up the stairs when she did so she could help you. You should have a little faith in me."

"Mike," she said, taking a few steps toward me, "I have faith that you'll have my back anytime I'm in danger. I know that you'll come to my rescue. But that is the exact opposite of what you needed to do there. You needed to stay where you were. And frankly, I don't think a real situation will be any different from this."

"So I'm supposed to be happy that you are going to Mexico with Bruce? That's going to be safer?"

"What am I supposed to say, Mike? I've told you this before. You're too protective of me, and it's tactically dangerous."

"'Tactically dangerous'?" I asked, letting out a snort. "That sounds like something that Bruce would say."

"So what if it does? Bruce is smart. He's been training with us all summer. He has experience, and he's seen the way you and I work together. And he's worried about it. He's worried about you."

"You're saying this was all his idea?"

"No. Why are you bringing all of this up right now? You've known about this change for six weeks."

I didn't know what to say. "I'm sorry. I'm just not ready for this. To leave you."

Mary stared at me, her lips a straight line. "We're going to see each other in Munich. This is just a bump in the road. We'll be back together."

She picked up her suitcase and left for the door.

"You need to wait for Barbara to get your ticket."

"I'll find her."

She stopped at the door, and turned. "Mike, I like you. I like you a lot. We have something good together. Just trust me, okay?" She grabbed the doorknob and walked out.

I was left all alone in the room, my heart racing and my stomach suddenly sick.

I wanted to trust her. I wanted to trust all of this. But it was getting harder. I just wanted to believe we'd get to the end and move on from all this, after Munich, after the Players had been stopped and Endgame was over. I thought Mary and I could find a new life in a new country. Somewhere far away from the violence, my crimes, my family, everything about my previous life. We'd start over.

I cared about stopping Endgame. I believed in what we were doing, and so did she. She made me believe. But while I'd thought we were growing together, she was leaving me to work with Bruce. Because she trusted him more. Were she and Bruce . . . ?

Had it ever been real? Or was she just an expert recruiter?

Was she sleeping with me so that I'd fully commit to Zero line?

"No, damn it," I said out loud. I had to trust Mary. I had to get all these thoughts out of my head.

There was a knock on the door, and for a brief moment I dared to hope that it was Mary coming back, but that thought was gone before I had time to walk to the door and look through the peephole. I knew she wouldn't be there.

I had my pistol in my hand.

The figure outside my door was turned to look down the hall, and I couldn't make out who it was.

With the gun in my right hand, I opened the door with my left and peered out.

"Hey, Mike," Eugene said.

I let out a breath.

"Hey," I said, letting him in. He'd spent a lot of time over the summer tanning, and with his stubbly beard he looked like he'd fit in well in the Middle East. I'd done the same, but I suddenly felt like I would be picked out easily. I had Greek ancestry on my dad's side, but I didn't know much about my mom's side.

I walked back to the bed and put the pistol back on my suitcase.

"I have our tickets from Barbara."

"Thanks," I said, anger rising up in me again. Every time I saw Eugene, all I could think about was Tommy crumpled against the cinder-block wall, a shotgun blast in his chest, his green T-shirt turned dark brown.

And I saw the sheriff, and each one of the five bullets I'd fired into him.

Now, today, Eugene looked like he didn't have a care in the world.

"Kat and I are ready. You and Kat are going to Istanbul, and I'm heading to Baghdad. We want the invitations to be delivered as close as possible to each other, so you'll prep in Turkey, set off your bomb,

134

then immediately come join me and I'll have the plans all made for Iraq."

And now I'd be traveling alone with Kat, who I thought was great, but she wasn't Mary. There was still a lot I didn't know about Kat. I knew she was a nurse at a hospital in Oakland. I also knew that she had left a boyfriend to come be in Zero line. She had tried to recruit him, but he thought it was a bunch of bullshit. Like I had at first, until Mary convinced me. Kat abandoned him instead of turning her back on the rest of us. As bright and sunny as she seemed on the outside, there must have been a fierce zealousness in her. I was glad I was going to have her covering my back in Istanbul.

Eugene, on the other hand, was trouble. I doubted his ability to set up a good scenario for our Sumerian invitation even if he had pulled off the bank job so well. But, as I was quickly learning today, I wasn't in control of anything that was happening.

CHAPTER SEVEN

We left the hotel, slipping out while workers were putting plywood in place of the broken windows. We went through a side door so we wouldn't have to deal with the front desk. Everybody had scoured their rooms for any evidence that we had been there.

Mary was in the van with me as we drove to the airport, but she was two rows ahead, and she didn't look back. Kat and Eugene were with me, Barbara was in the passenger seat, and all the other seats in the van were stacked with luggage. The others were crammed into our three other vehicles.

We drove in silence all the way to the airport. Bruce, driving the van, pulled to the curb of the loading area, and we all climbed out, making a large pile of everyone's suitcases. Bruce then drove off to long-term parking.

After a few minutes Eugene said he had to have a smoke, and he bummed a cigarette off the skycap.

I approached Mary, who was turned away from me, standing alone, waiting for Bruce to come back.

"Hey," I said. "Have a safe flight. Good luck. I'll see you in Munich."

"You too, Mike," she said.

"Mary . . ." I moved in front of her so she had to look at me. "Mary, I love you." I pulled the gold heart necklace out of my pocket and placed it in her hand.

She looked defeated, her shoulders slumped and her face blank. "It's beautiful. But we both have planes to catch. Please. Let's wait until Munich."

"Just take it."

She nodded, put the necklace around her neck, and fastened it easily. The gold heart gleamed in the evening light.

"It's beautiful," she said.

"You're beautiful."

She hugged me. "Be careful, Mike."

"You too."

"I'll see you in Germany."

And with that she turned from me and walked away.

Everyone from Zero line was going through the airport at the same time, though we all acted according to our cover stories. Kat and I perused the shelves of a bookstore and let Eugene go through before we did. I took a few minutes to pick up a *National Geographic* magazine and a chocolate bar, let a few dozen people go ahead of us. Then Kat and I walked as confidently as possible to the security checkpoint, holding hands.

She was my girlfriend. We both went to UC–San Francisco, and we were taking a semester off to see the world and go to the Olympics. It was a good enough story.

As I walked through security, a police officer watched me the whole time.

I was acutely aware that the cop's gaze was fixed on me.

I paused longer than I should have as the security guard checked my ticket, my mind completely focused on the cop, who was still watching me.

"All right," the guard said tiredly. "Have a safe flight."

As I walked past him, the cop approached. "Hey," he said. "Where are you heading?"

I handed him my ticket.

"Istanbul," he said, looking surprised. "What's in Istanbul?"

"I will be, soon," I said, smiling. "My girlfriend and I are traveling there to meet friends." It was the story Kat and I had agreed on.

"How did you get friends in Istanbul?" he asked, his voice low and even. I couldn't tell if he suspected me of anything.

"College."

"Which college?"

"Berkeley," I said. *Damn it.* I shouldn't have said that. What if he'd seen the article on me? What if he recognized me? We had rehearsed this, and I was supposed to say UC–San Francisco.

"What's your name?" he asked.

"Uh . . ." I reached into my pocket and showed him my passport. "Frank. Frank Finn."

"If you're from Berkeley, why are you flying out of Reno?"

"Look, is there a problem? I need to get to the gate."

He refolded the ticket but didn't hand it to me. "Why are you flying out of Reno?"

"I'm from here," I said. "School's out for another couple weeks."

"What part of Reno?"

"I've got to get to my plane," I said, trying to keep my voice calm.

"What part of Reno?"

"Sparks, actually. Near the golf course." I was making it all up, but I was banking on the hope that he, as a Reno cop, wouldn't know details about the streets in Sparks. In all honesty, I didn't even know if there was a golf course in Sparks.

Kat had made it through the checkpoint and came up behind me.

"Hey, Frank." She took my hand.

"You're with him?" the cop asked.

"Of course," she said.

"Okay," he said slowly. "Listen. I know why people your age go to the Near East. Hashish and opium, right?"

"We won't be messing with that," I said, and took my ticket out of his hand. "We have to go—we're going to be late." I started backing away from him, heading toward the concourse.

Behind the cop, I could see another officer leading John to a room just beside the security line. Had he been recognized? My worry must have shown on my face, because the cop looked over his shoulder. "You know him?"

"No," I said too quickly.

Calm down, I told myself. *You're acting defensive and stupid.*

He narrowed his eyes. A voice came in on his radio, and he answered it. Then he nodded at us.

"Go on, then. Have a safe flight."

As he walked away, I turned to Kat, feeling simultaneously relieved and panicked. Kat was grimacing.

The police were on high alert. What would happen if they arrested John? After all that hard work, our mission would be screwed.

We hadn't discussed any of this as a potential problem. My squad had contingencies in case we failed. If Kat and I didn't show up in Baghdad by a certain date, then Eugene was to try to do the job alone. But no one expected John to fail. No one was backup for him.

The same went for Walter. He was going to Omaha since he knew the Cahokian line so well, and he insisted he could get the job done despite being recognizable to them. He said he was able to get through their defenses. He said he knew them all.

If John didn't get on the plane, should I try to find other Zero line members in the airport and ask them if we needed to back up John? Maybe Barbara or Douglas had copies of the dossiers.

But I didn't know where Walter would be in the airport. He wasn't taking the same plane that so many of us were, since he wasn't going international.

I took Kat's hand. We made it to the gate in three minutes, just as the airline crew was closing the door.

Kat and I had seats next to each other, and I saw a few other members of our crew scattered around the plane. We were all pretending not to know one another. We were going to have a layover in Atlanta, and then Kat and I had another 10-hour layover in London before continuing on to Istanbul.

But the plane didn't leave.

I flipped absently through a *Time* magazine that someone had left in the pocket of the seat in front of me, knowing I needed to stay calm.

Were they on to us?

There was nowhere to run to, even if I dared. It didn't help that this was my first time on a plane—I felt claustrophobic, and my heart was pounding in my chest.

Two policemen appeared at the front of the plane.

Damn.

They started to very slowly walk down the aisle, looking at all the faces.

I wished I hadn't shaved my beard. Not looking like Michael Stavros would have been a big help right then.

The cops stopped. I was in the back of the plane, in a middle seat. Kat was by the window. She was reading a book in her lap, her head down and her long brown hair covering the sides of her face. I knew Eugene was up in front somewhere, but I couldn't tell if that was where they had stopped.

"What's going on?" I asked the man in the aisle seat.

"Cops," he said. "Do you think that maybe they were going to try to hijack this plane?"

"Who?"

"You know," he said. "The pinkos trying to get to Cuba. They're always in the news."

"Yeah," I said with a nod, trying to stay calm.

A stewardess walked past, and the man next to me asked her what was happening.

"Don't worry," she said. "Everything is safe."

Everything is safe. That sounded ominous, even though it was supposed to be reassuring. She should have said something like "Everything is fine." "Everything is safe" meant that something was unsafe, but the problem had been taken care of. Did that mean they stopped a criminal? Did they catch one of us in Zero line?

She left us. He blew out a long breath and pulled a pack of cigarettes from his shirt pocket. "I need a smoke. You travel much?"

"No," I said. "Not by plane, I mean."

"The name's Marty." He held out his hand to me. "Cigarette?"

I shook it. "Frank. No thanks."

"There they go," Marty said.

The police were pulling someone up from a seat.

"Shit," I murmured.

It was Eugene.

Did that mean they were onto us? Would Kat and I be next? And what had happened to John? He was supposed to be on our plane, but I hadn't passed him as I'd made my way to my seat. I'd never seen him come out of the room by security.

Had he been arrested?

Would we be able to manage with Walter in charge? Walter was working with John, but it was John we always went to with problems. Walter was focused tight on the objectives, not paying attention to the people who were supposed to perform all their duties. Walter didn't understand people who were struggling, or confused, or those who weren't as well trained as a Green Beret. He had no tolerance for problems. People were going to be scared now, and Walter was not the leader to calm anyone's fears.

"I wouldn't worry," Marty said, talking to me as if I was a kid. "They say planes are the safest way to travel. Much safer than cars."

"Yeah," I said. "I know."

Were the police just catching Eugene based on his other crimes? Or was this about the gun store? Or the bank robbery? My heart was pounding so loud, I was sure the cops could hear it.

What if they stopped Mary's plane to Mexico?

The captain came on the PA and announced that we would be departing in a few minutes, and he apologized for the delay.

I flipped through the pages of the magazine again, stopping on a photo of ancient Anasazi petroglyphs in Arizona. They were images somewhat in human form, but with circles around their heads, or horns, or antennae.

"Look like aliens, don't they?" Marty said with a laugh.

"Yeah."

"All this time we've been talking about aliens and seeing UFOs, wondering if they're real or not. Imagine if they really came to make contact with Earth, and they landed a thousand years ago with the Indians. Maybe they decided that we were primitives and they left thinking we were just living in tepees and not worth bothering with."

I forced a chuckle. He had no idea what was really going on. No one did. He had no idea that we were on our way to stop the aliens from destroying the world.

The police left, and a moment later John came on the plane, smiling broadly without looking at anyone in particular. He sat down, and the stewardess closed the door.

He hadn't been arrested. Relief flowed through my body. We'd lost Eugene, but at least we had our leader.

The low roar of the engines started up, and the plane began taxiing away from the terminal.

CHAPTER EIGHT

"This food is pretty terrible," Kat said to me, looking disdainfully at the ham sandwich in her hands. "Even the chips are bland."

We were sitting in the Atlanta airport during a three-hour layover, waiting for our plane to London. There were quite a few Zero line members waiting for the same flight—London was a hub that would lead many of us to our final destinations. But, besides Kat and me, no one else was supposed to know one another, and after the trouble at the Reno airport, we all sensed we should stick to our cover stories carefully. That only gave me Kat to talk to.

I ate the dry, stale sandwich I'd bought at an airport restaurant. From where I sat, I could see Rodney had one too, but he hadn't touched it. He used to run a deli, so this kind of prepackaged airport food must have seemed terrible to him.

They called his flight before ours.

Kat was reading a book. I debated asking her what we should do now that we didn't have Eugene. Just as I was about to, John appeared beside me and sat down.

He crossed his legs and slouched in his chair. "Ever been to Atlanta before?"

I stammered for a minute. I was four seats away from the next traveler, close enough that I didn't want to say anything important.

"I haven't. It's humid. Getting off the plane felt like walking into a Laundromat."

"It is. And this is nothing compared to outside."

I had bought a *New York Times* and a copy of *The Electric Kool-Aid Acid*

Test by Tom Wolfe. It didn't sound like my type of book, but John had recommended it several weeks ago. It was sitting on my lap.

"Any good?" he asked, pointing at it.

"Haven't started it yet," I said.

"It's missing a major character."

"Yeah," I said slowly and casually. "I wonder what it'll be like without him."

"The plot is still solid. You'll be surprised how well it all works out."

"How do you know?"

"I've been studying it all summer. Two great characters who work together well."

I nodded. "I hope you're right."

"Of course I'm right. I assume this edition has copies of all the notes? Details?"

"Yeah," I said. "I guess so." I had copies of all the Baghdad plans—the place where we were supposed to pick up the smuggled bombs, the thermite, and guns.

His voice lowered. "Do you need me to send you a third?"

"Who?"

"I could arrange Julia. Or Rodney."

I thought about it for several seconds. I flipped through the pages of the book, and then closed it again.

"No, we'll be good."

"Okay. Good. Don't worry. I know you're upset about Mary. But don't let that screw with your head. She'll be waiting for you."

"Okay."

"I'll see you. Be safe."

I didn't nod, just stared straight ahead. "Okay."

As it turned out, I started reading the book on the 747 and fell asleep, waking up to find it was the middle of the night in London.

I didn't know about the others, but I breathed a sigh of relief to be on foreign soil. There were no American cops to worry about the bank robbery or the protest at Berkeley or the gun store. And since no police were waiting for me at the airport, I figured that Eugene hadn't ratted us out. Not that he would, but my mind was wandering down a catastrophic road.

I checked my watch. It was set to California time. I mentally added two hours to it and tried to visualize where Mary was and what she was doing. Odds were she was asleep. Or staying up late, drinking with Bruce. Or they were—no. I had to stop myself from imagining the worst.

During our 10-hour layover in London, Kat and I ventured out of the airport. I'd never left the United States before. It was the middle of the night, so nothing was open, of course. After changing some money, we took a taxi into town and had the cabbie drop us off at Big Ben. I didn't know where any of the landmarks were, but we found Westminster Abbey and followed the signs to Buckingham Palace.

As I stared through the gates, I wondered what I'd gotten myself into. I was nineteen, a college dropout, standing in front of Buckingham Palace while I waited to get to Istanbul so I could plant a bomb. I was going to kill people. A Calling didn't need to kill people, Walter had said, but it could. If things didn't work out, I would die, Kat would die, and maybe a lot more people would die. Eugene might very well be the only one to make it out of this alive.

No, that wasn't true. If we failed, then the whole world would face apocalypse. My death would be horribly insignificant.

It was the surviving Player whose people would live, which made my mission almost laughable. Walter had guessed that I was part of the Minoan line—which was the line I was going to end. If any one of our squads failed in their missions, or failed in Munich, then I was signing my own death warrant.

With that thought, I joined Kat in wandering the streets of London, down a long road that was lined with trees, and, as the sun rose, we found ourselves in Trafalgar Square. I ate breakfast at a pub on a side street—the full English breakfast: sausage, eggs, beans, black pudding, and fried tomatoes and toast. I didn't know what black pudding was, but it tasted good. I wasn't a tea fan, but Kat insisted that I drink it, and the cup they brought with the breakfast was hot and satisfying.

We went back to the airport, and I broke the rules. I wrote everything down in the back pages of my book. Everything. I started by describing the Calling the best that I could, listing all the lines: Minoan, Shang, Cahokian, Aksumite, Sumerian, Harappan, and on and on. I wrote down where these lines could be found. I forgot the cities where some of the lines lived, but I narrowed the others all down the best I could: some got a city name and others got a city and street. I listed the specific addresses of the Minoan line and the Sumerians. And then I wrote about the aliens. Everything I knew. Everything that John and Walter had said. All the discussions we'd had around the campfires all summer, all the weird historical anomalies John preached about: the Pyramids, the Mayan artifacts, the Nazca lines, the Piri Reis map, the Annunaki. I wrote down how I'd been recruited, how Walter knew about this, how we'd lived and trained on Mary's ranch. I wrote about the meteor—how it flew harmlessly through our atmosphere, almost smashing into Earth and blowing out our windows with a sonic boom. I wrote about Mary. I didn't know how to end the section on Mary, so I left that page in the middle of a sentence.

I confessed to the gun store robbery, to killing the sheriff, to burning down the store. I wrote about Tommy. I wrote about the bank. It all came out, a manifesto of the Zero line.

And I left a paragraph of warning, saying that these 12 ancient lines needed to end, that we needed to imprison the Players, or kill them if need be, if we were to ever have a chance as the human race. We were not a game created by aliens; we were a planet filled with good people. Zero line wasn't intent on killing for the sake of killing. We were saving the world.

"What's that?" Kat asked, looking over my shoulder.

"Everything," I said. "In case this all goes wrong. Someone needs to follow in our footsteps."

"Is it safe?"

"Is any of this safe?"

"I worry about you, Mike."

"I'm not going to screw up our missions."

"That's not what I meant," she said. "I worry you won't make it. I don't want that to happen."

I reached over and took her hand, gave it a squeeze.

"We'll be okay. You and me."

Near baggage claim I found a locker. I used some coins to open it and leave my book. I put the key, clearly marked with the locker number and HEATHROW—in the pocket of my jeans.

Eight hours later I was waiting to pick up my luggage in Yeşilköy Airport with Kat at my side. We were here together, as boyfriend and girlfriend.

There was a cacophony all around us, but we ignored it and stared, waiting as the big, brown, hard-sided suitcase appeared and slid toward us. A few moments later, a burly man dropped Kat's smaller blue bag onto the sloped luggage rack.

I carried the big one, along with my backpack, out of the airport.

It was hot there in the Turkish sun, and humid on top of it. Kat immediately stepped out into the road and waved for a taxi. One stopped in front of us and the driver jumped out and placed our cases in the trunk.

CHAPTER NINE

The Minoan house wasn't a house at all. It was a compound. All the buildings in Istanbul were crammed together, and to get to the Minoan house you had to walk down an alley about twenty yards and then take a left into a parking area. A slim metal door opened into the compound, and from our vantage during a scouting mission, we couldn't tell if that door went into a building or a courtyard.

We'd been in Istanbul for a week, and only had five days left to figure out the best way to set off the bomb. So far, our trip had been careful and slow: we'd rented a truck, figured out where the Minoans were, and traced three different routes between their compound and our hotel (which we'd purposely gotten on the opposite side of the city). We visited the fish market, and a few of the tourist spots, just in case someone was following us.

Our scouting mission had the two of us holding a map and walking down the alley, arguing about where we were and which way we needed to go to get to Hagia Sophia and the Blue Mosque.

Following our cover story, we were dressed in normal Western clothes—jeans and a T-shirt for me, a long, casual sundress for Kat. We'd discovered that Turkey was a blend of Middle Eastern and European influences. Many of the men there were wearing jeans— even some women. In some ways it wasn't all that different from London.

When we were done finding the complex, we went to a café with outdoor seating, along a bustling street, about a half mile from the compound. I ordered four plates of mezes—something akin to appetizers—that we'd enjoyed the most since our arrival.

"It's going to be tough," Kat said. "We don't know what's on the other side of that wall. It might be a courtyard or it might be a roof. Remind me of the detonation time again."

I looked at my watch, doing the math to compare the current time to California time. "Two in the morning. So we'll have the cover of darkness. Much easier."

"I don't think so," Kat said. "I think they're always watching their place. I bet they have people watching that alley twenty-four hours a day. Couldn't you feel it, Mike? I could tell we were being watched."

"Yeah," I said. "I'm just saying that it'll be easier in the dark."

"Unless they have more guards at night."

I took a bite of something called borek, which seemed to be a savory cousin of baklava. "Do you still think that these guys are aware of the meteor?"

"Definitely," Kat said. "Look over there." She pointed to a newsstand. "There's an English paper over there with US news. And from what Agatha said, all of the Players watch for astronomical signs, just in case they represent the aliens. They'll have known about it, and they'll be waiting for an invitation to see if that was the true sign of the Calling."

"What if that meteor *was* a real sign, and they're going to get a real invitation? What if they already have?"

She frowned. "We need to Play as if this is the invitation. We need to stick to the plan. If they're already somewhere on Earth looking for clues, then we're screwed, but there's no way to know. I mean, we don't even know which person at the compound is the Player. Or if the Player is even *at* the compound."

I smiled. "You used the phrase 'we need to Play.' As if we're part of the game."

She rubbed the bridge of her nose. "I'm getting tired." She took a slice of pide, a kind of oblong pizza topped with cheese, egg, and diced beef.

"How big is the bomb? Yield, I mean. How big of an explosion?" I asked quietly. The busy street was overpowering our conversation, and I felt comfortable talking openly. There was no one at the tables beside us.

"Bakr said it was big," Kat said. "He said we needed to be at least 500 yards away when it goes off."

"Yeah," I said. "The whole thing weighs five or six pounds, and I've heard that a pound is pretty big. Like, half a pound is used in a car bomb."

We were supposed to pick the bomb up tomorrow. Bakr's connections had shipped the plastic explosives to a fish market down on the Bosporus Strait. We already had the detonator in our bag—all incorporated into a fully functioning clock radio.

"So," I said, "we don't need to worry as much about where we put it— on one side of their wall or not. If we put it in that small parking lot, it'll take out all the cars and knock down the walls on all three sides, you know?"

She shrugged. "I guess so."

"So do we even need to be in the parking area? We could put it in the alley, up against the compound wall."

Kat nodded her head emphatically. "Yeah. Yeah, I think that's smart. We're not trying to kill anybody with this thing. We're just trying to leave an invitation."

"Speaking of which," I said, chewing a piece of kofte—a sausagey meatball thing. I swallowed. "The thermite—what if we put it up on a wall and then the bomb destroys the wall?"

"We trained that over and over. We light the fuse on the thermite tarp at the same time we plant the bomb. If we secure it properly, it should burn itself into the wall before the bomb even goes off."

"You can use explosions to stop things from burning," I said. "You ever see *Hellfighters*? It's John Wayne fighting fires at oil rigs. He'd set off a bomb by the fire, and the bomb would suck up all the oxygen and put the fire out."

"Thermite supplies its own oxygen. It can burn underwater."

"Really?"

"We'll be fine," she said. "Bakr knows what he's talking about."

"Then where are we going to lay it out?" I said. "I wish we could ditch it altogether."

"Then how are we going to lead the Player to Munich?" Kat asked.

"Wait. Let's not even put it next to the compound. Let's not even put it there on the same day. We'll put it in the alley—that they all have to drive through—so they'll see it, maybe think it's a warning, and then the next day we'll plant the bomb."

"Do you think it'll go against our planned timeline?" I asked. "The other teams might be using their thermite signs on the same day as their bomb. Will this give the Minoans an advantage?"

"The only advantage is that he might go to Munich a day early, but that's fine, because not all the bombs are going off around the world at the same time. We still have to go through this whole mess again in Baghdad."

She chewed a bite of her kofte. "But from what Walter said, they're expecting the big bomb. They're expecting something big."

I looked over to the TV screen in the café. There was an Olympic report. It must have been some kind of preview since the games didn't start for a few more days.

"I've always wanted to go to the Olympics," Kat said, gesturing to the TV with her fork. "Not like this, though."

I turned to see the TV. "If everything goes to plan, we might be able to see an event or two."

"After we've possibly killed a bunch of teenagers?" she said, turning back to face me. "I don't think I'll be able to enjoy any of them."

"I checked the schedule," I said. "There are no medals being awarded on September fifth. It's going to be a quiet day, and I think that's good for us. There will be a lot of people in the Olympic plaza. We'll fit in, and no one needs to expect a thing."

"Unless the talks go wrong and we have to ambush them. The backup plan is supposed to have six snipers in place to take out the Players.

How are we supposed to hide rifles?"

"There's rifle shooting in the Olympics," I said. "We'll just keep our guns in cases and act confident. No one will be the wiser."

"So we're supposed to look like athletes?" Kat asked.

"Sure. What do target-shooting athletes even look like? We don't even have to look fit."

She raised an eyebrow.

"I wasn't meaning you," I said with an embarrassed laugh. "You look good—I mean, really good. I meant people like Walter, with a little too much weight around the middle. Speaking of which, what is on this pide? It's fantastic." I pulled another piece off and wolfed it down.

Kat did look good. She was beautiful, and any guy should have felt lucky to be having a fake vacation with her in an exotic city, thousands of miles from our real life.

But Mary was always in the back of my mind. And Bruce. The two of them together.

We changed the subject to other things—to the crazy traffic in front of us, which seemed so disorganized, to the food, and to the architecture that was so foreign and magnificent. At Kat's request, we stopped at the Hagia Sophia on the way back to the hotel. It was amazing: a huge building with a grand dome in its center, surrounded by four minarets. It had been a Christian church, then a cathedral, then a mosque—each conqueror recognizing its beauty and not wanting to destroy it, just remodeling it for his own religion.

While we were there, we heard the Islamic call to prayer, echoing from several minarets at once. We stood silently and listened.

Even though the Hagia Sophia was no longer a religious building—it had been converted into a museum in 1935—I sat down and silently prayed. I wasn't a praying man and never had been, so speaking to God fit me better in a museum full of tourists than in a church. But I poured out my heart. I knew what we were going to do, knew that people were likely going to die. And I knew how many people would die if I didn't go through with our plans.

If humanity was just the product of aliens, did that mean there was no God? I pushed that thought out of my mind and concentrated on my prayer.

But, even now, equipped with guns, C4, and thermite, I was starting to worry that all of this was a lie. I trusted Mary far more than I'd ever trusted John or Walter, or Kat or Bruce, but I wondered now if Mary had been brainwashed. Was *I* brainwashed? I hadn't seen over the wall of the compound, but I knew it housed far more people than just the Player we were targeting. We had a bomb with five or six pounds of C4, and that was going to be a big explosion. Was this going to kill innocent people? Was it going to kill children?

Could I turn my back on this now? Kat couldn't carry out the plan without me if I just ran away, could she? I'd walk away, and the Minoans would survive. So would the Sumerians.

But she might be able to do it all on her own. It wasn't going to be hard unless she got seen, and she was too smart to get seen. She could go into that parking area and plant the thermite without anybody's help.

In front of the Hagia Sophia, we held hands and walked casually. Kat had her camera hanging around her neck.

A man came up to us—we were surrounded by tourists, and he was obviously looking to make a buck.

"Ben bir fotoğraf alabilir miyim?" he asked. I thought that Kat and I had learned the basics of Turkish, but we both stared back at him blankly.

He made a motion with his index fingers and thumbs. *"Fotoğraf?"*

"Oh," Kat said. "Yes. *Fotoğraf. Evet lütfen.*"

She handed the camera to him, and we leaned close together. He snapped a picture.

"One more," she said. *"Bir tane daha."*

Kat looked at me. "Well, we are supposed to be on vacation." And before I could say anything, she turned and kissed me.

And I kissed her back. Because Mary was on the other side of the world. Because she was with Bruce. Because Kat was gorgeous. Because we could both be dead soon. Because, because, because . . .

Kat went back to the hotel, and I told her I'd join her in a while. I went to a café that was closer to the compound. I sat outside as the sun set, eating baklava and watching for any movement. I went through two more helpings of baklava and a plate of mezes. I recognized two of them—hummus and falafel. Those had made their way to Southern California. But there was also afelia, stifado, and halloumi cheese, all of which still felt foreign.

A big black Mercedes pulled out of the alley, turning away from me and heading north. No one in the car looked at me, but why would they? And besides, did the lines live in fear that someone would attack their houses? Did the Players declare war on other Players? Nothing Walter or John or Agatha had said implied that.

I wondered what Mary was doing right now. I checked my watch. It was just after noon in California, so two o'clock in Veracruz. Had they found the house yet? I was sure they would have. It was one Walter knew a lot about. It wasn't even a compound like this one. It was just a house. Expensive, to be sure, but just a house. Walter had even told that squad the name of their target.

Our only direction was that the Turkish Player was a teenage boy, a couple of years younger than me.

I ate the last bite of baklava, paid my bill, and left. I crossed the street, heading toward the alley and the compound.

The compound had a parking area for just three or four cars. The entrance was on the north side, the door just a blank piece of metal. The cars were extremely nice: an Alfa Romeo and a Bentley. It was dark, and I walked into the small area. It was probably 50 feet by 30. On the west and south sides were blank walls of a stone building that rose three stories. I was hoping to find a patch of weeds in the corner, or someplace where we could hide a shoe-box bomb, but there was nothing. If we could guarantee that the cars wouldn't move, we could leave the bomb under one of them, but that was a big question mark. The Player's house was short. I couldn't see any of it over the wall. I looked to the east, toward the alley. That was another stone building, but it had windows. I walked back to the street to get a better look. The wooden door had a metal gate in front of it. I tried it and smiled. It wasn't locked—the latch looked broken. Painted above the door was TOPTAN SATIŞ YERI. I tried the doorknob, and though the door felt flimsy, it was locked.

I closed the gate and then jogged back to the café across the street. The waiter who had been serving me was stacking the chairs outside and taking them back into the shop to close for the evening.

"Excuse me," I said. I knew he spoke a little English, but not much.

"Hello," he said, turning toward me, a chair in his hands.

"What does that sign mean?" I asked. "The translation."

"Toptan satış yeri?" he said.

I nodded.

"It is a . . . house. For things. To put things in."

"A factory?"

"No, not factory. It is"—he set the chair down and put his hands on his hips—"a house for putting things in."

"A warehouse?"

"Yes! Warehouse."

I pointed at the building on the other side of the alley—the three-story building that made the south wall of the compound's parking area.

"What is that?"

"Office," he said. "Closed."

"No one works there?"

"Office," he repeated. "No people."

CHAPTER TEN

I arrived at the Turkish fish market at four in the morning. I was wearing the traditional black *thawb*, a long-sleeved, ankle-length shirt. Kat was out in the rented truck, waiting for me to come out of the almost entirely male crowd of fishermen, auctioneers, grocers, and restaurateurs.

I felt completely out of place in this hectic, fast-talking mass of people. All around me was bickering and bartering. This was no place to be timid, but I couldn't assert myself without knowing the language better. Instead I stayed in the center of the aisles, arms folded as though in judgment of the fish, looking at the fishmongers who were holding up their prize catches, but engaging no one.

The man I was supposed to find would be wearing a red *taqiyah*, a round skullcap. It reminded me of a short, squat fez, complete with a top knot and small tassel. And, in case anyone else was wearing anything similar, he was going to have a long gold necklace with a large round green-and-black pendant that had Arabic writing on it. Lee and Lin had given me a photo of what the necklace looked like, and I'd memorized the symbol.

As I walked the aisles, my mind wandered again to Mary, and to Kat. And at that moment, both my head and my heart told me that my mind ought to be wandering to Kat, not Mary. When I thought about Mary, I thought about betrayal and jealousy and Bruce—even if I was just being paranoid. When I thought about Kat, I remembered that she had volunteered to be on my team, all those many weeks—months—ago. We were a team. We thought alike. We worked together so well. We finished each other's sentences. We finished each other's thoughts.

I could see the Bosporus just past the market. It smelled of fishing boats—oil, exhaust, fish, blood. All waterways were eventually connected. The water I saw out behind the market flowed into the Mediterranean, the Atlantic, the Caribbean, and to the beach Mary was on.

But that was the closest connection I could draw to her.

She was probably using the same cover story with Bruce that Kat and I were using—a young couple sharing the same hotel room.

And Mary had asked for us to be separated. To be safe. But maybe it was because she wanted to be with Bruce.

My mind snapped back into focus as I spotted the man. Red taqiyah, long chain with a green-and-black pendant. He was at the end of a row, lifting crates of large fish covered in ice.

I stopped in front of him, and he set down the crate and wiped his wet hands on his apron. *"Ne yapıyorsun?"*

"I'm looking for anchovies from the Black Sea," I said. "You are Salomao?"

He looked at me with no sign of recognition.

"No anchovies. Torik."

That was what he was supposed to say, but he was completely calm about it. It made me wonder how many times he had smuggled something.

"I hear that anchovies make the best lakerda," I said.

He frowned and made a face. "No. Best lakerda made from Bosporus torik."

I dug into my pocket and pulled out a prearranged bundle of Turkish lira and handed it to him. He grabbed a cooler from behind him and set it down in front of me. "Fresh torik. High quality. You like."

"Teşekkür ederim," I said. Thank you.

That finally got a smile from him, a snort at the poor accent. He patted the cooler. "You like."

I picked it up—it was heavy—and I carried it toward the street. Two of Salomao's workers carried the tarp, rolled up like a carpet. When I got to the truck, Kat and I put the cooler in the bed of the pickup, and the workmen casually tossed the tarp in after it.

It was still early in the morning, and we drove down a quiet road, then stopped under a cluster of shade trees. We climbed out and went to the cooler.

As expected, it was full of fish. We pulled them all out, tossing them aside. But halfway down the cooler, covered in torik and ice, was a false bottom. Under it, we found the shoe-box bomb.

On August 28, at 1:30 a.m., we dressed all in black, in Turkish robes that we'd bought at the market, and checked out of the hotel. I had parked the rental truck two blocks east of the compound. Our disassembled rifles now sat in our otherwise empty suitcase. Kat held the thermite sheet—it was folded and heavy. I didn't know what thermite was made from—it was the hottest-burning chemical on the planet, or so Lee had told me—but Lee had painted it on thick, with the hope it would burn the Olympic symbol into the ground or the wall, or wherever each of the various squads was going to put it.

I had a coil of fuse—Bakr had packed everyone's bags with 50 feet of fuse just in case the situation called for it.

I held the bomb. It wasn't heavy. There was five pounds of C4 in it, the clock, and the detonators. It seemed so innocent. I knew that this much C4 would make a decent crater, but I really had no idea what to expect. This was just a shoe box. It could have been holding a pair of loafers, not explosives that could level a building.

And we carried the guns we'd hidden in our luggage. They would be hard to get to in a fight, considering the big robes we wore, but at the hotel Kat had cut a slit in both our robes at our waists so we could access our weapons. Kat had a holster for her Beretta. I tucked my M1911 into my belt. We didn't expect to need them. We'd watched the compound since we arrived in Turkey, sitting at the same café. There was never anyone coming or going from either the warehouse or the office building. The lights never came on at night, and no one even tried the knobs.

Kat went to the warehouse and I went to the office. I stood on the empty street and watched as she smashed into the wooden door with her shoulder—once, twice, and then it broke open. She turned to pick up the thermite tarp and a small box of tools and then disappeared into the building, pulling the wrought-iron gate closed behind her. I knew the tarp was heavy, but she never looked like it was a burden.

I stood in front of the office building. Three cars were coming down the street, blasting music and swerving back and forth. I tried to look innocent and casual as they passed, but it was a good thing it was two a.m. Standing on the street, loitering in front of an abandoned building, must look suspicious. But they were too preoccupied with their race to care about me.

I set the box down and kicked in the flimsy wooden door. Shards of wood flew as the doorjamb split, and the knob was wrenched free, skittering loudly onto the cement floor.

I was expecting a musty smell—the odor that houses get when no one lives in them—but instead I immediately noticed the cigarettes. I'd cleaned more than my fair share of dorms, and I knew what old smoke smelled like, and this wasn't it. This was new smoke. This was someone smoking nearby.

I ran to the wall, knelt down on the concrete, and placed the box. *Watch your back,* I thought.

This wall was the other side of the parking area's south wall. My plan was to blow this building to bits and, with a little luck, have it collapse into the Minoan compound. It was sure to destroy the expensive cars out there and, at the very least, make an enormous explosion that they couldn't ignore. There would be fire and smoke, and they'd come running out of their compound just in time to see the sheet of thermite hanging from the warehouse wall, outside a third-story window. Kat should be doing that right now.

I opened the shoe box. Bakr had written the instructions on the inside of the lid, and I turned on a flashlight to read it.

I pushed the detonators into the bricks of C4 and attached the batteries to the clock. Immediately the display lit up and started counting down from four minutes.

"Durmak," a male voice said.

He sounded like he was just behind me.

It had to be just as dark for him as it was for me. I quickly replaced the lid, turned off my flashlight, reached under my robe, and readied my pistol. Slowly I turned around to face the voice.

There was a figure in the darkness, illuminated by just the dim lights out the door and in the street. *"Kıpırdama."*

If we were as concealed by darkness as much as I thought we were, the man shouldn't be able to see my hand pulling out my gun.

"I don't speak Turkish," I said.

There was a pause. "American?"

"Yes," I said. I was stalling for time, but I didn't know what he expected me to do. I started to stand up.

"Kıpırdama!" he shouted. "Do not . . . Hold still, please."

"Look," I said. "This is just a mistake. I thought this building was empty. I didn't expect you to be here. Just a mistake."

I was talking quickly, not expecting the Turk to translate and understand what I was saying. It was a distraction. But a distraction for what? I needed a plan.

"It's a mistake," I repeated. "I wasn't expecting anyone to be in here. Not that it makes much difference, I suppose. I haven't touched anything."

"Durmak!"

"I don't know what that means," I said, keeping my voice as calm as I could.

I had to make a move. I took a breath and turned on my flashlight, pointing it into the man's face while I pulled my gun out from underneath my robe. He immediately squinted at the light, and there was a loud bang. For a second, I thought I'd been shot. But as I waited for the pain to start, the Turk slumped to the floor.

"Shit," Kat said from the open door as she lowered her pistol, her voice wavering. She'd just killed a man. "There goes the element of surprise. Is that bomb running?"

"Yeah." I took off the lid and the red timer lights shined up at me.

"Three minutes, fifteen seconds. Are you done?"

"No," she said. "I saw him follow you in. Is this building part of the compound?"

"I guess so. We have to hurry!"

She ran out the door and I followed, sprinting down the street to the warehouse. The door was ajar, and we ducked inside, hoping that this place wasn't also part of the compound and guarded. It didn't look like it. There were rows and rows of boxes stacked to the ceiling. A freight-elevator shaft was there, but Kat didn't want to wait for it. She ran to the steps in the corner and climbed them, two or three at a time, until she reached the top floor. I was only a step behind her as we ran to the windows.

She was standing at an open window.

"This building could come down in the explosion," I said.

"I know," she said. "Don't have a choice, though. If it comes down, we're screwed." Kat reached out the window, holding nails in her lips. I held the heavy fabric up as she began pounding a nail into it. I could feel every second, as if the timer was giving me electric shocks as it counted down.

Working on the last nail, she spoke. "If they didn't hear the gunshot, they're going to hear this hammer."

"I haven't heard any alarm." Looking out the window, I could see down into the compound. Behind the wall was a squat, sprawling one-story house. There were no lights on.

I checked my watch under the flashlight. "We're all going to hear a lot in about sixty seconds."

"Did you lay the fuse?" I asked.

"Not yet," she said, smacking her head for forgetting it. She dug through the bag to find the coil.

"Forty-five seconds," I said.

"I've got it," she answered, twisting the end of the long coil of fuse onto the two-foot fuse Lee built into the thermite.

"Twenty-five seconds. Come on," I urged, and Kat started unrolling the coil, both of us retreating to the stairs.

"Ten," I said, and stopped looking at my watch. "Light it."

She pulled out a match and struck it against the wall.

But before she could light it, there was a tremendous crash, and our building shook, knocking Kat and me down the stairs to the landing at the second floor. Everything turned white and then black.

Kat was above me, looking down into my face, pointing my flashlight into my eyes.

"What happened?"

"You all right?" she asked.

"Yeah, I guess."

"Then let's get the hell out of here. You probably have a concussion. You got knocked out pretty good there."

I couldn't see straight, and I put my arm over her shoulders, and she held me around the waist.

"What time is it?" I asked. I felt like I was waking up from a deep sleep.

"You've only been out for a couple seconds," she said.

"What happened?" She helped me walk. I could feel wetness on my face as we descended the last flight of stairs. "I'm bleeding."

"It's not bad. Let's just get to the truck."

We got out of the building with no problems and found that the street outside was shrouded in dust. Kat was holding me around the waist, but I pulled away from her and stumbled, confused, toward the fallen building. It was hard to see because of all the white dust, but the office building was flattened. All three of the expensive cars outside

the Minoan compound—the Mercedes, Alfa Romeo, and Bentley—
were twisted mounds of steel. The wall with the compound door was
gone, revealing the house beyond. Half a dozen people had come out
of it, dazed and sleepy.

But there was a brilliant fire on the wall up to the east—the thermite
was burning. Kat must've lit it while I was knocked out. Right now it
just looked like a spiral, but once the fire died down, the logo of the
Munich Olympics would be obvious. I turned, about as stable as a
man made out of Jell-O.

Kat pulled a handkerchief from a pocket and had me press it to the
gash on my head.

"What about you?" I asked. "Are you okay? You fell down too."

"I'm fine," she said. "I'm going to be black-and-blue tomorrow, but
right now I'm fine. I kind of landed on you. Sorry about that."

"I'm okay."

"We need to find a clinic somewhere," she said.

"I'm going to be fine."

"But you don't look fine," she said. "Security will definitely question a
foreigner walking around the train station with a homemade bandage
strapped around his head. We have to look like regular, unremarkable
people."

I nodded as we hobbled to the truck. "Just buy bandages and gauze
from a pharmacy. We don't want anybody paying that much attention
to my face."

She paused, dabbing at the wound. "Yeah. It's probably not too
serious. It's a head wound, and head wounds bleed a lot. If you start
feeling worse, we'll take you to the hospital. For now, let's get to the
train station. We'll have time on the train to rest up before we have to
do this whole thing a second time in Baghdad."

Two police cars came flying past us, but the cops didn't look our way.
We were only a block and a half from the bombing—almost to our
truck—but they didn't stop to worry about us. We might show up
in a police report or witness statement later. But there was so much

confusion, and so much dust, that no one could be sure of what they saw. And we would be long gone by then.

The truck was right where we had left it, and I climbed into it and then slumped against the closed door. As we drove, Kat kept reaching across the seat to see how the wound was doing and whether or not I was sleeping.

We stopped at an all-night pharmacy, and she went in to get the things we needed.

Sirens blared in all directions, but they were far away. I ducked down anyway.

"Are you okay?" Kat asked me as she got back in the truck.

"I'm going to be fine. I just need to lie down."

She drove the truck and I wished I could recline the seat and sleep. But she forced me to keep pressure on the cut on my head. We finally ended up at the train station, and she stopped in the long-term parking lot. She told me it wasn't going to hurt as she treated my wound, and then she spent 10 minutes hurting me—scrubbing the wound with gauze and alcohol. She said it was full of dust and grit from the explosion, and she had to dig it out, and that normally something like this would be done with a toothbrush, which sounded awful. Finally she trimmed a bandage to fit the gash. It wasn't that big once it was cleaned—about two and a half inches long—and the bleeding had mostly stopped.

She had me hold it in place while she got the surgical tape.

"You know," she said, "we haven't made any plans for after Munich. Everyone is supposed to scatter. But we haven't bought any plane tickets. Some people have money tucked away—not everyone contributed all of their life savings. I kept some of my money, just a couple hundred dollars. But we really don't have any plans. Maybe you and Mary can find a place to live where no one will ever find you. We're all criminals now. We all need to go underground. I can go back to my life, but everyone will ask me where I went for three months, and what am I going to say? I joined a cult and sacrificed some teenagers to save the world? If we ever get caught, there will be a lot of explaining to do."

She taped down the bandage.

"Mary and I aren't going to settle down."

"What do you mean?"

"Well, she's not here, and you are."

Kat pressed the last edge down and leaned back to look at me.

"I thought that you guys were split up because you—" She stopped.

"What? What did you hear?"

She frowned and began putting the medical supplies back in the paper bag.

"John told me that both of you were too attached—that you wouldn't follow the plan if either one of you was in danger."

"Did he say that it was his idea?"

"Yes."

"He told me Mary asked to be separated from me for the raids. That's what Mary said too." I took a deep breath. "I'm starting to realize how naïve I've been this whole time."

"What do you mean?"

"Mary and I . . . I wonder if she's just using me."

Kat stared at me for a few seconds, then touched the bandage again, pressing down the edges of the tape. But this time her hand lingered on the side of my face.

I stared back at her.

And then she kissed me. Again.

CHAPTER ELEVEN

The Baghdad Railway was 1,600 miles, three days of travel with all the stops. Kat and I spent the time sleeping and reviewing the brief dossiers on the Sumerian line, making sure we had the plan down cold without Eugene. The planning in the dossiers had already been done by Bakr, who was from Baghdad, and we'd already studied it for weeks. The Sumerians' compound turned out to be a more public space than the Minoans'. The family ran a hotel and restaurant as a front for their secret activities. Bakr had gotten Eugene set up there, and now we would get a room at the Sumerian hotel as well. It sounded risky, being right under the noses of the people we were supposed to attack, but it also made everything easier: we could place the bomb nearly anywhere. We could just leave it in our room, if we wanted. Or an elevator, or a housekeeping closet. And there was a central courtyard ideal for our thermite stencil.

Even picking up the bomb and thermite would be simple: Bakr had had Lee and Lin ship it to his uncle's house. There was no need for code phrases or fake names.

Or so we'd been told.

So there wasn't much to do on the train.

We'd delivered one invitation, and it had nearly killed both of us. But we had done it. We had completed the first part of our mission. I'd been cracked on the head, and Kat had had to shoot a man, but we had made it.

Maybe we actually had the chance to succeed at all this. To survive, and go on with our lives. Everything felt renewed and reenergized. So when Kat wanted to introduce me to the world of wine in the plush dining car, I thought for a minute about my policy on drinking, and my insistence that I was never going to be like my father, and said, "Why not?" And when we'd gone through two bottles, laughing loudly and making a scene, we decided to take the third bottle with us back to the stateroom. And when we got back to our room, as the train was hurtling past Aleppo, we slept together.

Maybe it was the thrill of completing the Sumerian mission, or being nearly killed, or Kat patching me up, or the wine.

We were trying to save the world, so I didn't feel like holding back anymore.

We were going to live.

When we got to Baghdad, we enjoyed ourselves as much as we could. We were still riding high from the Sumerian raid and since we didn't have to do any recon on the compound, we sampled everything: the best food, the best wine, and the best bed in the hotel. Kat spent the money she had; I spent the money I had. And we had the best vacation anyone could ask for. Well, for a day, at least.

The bomb and thermite were easy to get, as Bakr had said they would be. We checked out of the hotel and walked through the plan dozens of times. I set the bomb in the middle of the street, in front of the building, and Kat laid out the tarp. And then, just like we'd discussed, she lit the fuse and I set the timer.

We watched as the thermite began to burn hot and white, illuminating the square in front of the hotel.

Backing up, I saw windows opening, someone throwing curtains aside and opening ornate shutters.

"Kat," I said. "Look."

"The guests are coming toward the tarp," she said, horror in her voice. I didn't know "Get away" in Arabic, so I started waving my arms, trying to get people's attention, trying to get them to duck and cover. But no one was looking at us.

"Mike," she said. "The bomb. We have to go."

Windows were lighting up all around the square, silhouettes appearing.

"Come on," Kat said, and grabbed my hand. "The bomb."

I stared at her in fear. We were having too much fun. We weren't taking this seriously. We were playing lovers while we were supposed to be playing terrorists.

"Run!" she screamed.

I finally found my feet, and we ran south down the street. Everyone was looking out their windows, watching the whole scene.

A moment later there was a flash so bright it lit up the neighborhood like it was noon, and I was lifted off my feet and thrown wildly across the road. Everything went black again.

CHAPTER TWELVE

"Mike."

I was blinking. I could feel the rough dirt in my eyes and my tears trying to wash it away.

They were dribbling down the side of my face. Tears—or was it blood?

"Mike."

Something was touching my chest. Cold and wet.

And then, as if a switch had been flipped, I could hear everything— the screams, the sirens, the scraping of rock falling on top of rock.

"Mary?" I called out.

"Mike. It's me."

"Mary?"

"Kat," she said.

"I can't see. Kat, I can't see."

"I've put my hijab over your face. Your head is fine. It's just one deep cut above your eyebrow. Nothing serious. I can stitch that up."

"Are we safe?"

"We have to get out of here. I've pulled you into an alley."

"Can I stand up?"

"I hope so."

"My chest hurts."

"You might have hurt a few ribs."

I felt her hands pressing on my side, and I gritted my teeth at the pain. I tried to stand. I was weak and hurt, but my feet were steady.

There was a searing pain near my sternum, and I yelped as she pulled my arm over her shoulder so we could walk.

"What happened?"

"What do you think? The bomb went off."

"Did people die?"

She was quiet for a minute. "Maybe. Yes. At least a few."

"We should have planted it in the hotel. Then at least we would have killed the Sumerians."

"And all the innocent people staying in the rooms."

"My chest hurts."

"Maybe you were hit by a chunk of cement—they came hurtling out of the hotel."

"Are you okay?"

"Scuffed up, but nothing worse than a few bruises. I think. It's a good thing we don't have to plant any more bombs. You have a tendency to get beat up."

We walked for another 20 minutes or so, but my pain wasn't letting up.

"There's a pharmacy up here. I can see the sign. I'm going to leave you here and go get some painkillers and something for the cut."

"Don't be long."

"I won't. You're going to be fine."

She lowered me down onto the stony ground of what must have been a dirt road. A dirt alley, probably.

I felt her kiss my cheek, and then she was gone.

I tried to raise my right arm again, but it felt like the muscles weren't even there. It didn't respond at all. It hurt like hell, though.

After what felt like an hour, Kat came back.

"We have to get out of here."

"Where is there to go?"

"Listen. I'm not wearing the abaya and hijab anymore. My hijab is wrapped around your head. The pharmacy wouldn't sell to a single white girl not wearing the right clothes. I had to shoplift. It's a good thing all the cops are busy with the explosion."

"Great."

"Let's just get out of here. I got what we needed."

"Kat?" I said, as she was helping me to my feet again.

"What?"

"I'm sorry I called you Mary."

She laughed, but there wasn't a lot of cheer in it. "Old habits."

After walking a long way, we checked into another hotel, where we had dropped off our luggage earlier. I got the feeling that Kat picked it because they didn't look too discriminating in their clientele.

In our bathroom, she unwrapped the hijab from my face. The bleeding had stopped, and my tears had flooded the dirt out of my eyes. She scrubbed out the wound—I took off my leather belt and bit down on it as she scoured the gouge in my forehead with a toothbrush. Once it was clean, she stitched it up with a needle that she sterilized by holding in the flame of a candle.

I showered, and the shower stall turned brown from all the dust I had covering me—in my hair, on my face, up and down my arms. When I was clean and dry—and she had taken a shower of her own—she bandaged my head with gauze and surgical tape.

We divided up the money that we had left, after factoring in plane tickets, which wasn't much. A couple hundred dollars.

We had guns waiting for us in Munich, so we discarded the pistols we were carrying—throwing them down the hotel's garbage chute.

We had originally planned to split up on our way to Munich, but we had stopped caring about that. We boarded a plane bound for Munich, with a brief layover in Belgrade.

What if we really did live through this? It occurred to me, then, that we'd also have to live with what we'd done.

Everybody was talking about the Olympic Games on the plane. From what was said—that I could understand—the USSR and East Germany were on a spree. The couple across from me was talking about gymnastics, where the USSR and East Germany had swept the floor exercises, the vault, the uneven bars, and the balance beam.

We had done our part. We had delivered our invitations. Munich was going to be a mess, but we made it this far, taking a beating, but with no serious problems. Now we would be getting to the heart of Endgame. We'd see who would show up for the Calling, and we'd try to get them to see reason. It sounded impossible before, but so did the invitations—and we did those missing our third team member.

I squeezed Kat's hand and reclined my seat.

We hadn't made any contingencies for Olympics security. Jim and Julia had been to the Mexico City games in 1968, and they'd said the security was slim to none, especially in the plazas—like the plaza with the sunburst symbol, where we were going to meet up with the Players, if we couldn't stop them at their hotels first. Mexico City had had a student demonstration turn into a massacre 10 days before the games—it reminded me of the People's Park protests where activists had died—along with the one where I hit that cop.

I looked at Kat. I imagined us heading toward some new, pleasant adventure instead of to Munich to possibly kill people. These Olympics were nicknamed "the Happy Games," and I wished we were heading there for another reason.

I missed Mary. And more than once on the plane, I wished that Kat's hand, which I was holding, were Mary's hand.

I hated myself for it.

It was all planned out. Agatha, the excommunicated former La Tène Player, was going to meet us at the sunburst spiral, where we would all play the role of tourists. Agatha insisted that all of the Players would come to the spiral when they got into the city, just to scope the place out, to make plans for where and when they would show up on September 5. From there, Agatha would ID them, and we would tail them to their hotels—just like we'd practiced in Reno.

I looked around the plane and wondered if the Player from Baghdad was here. There were a couple of guys who looked to be the right age, but neither of them looked like a trained killer.

But maybe that was part of the act.

I slept from Belgrade to Munich. It was the shorter flight, just over two hours, and I woke up as the plane descended into the city and the captain made an announcement.

The plane was crowded, all the seats filled. Everyone was going to the Olympics. A woman sitting next to me was eager to talk now that I was awake. She wore a T-shirt with the Greek flag on it.

"You know," she said, "the Olympics are Greek. We started the whole thing."

"I'd heard that."

"You are American?"

"Yes, you?"

"No, no, no. Greek."

"I've missed out on the Olympic coverage so far. How is Greece doing?"

She laughed, and took a bottle of mineral water from her bag. "Not so good. Not like America. Not like the Soviets. No medals yet. But we're going to win in Greco-Roman wrestling. It's named for us—we must win!" She chuckled to herself. "The Americans are doing well, but this is not their year. I am always amazed at the ... what's the word? *Tenacity?* Is that right? The tenacity of the Soviets. And the East Germans always surprise—they are such a small country, but they perform so well. Of course, they get help from the Soviets."

"Are you traveling alone?" I asked, mainly out of politeness. I should have been faithfully watching for tails or even for Players.

"Traveling, yes, but meeting friends."

"We are too."

"Meeting other Americans?"

"Mostly, yes," Kat said.

"Try to keep your chin up. The Soviets already have ten more gold medals than the Americans."

"There's still over a week left," I said.

She laughed. "See? That's what I'm talking about. Keep your chin up. We learn that in Greece. No medals in the winter Olympics, only one bronze at the summer games last time, in Mexico City. A Greco-Roman wrestler. It's what we're good at."

I looked at my watch. It was just past noon on September 2.

"Is that your luggage?" she asked, pointing to the backpack between my feet.

"Yes. And we checked two bags."

"You're going to be in for a long wait. That's why I don't bring much. The Germans check all the bags when you come into their country, and I've heard they're being extra careful this year. Terrorists."

"Terrorists?"

"Have you not read the news?"

"Nothing new. I bought a newspaper yesterday, but it was a couple days old."

"Terror attacks all over the world, all within days. America, Iraq, China, India." She reached into the pocket of her jacket and pulled out an Olympics ticket to see the wrestling matches later in the week. "You see that logo? It appeared at all of the bombings. There was even one in Turkey."

"Maybe someone is grandstanding—telling those countries that they will lose in the games. Taunting them."

"Maybe," she said, putting the ticket away again. "But they've killed people." My stomach dropped. We tried our best to avoid killing civilians, but sometimes it couldn't be avoided.

"So German security is tighter?"

"Yes, very much. They always check luggage, but now they're looking for bombs."

I looked down at my bag and at Kat, grateful we had ditched our guns.

It worried me that this woman hadn't mentioned a bomb going off in Ethiopia, or Japan, or Mongolia. If we'd missed anyone, we'd have to travel to their compounds and find a different way to stop them.

The plane hit the tarmac and slowed.

"Good meeting you," she said.

"Yes," I said. "You too."

I closed my eyes, seeing the images of the bombs again and again—seeing the man in the office building go down from Kat's bullet. He would have died in the explosion anyway. Hell, maybe other people had died in the explosion as well. But I knew for certain that I'd been part of two people's deaths now. I didn't feel like a murderer, but that's what I was, and it disturbed me how easy it had all been—and how little I felt about the second one. That first—the sheriff—had hit me hard. I'd had panic attacks, nightmares, and waking dreams plaguing me for months, but this second one was easier. I had trouble even remembering the details.

CHAPTER THIRTEEN

My squad was the second to arrive. We were renting a house about a mile from the Olympic Plaza—the plaza with the sunburst spiral, where we all would set about turning the Players. We took a cab to the house, left our luggage, and then headed for the plaza.

Agatha and John were sitting on a cement bench. Agatha was young, only 22 years old. But instead of youthful vigor, she had the posture and attitude of someone who had spent most of her life training to kill other kids like herself. She looked worn out, mentally and physically, and as she sat next to John, I could see the same look on his face. They were both tired of being who they were. They both wanted all of this to end.

John stood up to hug us as we reached him. "Tell me everything," he said, pointing at my head. "I know Eugene got nabbed. Did you get your invitations sent?"

"Yep," Kat said. "We might have killed the Baghdad player for all we know, though."

"I read about that in the paper. You guys are all right?"

"I got hit in the head a couple times, and might have cracked some ribs," I said. "Good thing Kat's a nurse."

"Well," John said. "Agatha and I are watching for Players. You up for tailing?"

"Sure," I said, and sat down next to him. Kat sat next to me.

Agatha knew the Players by sight—the lines all spied on one another, and she had a book of photographs and physical descriptions. We leafed through it, trying to familiarize ourselves with the faces.

"There," Agatha said. "Girl wearing a black abaya and head scarf. Ghaniyah. Sumerian."

John pointed across the plaza to where squad two—Larry, Lee, and Lin—were sitting on a grassy berm. The three of them stood up and gestured back to John that they had seen her.

They all spread out casually, Larry moving forward to be the lead, Lin walking close behind Ghaniyah, and Lee in the far-back position. She crossed the street confidently, seemingly unaware of the tail.

"She doesn't look like a killer," I said to Kat.

"Neither do we," she said.

"Don't get complacent," Agatha warned. "These people have trained their entire lives to be Players. They know how to kill and how to torture. They know how to shadow other people, and they'll be conscious of someone following them unless we're at our very best."

"Don't be afraid to screw the plan," John said. "If you think you've been spotted, then kill if you have to, or abort entirely. Don't let them get the jump on you."

We nodded, though we'd heard all of this a hundred times from Walter and John. We knew what we were doing—or, at the very least, what we *should* be doing. We weren't experienced in actually shadowing a real Player. But that was going to have to be enough. The time to prepare was gone, and it was time to act.

The pay phone at a nearby booth rang, and John jumped up and answered it.

I couldn't hear the call, but it was short.

"It was Douglas," John said. "He's back at the safe house. Phyllis, Henry, and Molly just arrived from India. They say Phyllis is hurt, but they came in on the same plane as their Player. Henry is following him. Molly's staying with Phyllis."

"I've heard Pravheet is very good," Agatha said. "I hope that guy you've got following him is one of the best."

"Pravheet is his name?" Kat asked. "The Indian?"

"The Harappan," Agatha said, nodding.

"Henry has his ups and downs," John said. "He can shadow, though. He did all right in training, anyway."

Agatha shook her head. "Doing all right is not enough. He's got to be good."

We waited there for another hour, everyone quiet. This was what we had been training for. Everything here—waiting for the Players, shadowing them to their hotels. This was real. This was where people were going to get hurt. Us or them. Probably both. Hopefully both, because I didn't expect us to come out unscathed—we just had to get them on our side or take them out. There were more of us than there were of them, and we'd need all the manpower we could get.

"Why don't you stay here and help, Agatha?" I asked, the waiting driving me crazy.

"I'll tell you what I told John and Walter: I'm out of the business. I'm done. Done with the La Tène line. I'm helping you because the world needs fewer Players. We need to stand up to the Makers and say we're not part of their game. But my method of doing that is to walk away."

I was about to speak when Agatha interrupted.

"There she is," she said. "Raakel. The Minoan. Gorgeous."

Raakel was indeed gorgeous. She was dressed in tight jeans and a loose shirt. Her dark hair was twisted into a knot on the top of her head, and she literally danced down into the concrete sunburst, her small backpack swinging in her hand before she pulled up on it and slid it on her back.

"She's excited about something," John said.

"She's one of them," Agatha said wearily. "Eager to Play. Excited to be the big winner. Everything I've been told indicates that she's cocky but deadly—she enjoys a fight. Bloodlust. Whatever you want to call it."

"Well," John said. "Mike, Kat, go shadow her. Take Barbara with you."

He nodded toward the grass where Barbara sat. She nodded back and stood.

I was in the lead, Barbara was back, and Kat was far back.

At the airport I had gone to a clothing store and bought everything that a certain mannequin was wearing, from its shirt to its shoes.

I wanted to wear something authentically German. It wasn't lederhosen or anything like that, but it was a slightly different look from American jeans and a T-shirt.

I hurried up the opposite side of the main road. Raakel was moving at a fast clip, and so I didn't try to sprint to get in front of her. Instead I walked parallel to her.

We followed her for five blocks when she suddenly turned on her heel and headed backward. I had to peel off. If she'd seen me in her periphery, she'd see me if I turned around and tried the same trick. I stopped at the traffic light and pretended I was heading the other way, but it just gave me a chance to stop and watch.

Barbara kept moving in the same direction, crossing paths with Raakel. Kat was the only one of us who could keep after her—she'd now become the lead.

Barbara turned and ran down the side street, while I hurried into an alley, furiously unbuttoning my shirt. Underneath was a yellow T-shirt.

I walked back out onto the street and searched for Raakel. I couldn't see her anywhere, but I told myself not to panic. I was just here to watch the Olympics and do a little shopping. I wasn't supposed to run. As I backtracked my route, I saw Kat, briefly, heading north—the same direction Barbara had gone. I turned at the next opportunity.

I walked down a block, amongst a large group of tourists. And, for just an instant, I saw Barbara turn a corner and disappear behind a building.

I followed her as quickly as I could, but as I turned the same corner, Barbara was kneeling down, tying her shoe. I walked past her, trying not to look like we were together.

"Mike," she said.

I froze. That wasn't how were supposed to shadow someone. We weren't supposed to talk.

"She went in that hotel on the left—the Hilton."

"Should we wait for her? See if she gets a room? A lot of hotels are full because of the Olympics."

"Kat went in," she said, standing up and moving next to me.

We sat down on the bench beside a bus stop and waited. The bus came, and we waved it past us.

"I'm not as afraid of them seeing us," Barbara told me. "The Players, I mean. They have no idea who we are. Why would she even care about us? I don't think anything bad will happen if she—Raakel—spots us."

"Either way, we don't really know what we're doing."

"For all the training we've gotten, all the weeks of shooting and fighting and shadowing, we're still just normal people. I'm a PR assistant. You're a student."

"And barely that."

Kat came out of the hotel a few minutes later, saw us, smiled, and took a different route. Barbara and I stood up and headed back to John. When we got back, Kat relayed the number of the room Raakel had gotten.

During that day we saw all the Players arrive except the Aksumite, and all the squads came back except for squad five—the one that was Rodney, Jim, and Julia, going after the Aksumite. It took two days, but Douglas managed to get forged press credentials to access the Ethiopian Olympic team. They had just won bronze in the 10,000-meter, and Douglas got a chance to sit down with the team's governmental delegate. The delegate was not familiar with any bombing in Addis Ababa. We had to assume that Rodney, Jim, and Julia were not coming back.

Mary arrived alone. She told me that in the lead-up to the bombing, Bruce had gotten some kind of virus. He was in a hospital in Veracruz and was in no condition to fly, let alone stand up and help with the bombing. Mary had laid the thermite on the Olmec's expansive lawn and set it burning. She'd had to place the bomb, too, by herself.

I was so happy to see her that I kissed and hugged her before I even knew what I was doing.

But then my mind flashed back to Kat and what had happened between us after Istanbul.

What was I doing?

CHAPTER FOURTEEN

On the morning of September fifth we rose at four a.m. We split back into squads. Kat looked angry. I couldn't blame her. I had shared a bed with Mary back at the safe house. We didn't do anything, but it still was wrong.

I didn't know what to do about that. But now wasn't the time.

Kat and I had been assigned to Raakel first this morning. We had to give her the talk. We had to hope that Raakel would be receptive to our message and not just kill us on the spot.

We entered the hotel, our pistols concealed beneath T-shirts and jackets. We had a walkie-talkie with an earphone so we could use it without the rest of the hotel hearing it.

We'd had a word of warning from Agatha that we needed to be perfectly accurate—the Players would scatter at the slightest sign of a trap. None of them knew what to expect; no living Player had ever gone to a Calling like this, and she said they wouldn't immediately start killing one another. They'd be waiting for a sign. But a hail of bullets was not that sign. They would scatter: they'd assume that one of the lines was breaking the rules by killing everyone before the Players could start Playing. Agatha said these Players were lightning fast, dangerous, and brutal.

I followed Kat through the Hilton lobby, walking across intricately cut marble floors. There was a stairway marked NUR AUTORISIERTES PERSONAL—Kat told me it meant "authorized personnel only." We went to the fourth floor, and then Kat led me back out to the hallway. We waited down the hall from Raakel's room for the call to go in.

"I don't like being exposed like this," Kat whispered.

"I'm sure it'll only be a minute."

"I hope you're right."

"Where will you go when this is over?" I asked, to cut the tension. "Switzerland? France?"

"I want to go home," she said, kneeling in position, but resting her Winchester on her legs. "If I make it out of here alive, that's where I'm heading."

"Go back to your job? That'll be some awkward explaining to do."

"I'm so good at telling lies now," she said with a sad, defeated tone. "I'll make it sound okay."

"About Mary," I said. Kat looked at me sharply. "What should I—"

She cut me off. "You're a big boy, Mike. You can figure it out on your own."

"No, I need to tell you. Nothing happened last night. It's over. There's nothing real about it. There never was. But you and I—that's something special. I'll go back with you to your job. Or we can go somewhere else—anywhere. I mean it."

Kat frowned. "You're so young, Mike."

"What's five years?"

"That's not what I meant."

Walter came on the walkie-talkie—I turned the volume down very low, even with the sound coming through the earpiece. "Something's going on. We're seeing a larger police presence than we saw when we did recon yesterday morning. Over."

"Are they on to us? Over," I said.

"I'll get back to you," Walter said. "I'm going to try a police channel. I'll need Kat to translate. Over."

I looked to Kat. "He wants you to translate."

"What? I had five years of German but haven't touched it since high school. I'm pretty rusty."

"You can do this."

Kat took the walkie-talkie. "This is Kat. I'll help if I can. Over."

"Walter says go to channel sixteen. There's a lot of static, but something is going on," I told her.

I unplugged the earpiece so we could both hear. What came next was five minutes of German chatter. I kept waiting for Kat to translate it, but she just shook her head. This was coming fast, from multiple people, probably using radio lingo she didn't know.

She flipped back to channel 23—our channel. "There's been a shooting in the Olympic Village. I'm really missing a lot of this. Something about Israeli team members and . . . a hostage situation? I'm not sure. They keep using a word that must mean 'terrorism.' *Terrorismus.* And they're activating everybody. But I don't really know. I don't have the vocabulary for this."

I looked out the hallway window to the street below at the entrance to the hotel. No one was moving.

"Keep listening, Kat," Walter said. "Over."

She switched the radio to the police channel, then back again.

"Shots are being fired in the Olympic apartments," she said after a moment. "Switching back. Over."

There was more chatter on the police channel, and we started to hear sirens, first to our east, but soon they were all around us, speeding to the Village.

Kat looked at me in horror as she switched channels again. "It's a group called Black September. They're armed, and they're murdering the Israelis in their beds. A guy managed to escape. He said they've killed at least two people, both coaches. Someone jumped out his window and alerted the authorities."

There were policemen everywhere now, combing the plaza.

I took the walkie-talkie. "Walter, this is Mike. Should we go ahead with the plan? Over."

"There are more and more cops here at the plaza," Molly broke in on her radio. She was watching the starburst spiral plaza. "And they're jumpy. If we stay here and if the Players come, it'll be a suicide mission. It'll be a shootout with police, and we don't have an escape route other than the way we came in. Over."

"Okay," Walter said. "All teams move out. Execute Plan Bravo. Over."

Plan Bravo. We weren't just staking out Raakel. We were going to knock on her door. It was going to be us versus her, and we had to convince her that she's wrong about everything she's worked for her entire life. And if she didn't agree, we were supposed to kill her.

"It's time," I said to Kat.

We double-checked our guns, made sure they were loaded, flicked off the safeties, and headed down the hall. We were either going to convince the Minoan Player or we were going to have to kill her. This was it. We stopped at room 412.

Ready? Kat mouthed.

I nodded.

I knocked on the door.

ENDGAME

THE ZERO LINE CHRONICLES

— VOLUME 3 —

REAP

CHAPTER ONE

"It's time," I said to Kat.

We double-checked our guns, made sure they were loaded, flicked off the safeties, and headed down the hall. We stopped at room 412. It was five in the morning.

Ready? Kat mouthed.

I nodded.

I knocked on the door.

This was it—what we had been preparing for all summer. We— just Kat and I—were knocking on the door of a Player. Raakel, the Minoan. Last week, Kat and I had planted a bomb next to her house in Istanbul, "inviting" her to come to Zero line's fake Calling. We thought she might have died in the explosion—the bomb was supposed to imitate a sign from the heavens, a message from the alien Makers.

And now we were supposed to reason with her, with this Player who was trained to be a killing machine. That's what a Calling was meant to be: the starting point of a bloodbath in which twelve killing machines, representatives of their civilizations, would each try to be the last one standing in a global fight that would decide the fate of the world.

And we needed to stop it.

My M1911 pistol was tucked into the back of my pants, covered by a long Munich Olympics T-shirt. Kat was carrying a Beretta in the front pocket of her sweatshirt. I had my backpack for our walkie-talkie and a few other supplies we might need.

There was the sound of the deadbolt being unlocked, and I tensed up, wishing my gun were in my hand. But no. We were here to talk to her, not to kill her.

Kat and I already had blood on our hands, and we didn't want more. The door opened.

Raakel stood there, fully dressed in a pair of jeans and a loose blouse. Her black hair was pulled back in a ponytail. There was a smirk on her face. Despite the early hour, she looked fully awake and ready for the Calling.

"I was wondering when you would show up," she said with very little accent. "You followed me with all the stealth of stampeding bulls. You're staying in a house with sixteen or seventeen others?"

I opened my mouth to speak, but no words came out. We were supposed to be surprising her, not the other way around.

"We're here to talk to you," Kat said.

"How do you know who I am?" Raakel asked. "For that matter, who do you think I am?"

Kat answered. "You're the Player for the Minoans."

"How do you know this?" she asked. "What line are you from?"

"Zero line," I said, finally getting my voice back. "We have important things to talk to you about."

"There is no such line." She opened the door an inch or two wider, just enough to let us pass. With her eyes trained carefully on us the whole time, she motioned us into her room. I caught a flash of metal at her side, and I realized she was carrying a blade that looked like a sword of some kind. My pulse was pounding so loud I was sure she could hear it.

"Consider us a group of concerned citizens," Kat said. I noticed the shake in her voice, and I wondered if Raakel could tell how nervous we were.

Raakel laughed as she closed the door. I walked to the table in the corner of the room, and when we sat, I got a better look at the weapon she was holding: a long, skinny machete. My heart jumped into my throat at the look of the sword.

"Oh, this?" she said with a cold smile, sitting on the foot of the bed and laying the sword across her lap. "It's called a yatağan. I assume you're both armed. I wanted to even things out. Now: talk."

Kat and I gave each other a look. Her tanned face was pale, or maybe it was just an effect of the lamplight. She was scared. I wondered if she could see the same fear on me.

I turned to Raakel. "We're here to tell you to give this up. Our group is talking to all twelve lines this morning. We want you to ignore the Calling, and to stop Playing."

Raakel laughed. "I am a Player. I've trained for this for seventeen years. My whole life. It's not just something I do; it's who I *am*. Why on earth would I give it up just because two strangers ask me to?"

"The Makers shouldn't be running the world. They shouldn't be toying with humanity like this. It's just a game they're playing."

"It's a game *I'm* Playing," she said.

Kat and I exchanged glances. We knew we were right, but I don't think either of us felt fully prepared to convince someone to give up everything that made them who they were.

"You have to give it up. All of you do—all of the Players from all of the lines. Listen: if you don't Play—if we can keep everyone from Playing— then there can be no Endgame. We can save the world." Raakel narrowed her eyes.

Kat jumped in. "The best way things can work out right now is that one of you wins and only your line will survive, and the other eleven lines on Earth get destroyed. Right? That's the best-case scenario if you Play Endgame. Millions of people will still die."

"And you two think that my not Playing will save those lives?" Raakel tightened her grip on the machete. "I don't know what you believe you understand about Endgame, but this entire world rests on the game. The history of the human race rests on the game. That's why we Play.

It's always been this way."

"But," I said, "what happens if no one Plays? If there's no winner, there will be no losers."

She shook her head. "If there's no winner, we *all* become the losers. If we defy the Makers, what's to stop them from killing all of us as punishment? Just wiping us off the face of the Earth and starting over?"

"Here," I said. I reached to pull several papers from my back pocket. Raakel jumped up, her sword ready in her hand.

"Sorry," I said, freezing. "I have something for you to read. Can I just pull it out of my pocket?"

"You read it to me," she said.

I had spent a year as a furniture salesman, and I knew when I was losing a customer. Usually they didn't threaten me with swords, though.

With trembling fingers, I unfolded the Xeroxed pages. "This is from an ancient document that we acquired from trusted sources on the inside.

"'This is the lie, the one that has fueled your life and the lives of all who have come before you. I have risked everything to remove the veil of mystery that shrouds the Annunaki.... It will all be for nothing....

"'The Mu had a choice. You have a choice.

"'To Play the game is to lose the game . . .

"'Prove to the Annunaki that you are not mindless animals, that you can think.... We, all of us, deserve a chance to live.

"'Choose to question what you have been taught.

"'Choose to be free, that we might all be free.

"'*Choose not to Play.*'"

Kat spoke. "That's from the Brotherhood of the Snake. We know at least two lines had this document in their archives. Maybe you recognize it?"

"The Brotherhood of the Snake?" Raakel scoffed. "Who are they to tell me how I should be Playing? I've never even heard of them."

"Just think about it," Kat said. "I totally understand what you're feeling right now. You're being confronted by two people you don't know, and you're being told to give up everything that you've ever been trained to believe. But this is real. It doesn't get more important than this."

I watched Raakel watch Kat, her eyes narrowing. Now that we were sitting there, facing a real Player, I couldn't help but see the cracks in our plan. We'd been thinking about this as a question of reason, that the Players would discuss it rationally. But I didn't realize until now what an emotional decision we were asking them to make.

What did it feel like to be asked to give up your entire belief system? I remembered how hard it had been for me to believe in what Zero line was doing. It took having my hand forced—realizing I had nothing left—for me to join them. I wondered: If I'd had a real choice, would I have left Berkeley to go on this crazy mission?

Raakel shifted the sword to her left hand.

"So what if I don't Play, and you can't convince every other line? I will have to Play, or my line will perish."

"We're out this morning to stop every other line," I said. "That's our goal."

"Why should I trust you? Maybe you're working for another line, trying to remove some of the Players."

"Look at me," I said, raising my voice slightly. "My name is Michael Stavros. I'm Greek. Odds are I'm a Minoan, just like you. If I believed that stopping you would cause the death of me and all my family, do you really think I'd be doing it?"

"What is this word you use? *Stop*? What is that supposed to mean?"

Kat's voice was pleading now. "It means that we want you to turn around and get on a plane back to Istanbul. Don't Play the game."

"Just 'don't Play the game'?"

"That's right," she said. "Don't Play the game."

"And what do I tell my family? My line? Their hopes are pinned on me. The lives of millions rest on my shoulders. And I should just turn my back on my responsibility?"

"You tell them just what we're telling you. That you don't believe in it. That you're walking away."

Raakel stood up. For what felt like several minutes she paced the room. The machete never left her hand.

"And if you can't convince me to do that, how are you supposed to stop me? Does your Zero line have a plan for that?"

Damn it. For a minute I'd thought we had her.

"We're supposed to stop you," Kat said. "That's all. Stop."

"You think it will be that easy? You underestimate me. I know some of the other lines," Raakel said. "We watch each other. The Harappan. You will not 'stop' him. And the Mu. And probably many others. You will fail. And then what will you do?"

"We will stop them," I said. "We will."

My heart rate was skyrocketing, and I felt sick to my stomach. We were going to have to kill her. One of us had to draw our gun and fire it before Raakel could swing her vicious sword.

I hadn't shot anyone since I killed the sheriff back in California. That seemed so long ago, but so present. I still saw that man's face down the sights of a gun, no matter how many rounds I had fired down the shooting range.

"Stop us how?"

Neither Kat nor I said anything. We sat, tense, staring at Raakel and the sword in her hand. This was not how this discussion was supposed to go. She was supposed to see reason. She was supposed to know that the game didn't have to be Played. But I saw now how naïve we were being.

One of us is going to die.

Raakel was going to swing her sword and kill one of us, and if we were lucky, the other one would draw their gun and shoot before she turned on them. And that was the best case. The worst was that neither Kat nor I would make it out of here alive. We were going up against people who had been trained by mentors like Walter.

The Players were too good for us. And they had been indoctrinated from birth. They weren't going to be convinced in a 20-minute conversation. They weren't going to give up on everything they'd been raised to believe.

"There's more to this book from the Brotherhood of the Snake," I said, trying to get Raakel to think about something other than killing us, and the meaning of "stop."

"What else is in there?" she said, but she was smiling, toying with us. This was the start of the game for her. She was enjoying it. Two easy kills before moving on to the real Calling.

"It gives the history of the game," I said. "It explains how the Makers started Endgame as just that: a game."

Kat jumped in. "You don't have to fight. The Makers started all of this as sport for themselves—initially they just hunted us themselves. Then they turned us on each other."

As I sat there and watched her, I realized something: this was real. I had had my doubts all summer, while we were at the ranch and hearing John and Walter talk to us every night about the Players, the Calling, Endgame itself. Even while we were delivering invitations, there was a voice in the back of my mind that said that Agatha, Walter, and all the others were delusional. That aliens weren't real. But now I had to face the facts. There really were Players. They really had responded to our bizarre invitations. They didn't just *have* to Play. They were eager to.

Raakel stood up, and we did the same. I felt the gun heavy and cold against my back.

"We are done," she said.

"Here," I begged. "Read the pages." I pushed the papers to her. If she took them and looked down, we could get the jump on her.

She glanced down at the papers, laughing. "I don't care what your book says. I don't know where it came from, and there's no reason I should believe it. Like I said: maybe you're from another line? Maybe you're trying to get rid of your competition."

"Just read the pages," I said again. "Please."

She laughed and took them from me, and immediately Kat and I both grabbed our guns.

There was a flash of movement, the papers dropping from her hands. She changed the sword back to her right hand—she wasn't ready; she had been too cocky.

I saw the Beretta in Kat's hand before I could draw my gun.

Raakel swung the sword just as Kat fired.

The sword hit Kat in the arm, and she screamed. Raakel grunted loudly, reminding me of a tennis player whose racket had just connected with a hard serve.

My gun was out and I fired. We were too close for me to miss her, but I was scared, trembling, and my shots were off target: my first hit her in the thigh; then I hit her stomach three times.

Kat dropped the Beretta from her injured hand, and Raakel dropped the sword.

"Aman tanrım," Raakel said, as she stumbled back and sat on the bed. There was blood everywhere—spatters all across the blankets, a sure sign that the bullets I'd fired had exited her back. She had her hands on her abdomen.

"Aman tanrım," she said again, sucking in air as the blood flowed.

"Bok. What did you do?"

"We had to stop you," I said.

Next to me, Kat ran for the bathroom.

"Kat?" I called.

"I need a towel," she said. There was a trail of her blood on the carpet.

"We have to get out of here!"

"You're fools," Raakel said with a wince. "You can't stop everyone. You can't stop the Makers."

"You should have listened," I said.

"Someone will take my place." Raakel's voice was weak. "Don't you know that? And someone will take their place. And it will continue. There's no way to stop us."

"We're going to stop everyone," I said.

She grimaced, hunching over. "Kill me," she said. "You want to stop me, so just do it. I'm going to bleed out."

I held the gun to her head.

There was the sheriff. There was Tommy. Staring back at me with lifeless eyes over the barrel of my gun.

Kat came back. "We have to get out of here." She had a white hand towel wrapped around her arm. "I need you to tie this."

"Just do it," Raakel repeated.

I couldn't force myself to look at her.

"Do it," Kat said.

I closed my eyes and fired two bullets into Raakel's head. When I looked again, Raakel was slumped over, sliding off the bed and onto the floor in front of me.

"You tried, Mike," Kat said, gritting her own teeth against the pain. "We both tried as hard as we could."

"Did we? Well, it wasn't good enough." I felt tears welling up in my throat, hot and painful. "Kat, I don't know if we're going to convince any of them."

"I need you to tie this," she said again, her voice shaking. I turned and looked at her. She was pale and scared.

"Come on," she said. "We're going to have police on us any minute now. We probably woke up everyone in this whole hotel."

I put my gun back in my waistband and took the ends of the towel in my hands. "How is it?" I asked, as I tied it into a makeshift bandage.

"It's the back of my arm," she said. "So no arteries or anything like that. But it went down to the bone. I need stitches."

I tightened it and then reached down to pick up her fallen gun. She took it with her left hand.

"There's a back stairway," she said.

"Okay."

She took a robe from the closet and pulled it on, putting the Beretta into a pocket. As we got outside into the hall, we saw a dozen other guests, most of them in pajamas or bathrobes; they all looked tired and bewildered, wondering where the noise had come from. Rumors of whatever was going on in the Olympic apartments had to be passing around. Kat and I played it cool, trying to take on the same look that the others had.

An employee of the hotel made an announcement in German that I didn't understand, but Kat did.

"Let's get out of here," she said.

"The back?" I asked.

"No, the lobby."

At the front desk Kat asked the clerk a question in German, and he nodded.

He opened a drawer, neatly organized with all kinds of toiletries: toothbrushes, shower caps, fingernail clippers. He pulled out a little packet and a book of matches and handed them to Kat.

"Danke," she said.

"Bitte."

We slipped out the front door and crossed the street to a park. It was still dark out, but the eastern sky was beginning to lighten.

"What's that?" I asked, as she led me to a picnic table.

"A sewing kit," she said, sitting down and opening the small packet, revealing thread, needles, and a couple of buttons. "You're going to stitch me up."

CHAPTER TWO

We had a first aid kit in the backpack and she opened it and took two painkillers. I opened an alcohol swab and wiped the vicious gouge. The Turkish blade had cut cleanly—a straight cut through the sweatshirt, skin, muscle, down to the bone. I lit a match to sterilize the needle and then tried to follow Kat's instructions to stitch the wound up cleanly. It took me a few minutes to get the hang of it—I was timid at first, knowing how much pain she had to be in—but I soon figured it out. It was going to be an awful-looking scar, but she said it had to be done.

While I worked, she got on the walkie-talkie and called to report in. She had the earphone in, so I couldn't follow most of the conversation. "We had to kill her," Kat said. "Yes . . . No, there was no other choice. . . . No. No. At least I don't think so. . . . Yes. Mike is stitching me up, but I'm not going to be able to use my right hand. It severed the muscle and tendons I think. I need a hospital. . . . We're in a park across from the hotel. . . . Okay. We'll see you."

There was a long pause, and she looked down at the slash. She was far more comfortable with blood and being stitched up than I was. I didn't know what kind of pain pills she'd taken, but they must have been strong. She'd been the one to make the first aid kits, and I'd have been willing to bet that she'd taken the pills from the clinic where she worked—these weren't over-the-counter medications.

"How are we going to explain this to a hospital?" I asked. "People don't normally stitch themselves up."

"You'd be surprised what people do," she said. "Lots of patients self-medicate, and do crazy things like try to remove teeth with pliers or try to close a wound with superglue. That one's not so crazy. It works pretty well for small stuff. Medics use it in Vietnam. I don't know if it's been studied for toxicity, though."

"You're not going to be able to use your hand?"

"No, since you're not suturing the tendons. That's going to need a hospital."

"Then what good is stitching?"

She smiled through her pain. "It stops the bleeding."

"What did John have to say?" I asked, gesturing to the walkie-talkie.

"Mary and Tyson had to kill their Player too. The Koori. Tyson took a bullet, and they're in the hospital. Walter is off meeting with the Cahokian. He thinks he'll be able to reason with him, since they know each other."

I concentrated on the last little bit of the wound, as Kat instructed me how to close it and tie the thread off. When I finished, I took her injured hand in mine. She moved her fingers a little, just to see what they could still do.

"I'm sorry," I said. "I thought that I could draw my gun faster than she could attack."

"It's okay," Kat said.

"You know what, though? I honestly thought she'd be a lot harder to kill. I thought she had some kind of trick up her sleeve. Walter and Agatha really made these guys out to be worse than they are."

"I don't know. You're not the one who got hacked with a sword."

I laughed a little. "Fair point. You know what's weird? No police are going to the hotel. We fired, what, five shots? Six? And nobody is there to investigate."

"Maybe they came and they just don't have their sirens on. I can't see the entrance to the hotel from here."

I nodded. They could be going room to room with a SWAT team, searching for bullet holes, looking for bodies. They'd find Raakel and her sword and that would be that. It would be a puzzle that they never solved.

At least I hoped they'd never solve it. No police department would ever believe in Endgame, would they? Not even when they found Raakel and the Koori.

"What are we supposed to do about the Aksumite?" I asked, suddenly worried about everybody. "Rodney and Jim and Julia never came back from Ethiopia. Agatha never spotted the Aksumite Player. I think we have to assume he killed them?"

"Maybe the bomb went off too soon and killed them."

"Either way, that's a loose end we need to tie up."

"Maybe." Then she stopped. Her face grew even paler than it already was. "Wait. Mike. Did you get the pages off the floor—the Brotherhood of the Snake stuff?"

My heart dropped. "No. And that's my only copy."

"That's *our* only copy," she said. "But that's not what I'm worried about. Our fingerprints are all over that thing."

"They'll be all over the table and chairs too," I said.

"Yeah, but there will be a thousand fingerprints on the table, from everyone who has stayed in that room. But those papers lead directly back to us—just our prints and Raakel's. We'll get put into a database from Interpol or something."

"But they can't connect us to anything," I said. "Right?"

"What about the gun store robbery? The bank robbery? Both our prints were at the bank."

"There'd be no reason why a shooting at the Olympics in Munich would ever be connected to a bank robbery in California. No one would make the connection. No one would compare the prints."

She pulled the robe closer around herself, as if she was cold. "Except that there's some kind of terrorist attack going on at the same time we're killing people in their hotel rooms. And how many witnesses saw us come out of that door?"

"We can't just go back there," I said. "There's no way we can get them back. We're screwed, Kat."

"Yeah," she agreed. "We need to talk to John and Walter. They're all coming here, after Mary gets done with Tyson."

"Why here?"

"It's kind of a central location. We're all going to meet up and try some new tactics."

I nodded. "Good. Because Raakel was totally unswayed by our arguments."

Kat stood, but she was a little unsteady on her feet. "You okay?" I asked. Kat was stronger than most people I knew, but everyone had a limit. I couldn't believe I hadn't reached mine yet.

"Let's get to a more concealed part of the park."

"Right. And you need to get out of that bathrobe."

"Everyone else is in robes," she said, gesturing to the hotel guests who had filled the street after the alarms went off. "You wear it."

"But we don't want to look like we came out of that place."

Kat set her face in a grimace. "You need to get in there, fast," Kat said, with a slight slur. "Go now, while everyone is outside and the police haven't arrived yet. I'd go with you, but I think I'm not fit for service right now."

I helped her down on a park bench, farther from the street now that it was getting light.

"Stay here," I said.

I took another look at the slice in her arm and my poor, uneven stitching. She was definitely going to have a scar—but hopefully she'd regain the use of her fingers. At least the bleeding had stopped.

She took a pouch of something out of the first aid kid—some kind of antibacterial something—and squirted it all along the cut.

"Can you help me with the bandage?" she said, pulling two-inch squares of gauze from the first aid kit.

She held the cotton down with her left hand, and I taped it on. I was no surgeon—I wrapped a strip of tape all the way around her arm twice.

I took the robe from her and put it on myself. I left her gun with her, in the backpack. The robe was snug, but no one else looked particularly well dressed. They'd been awakened by a fire alarm early in the morning. The fact that my robe had blood on it seemed to go unnoticed by anyone in the crowd. There was a lot, but it mostly stained the inside of the fluffy material, not soaking through.

Despite the fire alarm and the noise of bullets, there were only two fire trucks—no police at all yet.

"Absurd," a man next to me said in a proper English accent. "To be awakened at this hour is absurd. They don't even know what they're looking for. I don't see any smoke. Do you?"

"No," I said. "And I have to get inside. If there is a fire, I have documents in there that can't be destroyed."

"Good luck. The concierge is turning everyone away at the door."

I hadn't had a good look at the entrance, so I bade good morning to the man, and walked around a fire truck, the word FEUERWEHR emblazoned on the front. There was a single man at the top of the stairs—a balding man in a suit and tie, who was giving his assurances in English and German to the guests that everything would be fine. He said it was likely a false alarm.

"Wait to go in," a voice behind me said.

I startled and looked back. It was John.

"How did you get here so fast?"

"I was only down the street at the Staatlich hotel. Say good-bye to the La Tène."

"I thought that Agatha was going after the La Tène?"

"Agatha talked to the La Tène last night. But he wouldn't get on board. Agatha left him for us—he wouldn't agree to stop Playing, and she said she wasn't going to kill anyone."

"You had to kill?"

He nodded, his lips forming a thin line. "I think we're going to have to kill more today."

I sighed and shook my head. "The Minoan got Kat pretty good," I said.

"I had to kill her—" I laughed tiredly. "Kill the Minoan, not Kat."

"I knew what you meant. Where is she?"

"In the park. I stitched her up, but she won't be using her right hand anytime soon."

"Damn."

"Yeah. And I left evidence in the room. I've got to get in there."

"What did you leave?"

"The Brotherhood of the Snake papers."

"Some good they did, right?"

"Yeah," I said, annoyed by how casual John was. He was always like this. Walter was the one who barked orders. John just talked like a normal person. He talked like a peacenik half the time, and I'd rarely seen someone get a rise out of him.

"Who says you need to go back inside and get them?"

"Our fingerprints are all over them."

"It's a risk we have to take. You can't go back in there."

"But they're what's supposed to convince them to join us," I said, my panic rising. "We only have so many copies."

"Mike," John said, "I think it's time that you face the facts. Negotiation hasn't worked. We need to just get in there, eliminate them, and get out."

"We can keep trying," I said.

"Mike," John said, grabbing my arm. "You didn't really ever expect that to work, did you? These Players are trained killers. Their whole lives have been built on the idea that Endgame is real and they're saving their entire line—that everyone they know and love will be killed if they don't win. Negotiation was idealistic, and it's not working."

"They're not that good," I said. "You made them out to be half kung-fu master and half gunslinger. And so far we've killed the Minoan, the

Koori, the La Tène, and the Cahokian. These Players aren't what we expected them to be."

"We haven't heard from Walter on the Cahokian yet. Barbara and Douglas haven't called in yet from the Olmec, either. Tyson took a bullet. We haven't heard from Larry, Lee, and Lin, either, or Molly, Henry, and Phyllis. Bakr too. Don't make the mistake that this is going to be easy."

"Mary's okay?" I asked.

"She's fine. Cuts and bruises."

"We need to rethink this. We're not getting any of the results that we set out to get. This is going to turn into a bloodbath."

"Yes we are, and it already is," John said, with a fierceness in his eyes that I hadn't seen before. "Tell me you never thought that this was going to end peacefully. We warned you: the Players are trained killers, not diplomats. They're here to do one thing: kill everyone who stands in their way. We need to move to Plan Charlie."

"Plan Charlie? Go in guns blazing? What about Bravo? What about talking to them?"

"We're losing," he said. "We've killed three or four of them, and they may have killed as many as half of us. And it's barely even dawn."

My head was swimming. I couldn't think straight through the panic.

"Just let me get back inside and get those papers. John, please. My prints are all over them. I can't be connected to this. I can't." Kat had reached her limit; maybe I was reaching mine.

John grabbed my shoulders and looked me dead in the eye. "Mike, have you been following what's going on here today?"

"What do you mean? The shooting at the Olympic hotel?"

"It's not just a shooting. It's terrorists. Black September, a faction of the PLO. You know the PLO, right? Blowing up buses in Jerusalem and hijacking planes. Do you remember two years ago—the big hostage crisis when those airliners were held full of passengers? Three hundred and ten people on four jets, out in the desert?"

"Yeah, I remember." My vision was blurring. I couldn't take in all this information right now. This was getting so far out of control.

"It's those guys. This morning a number of them—some say as many as twenty; nobody's sure—they barged into the Israeli hotel rooms. One guy, a wrestling coach, was able to escape through a window, but that's all we know so far. There have been gunshots."

"They're going after the athletes?"

"They are. And it's going to be a huge disaster. It might derail the whole Olympics. And you have to think about it: these guys didn't come to Munich because they thought they were going to escape. This is a suicide mission, and they have the whole Israeli team. This could be the start of a war."

"But what does that have to do with us?"

"You haven't seen police response like we're going to have here. It's going to make the protests at People's Park look like a picnic."

"Then all the more reason for me to get up into the hotel and get those papers. They're the only clue we left in the room, and when the police find them, they're going to dust them for fingerprints."

"Are your fingerprints on file?" he asked, looking over my shoulder at the concierge at the entrance to the building.

"Yes. It was part of becoming a park ranger."

"But you're not on some national fingerprint list, are you? Who is going to compare those papers to fingerprints in southern California? You're panicking, and you're not thinking straight."

I ran my hand through my hair. "The more time we talk, the less likely I am to get safely into the room."

"You're not going back in there, Mike. I'm sorry, but I can't let you do that."

"You can't *let* me?"

He pulled back his jacket a little, flashing just enough of his gun for me to get the idea.

"I can't let you," he repeated.

I couldn't believe what was happening. Peaceful, hippie John was threatening me. Maybe he wasn't really into peace and love and all that. Maybe that was just a ruse, and this was his real personality. It was like half the training we'd gone through had been a bluff to trick us into thinking we were more than just assassins.

"I'm going in," I said. His hand grabbed my arm, but I wrenched free and ran inside.

CHAPTER THREE

At the top of the stairs, the concierge stopped me. "You can't enter," he said in heavily accented English. *"Sie können hier nicht reinkommen."*

"I will only be a minute," I said.

"But sir, it's not safe. *Sie sind in Gefahr. Achtung!*"

"I'll be right back," I said, pushing past him.

"Sir!" he called after me. "Sir!"

I turned a corner and raced up the stairs. There were still no police here, only firemen. Even so, I switched my gun from the back of my pants to the large pocket of the robe. It was heavy and made the bathrobe sag. I moved quietly and swiftly up the steps until I reached the fourth floor. We had done so many runs up the mountains at Mary's ranch that I wasn't even winded when I got to the right door. I knew the room was down the hall about forty yards. I didn't relish seeing Raakel again. Her face was stained into my memory now too. Her brains and blood were sprayed across the blankets. I would never be able to unsee that.

I could see the door. It wasn't closed all the way, but there were no firefighters, no crime-scene tape. I pulled out my M1911 and moved quietly to the door.

I shouldn't have felt so afraid. Kat and I had gone head-to-head with a trained killer, and we'd won. It was a complete victory, with the exception of Kat's arm injury. But stepping into the dim room made it look like a disaster. There was blood everywhere. It wasn't like a shooting in the movies, not a simple hole in the forehead and a pool of blood under her body. No, she had slumped down, her face turned toward the floor, and I could see the enormous holes in the back of her head. There were tufts of hair and scalp on the bed, and the blood had spilled onto the blanket, soaking and spreading into a wide patch.

I could see the sheriff, but this was worse than the sheriff. He'd been a middle-aged fat guy carrying a gun. Raakel was a 17-year-old elite athlete. Sexy. Armed only with a Turkish sword. And I'd talked to her. I'd pleaded with her. This hadn't been a simple execution. It had been a negotiation. I hadn't realized how quickly it would escalate, but it had, and there was nothing I could do about it now.

I should have been less hopeful. It had been my hope to be able to talk her into a peaceful resolution, and I'd stuck to that so firmly that I hadn't realized I had lost. It was my fault that Kat got injured.

The papers were lying on the floor, with only a spot or two of blood. I bent down to pick them up.

"Don't move." An American accent. I heard the sound of a gun cocking.

My heart sank. I hadn't heard the door, hadn't seen a shadow. But the voice was close behind me.

I raised my hands. I still had the M1911 in my hand. "What do you want?"

"Take a guess."

"I just got here. I didn't do anything."

"Look in front of you," he said. "You wonder what I want?"

"I don't know anything about this."

"Right." He moved closer to me and took my gun. I heard him pull back the slide and eject the round.

"Look," I said. "I'm not who you're looking for."

"Why are you carrying a gun?"

"Look at this room. Why do you think I'm carrying a gun? We're all in danger."

"Danger from who?"

I started to turn around, to find out who I was talking to. Maybe a Player? He was American. Maybe a partner with the La Tène? Maybe a

Minoan with a really good accent?

"Keep your face to the front."

I stopped. "Who are you?"

"I'm the one asking the questions."

He grabbed my hand and twisted it down to the hollow of my back. I felt the steel of a handcuff snapping into place. I had to get away. I couldn't have him stop me here and take me away to a jail cell. I had to get back to Kat and John.

I yanked away from his grip and spun around, the cuff flying out of his hand. But as I made a motion toward him, his revolver pointed solidly into my chest. He had both hands on it now, finger on the trigger.

"Stop," he said, "or you'll end up dead on the floor next to your Player."

I stared back at him. The room was dark, with the only light coming from the hallway, making him a silhouette. I gazed into his face and fell silent, knowing he could squeeze off a shot faster than I could move.

"How do you know about Players?" I asked.

"Put the other handcuff on your own wrist."

"Tell me how you know about this. If you know, and you're stopping me, you'll be as guilty as the Players themselves."

"Put the handcuff on."

I did as he ordered. I was restrained, my hands in front of me.

"Let's get to another room," he said. "Somewhere we can talk." He took the Brotherhood of the Snake papers and stuffed them into his suit pocket. He directed me out the door. Instead of going downstairs, we went up. No one was around, not the fire department, not housekeeping—nobody.

"Who are you?" I asked as we walked, me in front, him telling me where to go.

"I work for the American government. Security for the Olympians. They sent me over to find you."

"Shouldn't you be protecting the Olympians, then?"

"Just walk."

"If you know about the Players," I said, "you have to understand why we're doing this."

"All I understand is that too many people are dying today. Are you a part of this? Are you killing Israelis too? Are you Black September?"

"I have no idea about that. You probably know more about them than I do."

He opened the door to a hotel room and pushed me inside.

He sat me in a chair at a small circular table, handcuffing one of my hands to the armrest, then sat on the bed to use the phone, his eyes still on me. He was on for a long time—maybe an hour, maybe more. I tried to catch parts of his conversation, but it was hard to follow only one side of it, and the person on the other end was doing more talking than he was. He was listening or waiting on hold or something.

At long last he hung up and walked over to the window.

"I know you killed a sheriff in Redding, California. I know that you've been part of a militant terrorist group called Zero line. I know that you've spent the summer practicing to kill twelve kids—like that girl back there."

"She's a trained killer."

"She was. So are you."

"Listen," I said. "You seem to know a lot about this. You have to know the danger we're in if we don't get to all the Players."

"If you don't kill all the Players, you mean."

"No, I don't. You have to understand: we're trying to talk to them. Our goal is not to kill a bunch of people. We're trying to get them to stop. To stop Playing."

He smirked. "Because that's how to stop the aliens, right?"

"Yes," I said angrily. "I know it sounds crazy, but it's true."

"Prove it."

My mind raced. I had no idea how to talk my way out of this. He had that gun trained on my chest.

"We faked a Calling," I said. "Do you know what a Calling is?"

"It's when they all get together—the twelve Players."

"Yes, but it's when Endgame starts. When they all try to kill each other, to fight for survival. The fact that they're here, that they're prepared to kill, that should be plenty of proof that this is real."

"Nice try," he said. "So maybe they're as delusional as you are. Two sides of the same cult. What I want to know, Michael—"

"My name's Frank Finn."

"That will come as a surprise to your parents in Pasadena. Come now, you don't think I haven't done my homework? We've talked to your parents. They know about the cult. They know about killing the sheriff. Now just talk to me. Tell me about him."

"The sheriff? He wasn't supposed to be there."

"So that was your first murder?"

"No. It was my first kill," I responded, pissed off. "It wasn't planned. I'm not a murderer. I killed him, but I'm not . . . it's not what you think."

The American sat down across from me at the table in the corner by the hotel window. My left wrist was handcuffed to the armrest, but it was an old wooden chair, and when I leaned back, the arm came out of joint. I thought that I could get the handcuffs loose if he looked away. I had to be ready to move when I did that. I only had one shot at escape.

"How is that not murder?" he asked, his face a mask. "Tell me what I'm misunderstanding."

"It was self-defense." My heart was pounding in my chest. I couldn't even tell if I was bluffing anymore, or if it was the truth.

"You had just killed two other men. Was that self-defense, too?"

"I didn't kill two men."

"Your friends did." The agent—was he CIA, FBI maybe?—stood up from his chair and paced the room. I had no idea how he had tied me to anything in California. The papers from the Brotherhood of the Snake were on the table—no one had even run prints, and now the man's fingerprints were on them as well.

I didn't know what to say to him. All I knew was that I had to get out of there, fast. The team was counting on me. Kat was counting on me. We didn't have much time.

She was probably already gone. I'd been in the hotel far too long. She couldn't just be waiting in the park, like I'd left her. John had been there. The two of them might have written me off as captured, a lost cause. John had shown his true colors. He was ruthless. He didn't care about any of us.

Kat wouldn't abandon me. And she knew I wouldn't abandon her. She had to know that something had stopped me from getting back to her. She'd wait.

No, Kat needed to get to a hospital. Would someone still be waiting for me? The fire department was likely gone. It was up to the Munich police to worry about Raakel's body, and they were so busy with the Olympics that they might not come for hours. John said we would all be meeting at the park, but they would have had to leave without me. They couldn't wait this long.

"The cop," I said, thinking fast, "had just shot my friend in the chest."

"Your *friend* was shot in the chest while you were robbing a store at gunpoint. You face charges of grand larceny, assault with a deadly weapon, and murder, and that doesn't begin to address what you're doing here in Germany."

He was the only agent there—alone and stupid. Maybe he was just from the US Consulate. He clearly had no idea who he was dealing with. He thought I was just a run-of-the-mill terrorist. But I wasn't. I was Zero line. What we were doing was so much bigger than one California sheriff's life. So much bigger than an FBI or CIA agent. So much bigger than me. He was wasting my time, and time was the one thing we needed on our side.

"Listen," I said. "Can I use the bathroom?" I'd scanned the place for anything I could use to escape. It was no prison—it was just a hotel. Someone had slept in the bed last night. It wasn't made. "We've been sitting in here for hours."

He stared at me through narrowed eyes. "I'll let you get up when you're finished answering my questions." He leaned forward, trying to intimidate me. "Why are you in Munich? What's your plan here?"

"I want a lawyer."

"We're not in the United States," he said. "Different rules."

"Different rules?" I said, nervously laughing a little bit. "You're an American; I'm an American. The Constitution guarantees my rights."

"Here's the passenger manifest from your flight out of Reno. I'm going to read through the names, and you're going to tell me who else is in your group."

"Seriously?" I said, and laughed. "I thought you already had all the answers. You obviously have no idea what is going on. No idea."

While the agent talked, I leaned back in my chair. The armrest wasn't moving enough. The joint was loose, but the back of the chair hit the wall, and I wasn't able to squeeze the handcuff out through the gap. I gripped the armrest, trying to guess its weight.

He sat again, his chair scooted all the way in to the table. "I know you're not here alone. Who else from the plane is working with you? I've heard about Katherine McKnight—Kat."

"You're wasting my time," I said. "I need to get out of here. I don't have time."

I gripped the arm of the chair with my handcuffed left hand.

"If it's so important, why won't you tell me what it is?"

And then it hit me.

"Eugene," I said, looking at him. "You've been talking to Eugene. That's how you know about all this stuff."

He smugly straightened his tie. "Eugene West. We were told to watch for you. I knew you'd start your killing today, but I didn't know the magnitude. Tell me: How did you get involved with Black September?"

"You have no idea what you're talking about," I said, shaking my head. "We're not with Black September."

214

He leaned toward me, our faces only inches apart. "Then explain it to me."

I shoved the table with my right hand, tipping it into the agent's stomach. I leaped to my feet, yanked up the chair, and smashed it into him. It lost some of its momentum as it scraped against the wall, but I was still able to bring it down on him hard. The chair broke as it hit his shoulder and the table, but the armrest was still in my hand. I beat him across the face with it until he went down. He was dazed, and I scrambled out from behind the table and pieces of the broken chair. He went for his gun, slowly pushing the broken chair away. He was bleeding from his head—a lot. I hit him again with the armrest and then gave him a right hook. He wasn't struggling anymore, and I grabbed his pistol from his holster.

I pulled the broken armrest out of the handcuff and knelt down next to him to find his keys. I grabbed them just as he tried to throw a weak punch. It caught me off guard, and I stumbled back slightly. But I had his keys and gun, and I held the pistol in my left hand while I unlocked the cuffs.

CHAPTER FOUR

I put a handcuff on his left wrist and locked him to the radiator. Then I grabbed a hand towel from the bathroom and used it to gag him. "You want to know what we're doing here?" I asked as I rummaged through the closet. There was a suit there, but I didn't want that. All I needed was a shirt that wasn't covered with Kat's blood. I knelt down and unzipped a gym bag.

"We're saving the world," I said. "You probably thought Eugene was crazy, or maybe he told you that we're crazy, but all of it's true. If it wasn't true, then why would Raakel—the girl in the other room— why would she be here? We sent out invitations, and she understood what we were doing, and she came here. Because of this goddamned Endgame. I hate it just as much—no, I hate it more than you do. Because I know what it is. The Players fighting for the end of the world. They're fighting for survival, and we have to stop them before they come after each other."

I found a plain gray sweatshirt and pulled it from the bag.

"If we don't do this, the entire population of the world could be wiped out. Well, maybe a twelfth will live. But billions will die. Billions. Can you even comprehend that? We don't know how it will happen— disease, nukes, maybe just hunting us down like animals—but it will happen. That was the contract signed thousands of years ago. By killing Raakel, I just stopped the Minoan line from Playing. Now we have to stop the rest of them, if we want to stop Endgame from happening."

I pulled the sweatshirt on and checked the agent's Colt Lawman revolver. I opened the cylinder to see if it was fully loaded. It was, and I put the safety on and tucked it into my belt.

"When this is all over, you can hunt me down. I know I've done a lot of illegal things in the last four months. But you'll have to wait, because there's a job to be done. Who knows—maybe I'll die and you won't need to look for me."

I gave him one last look, took the papers from the table, and then exited the room. I put the DO NOT DISTURB placard on the door.

The corridor was empty, and I looked for the nearest stairs. I wanted to find a back way out of this place and stay as far from Raakel's room as I could. From what I was able to pick up from the one-sided phone conversation, the agent hadn't informed the Germans about Raakel yet. He only spoke on the phone to other Americans.

That could mean backup was coming. Or maybe there was no one to send. Maybe the agent was bluffing, and he was alone. I looked at my watch. I'd been in this damn hotel for more than two hours. I needed to get out and find Kat or John. Or Mary.

I ran down the stairs, as fast as I could.

I was flooded with confidence. Not only had I killed a Player, but I had successfully escaped from an agent. Of what agency, I didn't know, but he was some kind of cop. State Department, maybe. From the consulate, perhaps.

At the bottom of the stairs there were two doors, one to the hotel's main floor and another to the back of the hotel. I cautiously stepped out a side door. It was lighter now; the sun had risen. There were still people in the street and in the park, but no sign of Kat or John or anyone else. I was going to have to go back to the safe house if I was ever going to find them. Odds were the safe house would be empty by now, and I'd have to call on the walkie-talkie. We hadn't made contingency plans for if we got separated.

I made a beeline for the closest train platform and started jogging. They'd be at the next targets now—other hotel rooms somewhere. Or would the Players all have gone to the plaza already? That's where we had talked about eventually meeting them—we'd talked of getting snipers up on the roof of the buildings surrounding the spiral sunburst. But could we do that now? I was seeing cops all over the place, in cars with flashing lights or on street corners trying to do crowd control.

There were clinics everywhere—or pharmacies, maybe. They were small, with neon crosses glowing. I wondered if Kat could be in one of them, getting better stitches than my uneven, crooked attempt. She'd need major surgery eventually. She'd told me that. Raakel's sword had cut through at least some tendons—Kat couldn't move her fingers more than a little painful twitching.

The train stop was crowded, with Olympic guests everywhere. They were all speaking in different languages, and I could only catch a little. *Terrorism* seemed to be the same in every language, and I heard variations of *Israel* a lot.

I waited in the warm morning air for several minutes before the lights of a train appeared down the line.

"Have you heard?" a woman behind me said. "At the Hotel Vier Jahreszeiten. They found two people dead. There were others there too. A Japanese girl, they said, and an American."

"What?" another woman replied. "That's just down the street from us."

"I know. I talked with a policeman and he said that there was a tremendous gunfight. A young woman managed to evade capture and is at large."

Mary, maybe? John had said that Tyson had gone down. And the Japanese girl—was she Mu? What could have been happening in the last two hours?

"Is it part of the dreadful attacks on the Israelis?"

"He didn't know," she said. "Or perhaps he just wasn't going to tell me. No one has made an official statement about any of this yet."

"If they don't have the terrorists contained, one would think they should issue a warning to the public."

"I do wonder if it's something else entirely," the first woman said. "The hostage situation would seem to have nothing to do with the Japanese or the Americans."

As the train drew closer, their conversation moved to a discussion of whether events would be canceled and if it would disrupt the schedule of the games.

We had to cram inside the crowded train, and I stood in the center, clutching a strap to keep my balance. I listened for more news, but no one had anything solid to say. A few people griped about having been awakened by sirens, and someone else said there'd been a rumor of a man running through the plaza carrying a rifle. But officials were still being tight-lipped and didn't know the extent of what was going on. Most people got off the train before I did, and when we finally reached my stop, only a handful of people were left.

"Geht es dir gut?" an old woman asked me, and tapped my hand.

I looked down. There was dried blood on the back of my hand and fingers. Kat's blood, from while I was stitching her up.

"I'm okay," I said, and smiled.

She gave me a suspicious look, but she turned her head, and I got off the train.

I climbed the stairs up to the front door of our safe house. There was no secret knock or even keys. I just let myself in and saw Mary sitting across the room, pointing a pistol at me.

"Oh my God," she said. "What are you doing here?" She jumped up and gave me a long hug. I hugged her back, but things weren't the same as they'd been. I'd changed. Maybe it was planting the invitations with Kat at my side. Maybe it was the train ride to Baghdad. But somewhere along the line, I had changed, and I wanted to see Kat in front of me, not Mary.

"I got caught at the hotel. Someone in the government—the American government. I don't know who it was, but I had to sit there for two hours while he interrogated me." I let go of her and slumped down into a chair.

"What did you tell him?" she asked, sitting across from me.

"There was nothing to say that he didn't already know. Eugene ratted us out. He spilled everything. This guy knew about Endgame and the Players, and he knew our plans to meet at the plaza."

"How did he find you?"

"He found the Minoan—I don't know how. Maybe Eugene still had the dossier on her. He was supposed to go with me and Kat." I looked around the room, frustrated, and then stood up and walked to the kitchen sink to wash Kat's blood off my hand.

"Well, everything has gone to hell here," she said. Her voice was ragged, and she didn't look much better. "John was supposed to find you—"

"He did."

"So you know about Tyson?"

"Yeah. Someone on the train heard about you and Tyson. You're wanted."

She seemed shaken, not her calm, happy self. "Lee died too. That was just now—well, maybe an hour ago. Tyson died at the hospital after getting shot while we went after the Koori, and then Lee went with me and died fighting the Mu."

"You've killed two Players?" I said. "Wow."

"Yeah," she said. "The Mu was staying at a hostel next to one of those small neighborhood police stations. She got Lee right in the head. He didn't have a chance. It was just the blink of an eye and she got him. I got this." She pulled up her shirt to show me her stomach. There was a white bandage with a red spot in the middle.

"You got shot?"

"Grazed. And then I killed her, and had to escape past the police. I killed the cop, too. He never saw it coming. He thought I was just one of the kids staying at the hostel."

"You just shot a cop?" I asked, my stomach turning and visions of the sheriff coming back to me.

"Of course," she said. "I was fighting for my life. She killed Lee."

"But you said the cop thought you were just one of the kids at the hostel. Innocent."

"But he saw my face," she said. "What was I supposed to do? Bruce and I learned in Mexico that you don't leave witnesses."

"But you said he didn't witness you."

She stood up and came over to me. "Mike, what is this all for? You knew we were going to war with these guys. You can't have imagined that we were just going to talk our way out of anything."

"Couldn't I?" I yelled. "You kept emphasizing that this was not about *killing* Players; it was about *stopping* them. John had me write up the sales pitches. Did you even try that with the Mu? What about the Koori? Or did you just go in shooting first and asking questions later?"

"Come on, Mike," she said. "Grow up. We did target shooting every single day. We practiced stacking up at a door and making a hostile entry. We ran the mountains. We did obstacle courses. Did you really think all of that was so that we would be in better shape to *talk*?"

"Yes," I said. "Yes, I did think that we were going to talk, because that's what we said we were going to do. That's what John said, and it's what Walter said, and it's what you said. And you know what? It's what Kat and I did with the Minoan."

"And how did that go for you?"

"We ended up having to kill her," I said, turning off the water and drying my hands. "But we gave her a fair chance. She knew why we were there, and she had a choice. We didn't just ambush her."

"And now Kat is at the emergency room," Mary said. "And we still have seven Players to kill. Still no word from Barbara and Douglas—they were going for the Olmec—or Molly, Henry, and Phyllis—they were going for the Harappan. We're getting murdered out there, so maybe you'd better start to act like this is the war that it is."

"You lied to me."

"Lied? Mike, you are such a—"

"What? Such a what?"

"A child. I used to think that you joined Zero line for me, but I was wrong. You joined because you're a Boy Scout. You really thought we were going to end this all peacefully, and you could go back home like nothing had happened."

"I didn't think that. I killed that sheriff. I robbed that bank."

"Then what? You thought that you were going to retire on some remote farm somewhere and live the quiet, peaceful life of a hero? You probably imagined me right there beside you."

"Mary," I said through gritted teeth, "you're old news. Kat and I are together now. I don't need—I don't *want* you."

"Oh," she said, and then stopped without saying anything else.

"Yeah."

Her voice was quieter now. "What did I ever do to you?"

"You left me. When I thought I needed you most. And . . ." I looked out the window and then moved back to the chair by the door. "And then I realized that I didn't really need you. You did your job. You got me into this mess. You got me to believe, and you were right—Endgame is real. But we have very different ideas about what to do about it."

"The Players are killing us," she said, still standing where she was, not turning to look at me. "I wish we really could talk our way out of this."

"You weren't expecting that?" I asked. "You thought that going in like cowboys, shooting everyone we see, was going to work? At least Kat and I had realistic expectations. We knew that we were going up against killers. Assassins. We knew we were outmatched. You had too much faith in a couple of ex–Green Berets."

"Bruce was a vet. He wouldn't tell me how many he killed, but he said he could remember every face."

"I always see the sheriff."

"The Mu didn't look like a killer. She looked like a kid." Mary turned to face me. "We thought it would be easy. I had a clean shot and I didn't take it. I didn't want to shoot so close to the other people in the hostel.

I thought I was being kind."

"What hospital is Kat in?"

"I don't know the name of it," she said. "Walter found it on the map. He said it was just a mile north. John took her there in a cab."

"Is John still with her?"

"No," she said, and crossed the room to pick up the walkie-talkie. "They're trying to kill the others. Walter and John are. I was supposed to wait here and alert them if anyone came back."

"Where did they go?"

"John is after the Olmec, and seeing if he can find out what happened to Barbara and Douglas. Walter is going for the Shang. I was supposed to tell the next group back to go to the Nabataean."

"Call them and tell them I'm going for Kat. I'll call you when I know more." I picked up someone's backpack and dumped out its contents onto the floor, and then I put one of the spare walkie-talkies inside. "Okay."

CHAPTER FIVE

"Mike!" Kat said, sitting up on her hospital bed. "I thought . . . We thought you'd been caught."

"I was," I said. "Eugene ratted on us. There was somebody waiting for me. He knew everything."

"If he knew everything, why did he let you go?"

"He didn't. I escaped." I sat down on the stool next to her bed. "How are you?"

Her arm was splinted and wrapped in an Ace bandage.

"They say I'll need surgery. I still can't move my fingers very well, but I was afraid all the tendons were cut. They're not. Well, not all of them. And either way, I'm not supposed to try to move them. That's the reason for the splint."

"Where are the others? Mary told me that John had been here with you."

"He brought me in, but we have to get to all the Players. We might have missed some already. What time is it?"

I checked my watch. "A little before ten."

She shook her head. "We still have so many Players to stop. We can't be sitting around here."

"You need to heal."

"I'm done here," she said. "I've already been stitched up, and now all I'm waiting for is to be discharged."

"What did they say about my stitches?" I asked with a little laugh. "Do I have a second career as a nurse?"

She rolled her eyes. "They weren't happy. They didn't know what to make of it. They asked why I would have you do that instead of coming to the hospital."

"Were they suspicious?"

"No," she said with a little shrug. "I think they just thought I was a stupid American. I pretended not to speak any German, or even understand much of their English, blaming it on their accents. And you know John—he can lie his way through anything. He made up something about being foreigners and not understanding the German health-care system. He took the blame on himself, and they believed every word."

"What did you tell them about how you got hurt?"

"Kitchen accident. He was holding a knife and turned quickly and didn't know I was standing there. Again, they just thought we were dumb."

"Well, can you go?"

"I want to, but I need the pain meds that they're going to bring me when I get discharged. Then we can get back into the action. According to John, things aren't going too well."

"They're not," I said. "We're being taken apart piece by piece. But we've got five, maybe six—John and Walter are out again. We're still waiting for the others to report in, but I don't have high hopes. Douglas and Barbara are out together, and they haven't had as much training as the rest of us. John went out after them. They were the business managers and forgers. I don't think they're as prepared. Molly and her team haven't come back either."

"Damn," she said. "Barbara and I were close. She's not going to make it; I can feel it."

"Don't think about that. I've got a walkie-talkie in my backpack. I don't want to pull it out right now, but when you get discharged, we're supposed to check in and get our next assignment. My next assignment, I mean. You're going back to the safe house."

"No way," she said. "We started this insanity. We're going to get it done. I don't want to let all of our efforts go to waste."

"You can't even hold your gun."

"I'm coming with you," she said. "We'll figure out what we're supposed to do, and we'll make a plan, and I'll do what I have to do."

I looked at her arm and her pale skin. She didn't look well.

"Hey," she said, gesturing to the TV. "Turn on the sound."

There was a news anchor sitting at a desk, the words MÜNCHEN GEISELKRISE on the screen next to him.

I turned on the sound, but he was speaking in German and I couldn't understand anything.

Kat was watching intently, and she began to translate for me as we watched.

"They're saying anywhere between three and twelve Israeli athletes are being held hostage. The terrorists are members of the group Black September—Palestinians from Jordan. The body of Moshe Weinberg was found naked in a hallway. He was shot to death. He was a coach. Another person—*ringer*? I don't know that word. He was also shot. Black September demanded the release of two hundred and something Palestinian prisoners. They gave the deadline of nine o'clock, but that time has passed, and this is still going on."

"What about our attacks on the Players?" I asked. "Have they said anything about that?"

"Not yet," she said.

"It won't be long."

As we waited, I told her everything that had happened to me this morning—told her everything that I knew about the agent who'd detained me, and told her about meeting Mary back at the safe house. She told me about how she and John had decided to leave the park and go to the safe house. After he unwrapped the gauze on her arm to wash it, he saw how bad it was and made her go to the hospital.

"I wanted to wait for you," she said. "I wasn't going anywhere, but I started to get really dizzy, and John said he thought I was losing too much blood. I don't know if that was it. It might have been shock."

"It's okay," I said. "I'm glad you came here. I'm glad you're getting help."

A few minutes later the doctor came back in. The two of them talked for a while in English, and she sat up and smiled. She didn't look nearly as sick as she had when I'd first gotten there. He gave her a bottle of pills and told us we were free to go.

Outside, we stopped on a park bench, and I pulled out the walkie-talkie and called in. Mary answered almost immediately.

"Kat's out of the hospital," I said. "Where do we stand?"

"John couldn't find the Olmec," she said. "No word from Walter. Bakr is gone. He wasn't assigned to any team yet, but I get the feeling he skipped town. Molly came back." There was a pause. "Henry and Phyllis are dead, and they weren't able to kill their Player."

"Who were they after?" I asked.

"The Harappan," she said. "He's still at large."

Kat took the radio from me. "Mary, this is Kat. Any word from Barbara?"

There was a moment of heavy static, and then Mary spoke. "Barbara and Douglas haven't reported in yet. John was going to look for them when he went after the Olmec, but he hasn't found any trace."

"We'll go to the plaza," Kat said. "See if we can find them."

"John told me to send the next group after the Nabataean."

"Don't you think the Players are going to be at the plaza?" Kat asked.

"That's where the invitations told them to go. It's a little late in the morning for them to be still waiting in their hotel rooms."

"You can go for it," Mary said. "But be aware that there will likely be a heavy police presence there."

There was more static, and then we heard John's voice. "Just off the plaza is a café called Siegfried's. Come here, Mike, Kat."

"Ten-four," Kat said.

She handed the walkie-talkie back to me, and I collapsed the antenna and turned it off.

"If we're just going to the plaza to wait for Players to show up, this is going to get violent and dangerous. I don't even know where the sniper rifles are—probably back at the safe house."

"I left my gun there," Kat said.

"Here."

I looked around to see if there was anyone watching us. No one was. I took out the Colt revolver I swiped from the agent and handed the gun to her.

"I haven't ever practiced shooting with my left hand," she said.

"Neither have I," I said. "But this is just in case. Don't plan on being the one who needs to shoot."

She put the gun in the large pocket of her jacket. It wasn't a great option—the gun was heavy, and it was obvious that she was carrying something in there—but at least it was concealed.

Kat stopped someone on the street and asked the fastest route to the plaza. We followed the directions to a bus stop and waited about fifteen minutes. By noon we were being dropped off at the Olympic center. It was eerily quiet, and a sign posted at an information kiosk said that the games were being delayed due to the ongoing crisis. There were still a couple dozen tourists walking around, and some were even sitting at the concrete sunburst.

"Who's that?" I asked Kat, taking her good hand in mine. "The kid in the red hat."

"It could be the Harappan," she said.

He was just sitting there. Not moving. Not reading. Just observing. Our eyes met for a minute, and it was all I could do not to look away. But I kept my eyes on him for a few lingering seconds, trying not to appear suspicious.

"What do we know about the Harappan?" I asked.

"That's where Molly, Henry, and Phyllis went. I haven't read his dossier. He killed Henry and Phyllis."

There was another possible Player sitting on a patch of grass beneath a large pine. She didn't appear to be paying any attention to us, or to the Harappan. She was just reading a book casually and calmly.

"Who's left?" I asked.

"Well," Kat said, thinking. "The Harappan. The Donghu. Nabataean. Sumerian. John was supposed to take the Olmec and Walter was going after the Shang. Agatha didn't spot the Aksumite at all yesterday; Rodney, Jim, and Julia are likely dead. They never came back. Who am I forgetting?"

"We got the Minoan, and we know the Mu, Cahokian, Koori, and La Tène are dead. That's everybody."

"And we're cut in half. We don't know where most of our group is."

A door to a café—a café that was closed—opened and we saw John. He waved to us, and we turned and went toward him, leaving the possible Players in the plaza.

"Hey, guys," he said as we got close. He looked awful. Exhausted, sweating, and covered with little droplets of blood.

"What's going on?"

"We tried to get you on the radio. We have the Aksumite."

I frowned. "I thought the Aksumite didn't come."

"That's what we thought," he said, closing the door behind us. He was out of breath. "But he showed up. Looking for us too. He knows all about Zero line. He must have killed Rodney, Jim, and Julia, and then came after the rest of us."

"Did you kill him?" Kat asked.

"Not yet," John said. "We want to know what he knows."

"You're interrogating him," I said.

John led the way to the kitchen of the café. The Aksumite was there, bleeding from his head. He was young—younger than Raakel. I guessed maybe 15. Hands and feet both tied. But he was wiry and looked tough. And he was smiling at us as we entered.

Walter had his sleeves rolled up, showing the Green Beret tattoos on his arms.

"I'm going to ask you again," Walter said, perfectly calm. "What happened to the three people that came to see you in Ethiopia?"

The kid grinned. "You are all fools. Interfering in Endgame. You will all perish in the fire of the gods."

Walter turned to the counter and picked up a meat tenderizer.

Kat grabbed my hand.

He smacked a pane of glass with the mallet and it shattered into pieces.

"What do you want me to say?" the Aksumite said. "That your friends are alive and waiting for you somewhere? You sent them to me to kill the people of my line and bring me to this counterfeit Calling. My people are not the kind to sit idly by."

John spoke. "So you killed them?"

"We have eyes everywhere."

Walter grabbed the kid's laughing face and picked up a piece of glass a little bit smaller than a playing card. He shoved it into the boy's mouth, slicing the edges of his lips. The boy began to choke, and John swung a fist into the kid's chin. Walter let go of him, and the Aksumite spewed out glass shards and blood. He struggled for breath, and moaned at the broken glass in his mouth and throat. He hacked and coughed, and then began to vomit.

"You . . . ," he panted. "You will burn." Blood was pouring from his mouth.

"You won't be around to see it, kid," Walter said, and punched him.

"John," Kat said. "John, we don't need to do this."

The boy spit again, and I could see the tiny slivers of glass in the blood on the floor.

"He doesn't have any information," I said.

"Stay out of this, Mike," John said.

"You can't just torture a kid," I said back.

John jumped up and grabbed me by the shirt. "He's not a kid. When are you going to get that? These people do not deserve our pity. They deserve pain and death. And when he has experienced enough pain, I'll give him death."

"This is not what I signed up for," I said.

"Me either," Kat said.

"You wanted to stop Endgame, didn't you? Wasn't that what you signed up for? Because that's what we're doing."

"You're torturing him," Kat said.

"And what about Rodney, and Jim, and Julia?" John said. "They were my friends."

The Aksumite spit again, and formed as much of a smile as his torn face allowed him to. "They were p-p-poisoned before they ever . . . before they got off the plane."

Walter grabbed another piece of glass, but I didn't give him time. I pulled the Colt Lawman from my belt and fired two rounds into the young boy's chest.

John pushed the gun away and shoved me backward. I slipped on the tile floor and landed on my tailbone, pain shooting up my spine.

"Are you trying to make the other Players run away?" John shouted. "The Harappan's been sitting out there for an hour. The others will be coming!"

Kat answered for me. "Then shouldn't you be focusing on them instead of torturing him? We were supposed to be stopping these guys, not even killing them. Just stopping them. And you're torturing him for information you already knew? Tell me that you had any doubt Jim and Julia and Rodney were dead."

John stepped toward her, and I raised my gun again. "You do not threaten her."

"Keep it up, Mike," John said. "Keep thinking with your dick. First Mary and now Kat. Is that the only thing that motivates you?"

"Back off," I said.

We stared at each other for a long, silent minute. John could make any assumptions he wanted to, but I was here to save the world. Sure, I'd gotten into Zero line because of Mary, but now Kat and I had found something special. I was determined that, no matter what happened here in Munich, Kat and I were going to survive. We were going to stop the Players, and we were going to live.

Just then a little bell jingled. The door to the café had opened.

I turned my gun away from John and moved to the kitchen door.

It was Mary.

CHAPTER SIX

"Harappan, Nabataean, Donghu, Sumerian, Shang, Olmec. We've killed half of them," I said. "The rest are all out there, waiting for whatever is supposed to happen at a Calling."

We were still in the café, the place still heavy with anger and the smell of blood and gun smoke. Through the big glass windows, we could see the six remaining Players. A few were looking in our direction. They must have heard the gun.

But, instead of coming toward us, they all moved toward the sunburst, forming a circle around it. I moved to the window and opened it, hoping I could hear what was happening.

"So this is it?" the Sumerian asked. He was a short kid, maybe 16. He wore a red tunic and pants that reminded me of the clothes I'd seen people wear in martial arts classes. In fact, almost everyone appeared to be in fighting clothes, as if this were the Olympic judo trials. Most of them appeared to have a weapon of some kind—concealed, so as not to draw attention, but I knew what I was looking for.

There were four boys: the Sumerian, the Harappan, the Shang, and the Nabataean. The Olmec and the Donghu were girls. The Donghu was bouncing from foot to foot as if she were preparing for a boxing match. The Olmec was gorgeous—a tall, tanned girl with long, black, curly hair. She looked about my age—19, maybe.

She had a confused and angry look on her face.

"Who is that?" she said, speaking to the other five Players but pointing over at our café. She had virtually no accent. "The girl who just went into the restaurant. Who is that?"

"What are you talking about?" the Nabataean asked. He had a low voice, and he spoke perfect English, but with a British accent, and he stood as still as a tree, his arms folded. "This is about us."

"Have you noticed there are only six of us here?" the Olmec said. "That girl who just went into the café was in Mexico. She was there right before the sign from Huitzilopochtli. The explosion."

"Someone has already started Playing," the Harappan said calmly. "And I don't think that it's Player versus Player. I think someone—one of you—has brought assassins from your line. They're watching right now. Maybe they have us in their crosshairs. This is not in the rules. The Makers are watching us, and they know who is a Player and who is not. They will not tolerate cheating."

"I didn't do this," the Shang said. "I don't need help to defeat the rest of you."

"Perhaps should go see who in the café," the Donghu said in broken English.

"Perhaps you should," the Harappan said.

The Olmec girl pulled an obsidian knife from her belt. "One of you is lying. But it won't help you win. Let's get this started."

"Do we wait for another sign?" the Shang said. "Or has the game begun?"

The Harappan spoke. "Someone thinks the game has begun. I do not know what the Makers will rule about this breach, but I do know that you will not need to wait long."

The Shang, barely five feet tall, pulled a saber from his belt, eyeing the Olmec on his left and the Nabataean on his right. "Your lives will end on my blade." The Harappan was directly across the circle from him. The Nabataean held out the walking staff he was holding and removed a leather cover that hid a spearhead. In response, the Harappan drew his sword—short, with a wicked curve.

The Donghu laughed. "What is this? Middle Ages?" She reached into the folds of her clothes and pulled out a pistol. "Sorry. I prepared." She aimed at the Shang.

Next to me in the café windows, both John and Walter pointed rifles out the window, waiting for the action to start.

The Sumerian was the only one who didn't draw a weapon, but he was still smiling.

"Wait for them to kill each other," Mary said. "We don't need to shoot if they're going to settle this here themselves."

"We have clear lines of sight," John said, "and there aren't many tourists right now."

I heard a whistle, and then a Munich police officer came running over, pulling out his pistol.

"Halt! Nicht bewegen!"

Before I even got a look at the cop, the Sumerian flicked his hand and a knife buried itself into the policeman's chest.

To my side I heard glass break, and for a split second I thought John and Walter were firing, but it was the opposite: Walter fell back, a bullet in his forehead.

"No!" Mary shouted, and I grabbed Kat and pulled her down, out of sight. John fired his gun—a fully automatic AK-47. He had dropped low and was firing in long bursts, barely looking out the window.

"Who shot Walter?" Mary cried, on her knees next to him.

John ducked down and swapped out the magazine. "Shit. I think it was a sniper. Or it was that Donghu girl with the Sig Sauer." He was scared. I'd never seen that look on John's face before. He was the one who was supposed to keep the rest of us calm. "But it couldn't have been the Donghu. Or it was just a really lucky shot."

"Why would there be a sniper?" Kat asked.

John shook his head. "It's like they said. Maybe one of their lines really did send someone with them."

"Isn't that cheating?"

"I . . . I don't know. Walter would know."

"We're going to lose them," I said. When no one responded, I peeked out the window.

"Don't!" Kat said, grabbing my arm. But I stayed where I was.

"I don't see anyone on the roofs," I said. "No snipers. And we're safe."
The Donghu with the pistol was dead, lying in a crumpled heap,
the Harappan standing above her, sword fighting with the Shang.
The Olmec was running, no knife in her hand anymore—I didn't
know where it had gone. She leaped for the Donghu's gun, but it was
knocked away from her at the last minute by the back end of the
Nabataean's spear. She turned the leap into a roll and was up on her
feet in an instant, dodging the sharp end of the spear and trying for
the gun again. The Sumerian was all alone, hunched over the dead
cop's body.
The Olmec ran for the gun again, but the Nabataean was too fast
and hit her in the face with the spear shaft. She fell to the ground,
unconscious. The Nabataean looked at the fighting all around him,
spotted the Sumerian, and threw his spear.
He had good aim, but, it seemed by luck, the Sumerian turned at
the last minute, the blade slicing his clothes and skittering to a stop
several yards away.
"We have to get out there," John said. "We have to kill them all."
Mary grabbed up Walter's rifle—an M14. That was what I'd trained on
all summer. I knew the gun inside and out, but so did she. I grabbed
for the pistol at Walter's side—a Beretta. I gave it to Kat, and took
back my M1911. I kept the Colt Lawman with me, too, tucked in the
back of my pants. It only had four rounds left.
John opened the door, ran into the square, dropped to one knee,
and—didn't fire. He was searching for the sniper, if there even was
one. Mary ran out and crouched behind a cement planter full of
yellow and red flowers. She too looked for the sniper.
The Sumerian was up from the cop, holding his pistol. I aimed at him
with mine, but he was at least fifty yards away, farther than I ever
trained for.
I fired twice, from a standing position, both hands on the gun. But
I missed. He ducked back into a crouch and shot back at me. I dove
down next to Mary, trying to catch my breath. We had them vastly

outgunned, but they were moving with the skill and grace of Players, not wasting a motion, not ever unfocused.

I could hear the rat-a-tat of John's gun. He was taking short bursts now, but shooting up into an empty window.

"Shoot the Players!" I called to him.

"There has to be a sniper. That's the only open window."

"You can't see a sniper," I said. "And we need to kill the Players."

"I will," Mary said, taking a deep breath and then peering up over the planter to shoot through the flowers. Petals exploded into the air as she fired the semiautomatic rifle. I dared to look out to see what she was hitting.

Nothing. She couldn't see anything through those flowers. She was firing blind.

"Mary!" I shouted. "Give me the gun."

"No," she said, ducking back down.

"You're not hitting anything. You can't see."

"It's suppressing fire," she said, as she tremblingly fumbled with loading a new magazine—the last magazine we had with us, unless there was more ammunition on Walter's body I hadn't seen. "I'm fine. You shoot."

Kat was using an upturned outdoor table as cover and was firing at the Sumerian, but because of her injury she was forced to use her left hand, and she wasn't hitting anything.

I took aim at the Harappan, who was still struggling against the Shang, their swords swinging and clashing, parrying and lunging. I squeezed the trigger and the gun jumped up. I wasn't good at these distances. I fired again and hit the Shang in the leg. He stumbled, and immediately the Harappan swung at his neck and practically beheaded him. The Shang fell to the ground, blood spurting out of his severed arteries. The Harappan was close to the unconscious Olmec, and he ran over to her and stabbed her in the chest.

The Nabataean was running to the Sumerian, or to retrieve his spear—I wasn't sure. I didn't even try wasting bullets on him while he ran. Instead I focused on the Sumerian. I tried to follow all my training—sight the target, pull the trigger, don't squeeze it, and let out a long slow breath—but by the time I had let out the breath, the Sumerian was on his feet, running. I fired one shot at him and missed.

"Sniper!" John called, and started firing again.

I looked all around for him, trying to see what John was shooting at. "Where?" I asked.

But he couldn't hear me over the noise of his gun. I turned to Mary. "Mary."

She was lying next to me, still bent at the knees but lying on her back. She'd been shot in the eye, and there was a spray of blood out the back of her head, splattered across the cobblestones.

"Mary," I said, tears immediately springing to my eyes. I reached a hand out to touch her cheek, but then recoiled. Her face was distorted and broken. The bullet hadn't gone cleanly through her eye but had hit her cheekbone and torn a hole through her face, fracturing the bones. It was too much, too horrible to see, too horrible to remember. But I knew I was going to remember this every day of my life. It was burning into my mind, searing my eyes like a cattle brand.

"I got him," John said, letting out a long breath. "I got the bastard."

"Where?"

He pointed up at the roofline. "Behind that chimney."

"Are you sure?"

Kat answered. "I saw him fall. He's over there. By the Olmec."

"Where did they go?" I asked, numbly noticing that the Players were gone.

Mary was dead.

"The Sumerian ran, and the Nabataean followed. The Harappan, calm son of a bitch, stabbed an extra time into all of the bodies. Made sure they were dead."

"I'm sorry," Kat said, eyes wet. "I tried to shoot him. I really tried. But my hand. I couldn't hold the gun steady. I'm so sorry."

"It's okay," I said.

"We don't outnumber them anymore," John said, dropping his gun. "We need to move, and fast."

"Don't we have to follow them?" I said.

"Of course," John said, visibly shaken. "Who has bullets?"

"I have some," Kat said, standing. "I wasn't counting my shots."

"I've got three or four," I said.

"Hide your guns," John said. "I've got a Walther. One full magazine."

"Then we're going to have to figure this out. But first we need to follow them. Hopefully they'll kill each other."

I took Mary's hand and squeezed it one last time. I didn't care what she had done to me at that point. She didn't deserve to die, and not like this. And she deserved more than my just leaving her on the side of the road for some paramedics to find.

But like so many things in my life lately, I had no choice.

We ran after the Players.

CHAPTER SEVEN

I helped Kat check her magazine and saw she had four bullets left. She was bleeding through the bandage on her arm—it was dribbling down her wrist and hand—but there was nothing we could do about it. We needed to follow the Players, and we needed to stay away from the cops.

All of us concealed our pistols.

"Will they split up?" Kat asked.

"No," John said, speaking softly. "They were expecting the beginning of the game. But they didn't get any direction, any puzzle to solve, any answer to look for. So all they have as an objective is to kill each other. They have to do it now, today, because there's nothing else."

"And we can't let them get away because we'll never track them down again," I said.

"And they'll stick together, because there's nowhere else to go."

We heard a whistle, and John stopped running. Kat and I did too. I took her good hand in mine. Moments later two policemen jogged past us toward the plaza.

"Are we still in this?" I asked. "I mean, do we even have a chance anymore? We've lost everybody. Kat can't shoot because of her hand. We are almost out of bullets, and we're going up against these guys? Did you see how they fight?"

"It was unbelievable," Kat said. "Who can move like that?"

"And what if they have more backup, like that sniper?"

John took a deep breath. "We knew it was going to be hard."

"What?" I asked, incredulous. "We knew it was going to be hard. We didn't know that it was going to kill us all."

"Walter and I tried to prepare you," he said, but the words sounded hollow. "We're trying to save the world, remember? We trained all summer. Were you expecting this to be easy?"

"We trained all summer as a group. We were hunting as a team, in everything we did."

"We're still a group."

I rolled my eyes. "I meant we practiced as if we were outnumbering them. Like there were going to be more of us, like this morning when Kat and I went after Raakel. We only beat her because there were two of us."

"Guys," Kat said. "How do we even know we're going in the right direction?"

"Blood," John said simply, and pointed at the roadway. "The Sumerian is bleeding."

I hadn't noticed, but now that I was looking for it, I could spot it on the street. Not a constant trail, but every ten steps or so there was a drop. As we went farther, the drops got bigger, more the size of smallish puddles. And then they turned into small, patterned impressions, like the blood was now on the bottom of his shoe. He would have to stop somewhere soon and wrap the wound, but—

Mary's face came back to me, unexpectedly, filling my mind—just that image of her broken face, a face that I had kissed so many times. A girl who I once thought was mine. I'd been wrong. She'd played me for a fool, but I had still loved her. And now all I could see was her lifeless body, the gaping hole in her cheek.

I looked over at Kat, who glanced back at me and gave a weary smile. The trail took us out of the Olympic Village and into the streets of downtown Munich.

"Look," Kat said, pointing down a side street to where an ambulance was parked, surrounded by paramedics and one police officer. There was the Sumerian, sitting up, his back against the stone foundation of an old government building.

"Damn it," John said. "Shit."

"What?" I asked.

"The trail only leads to him. We don't know where the others are."

"Is he alive?" Kat asked.

We looked down at him, waiting for some movement. The Sumerian lifted a hand wearily. He seemed to be desperately signaling for help. John immediately started walking toward the emergency team, and Kat and I followed.

"What are we doing, John?" I asked. "There's a cop there."

"We have to kill all the Players," he said, anger in his voice.

"Yeah," I said, "but won't it be easier to track him down at the hospital? Besides, look at him—he's not going to make it much longer anyway. We should go after the others."

"Don't talk," he said, and put a finger to his lips.

I exchanged a look with Kat and let go of her hand, getting ready in case I needed to pull the gun from my waistband.

"The Nabataean and the Harappan can't be far. They're trying to kill the Sumerian too, remember."

I nodded. The two of them seemed the calmest under pressure. I didn't imagine one of them would run from the other. They'd face off, sword versus spear, somewhere nearby. An alley, maybe, or a parking garage—somewhere out of the way, out of sight.

I didn't know what John expected to do here. Kat's hand was red with blood and the paramedics would likely want to treat her too. And the cop would be suspicious of the three of us.

If there was anything helping us today, it was the hostage crisis with the Palestinians and Israelis. The police probably had a lot of manpower surrounding the Olympians' apartments, which would take a lot of cops off the streets. They were overwhelmed and couldn't chase Players across the city.

"Where are we going after this?" Kat asked.

"We're going to find the other two," I said.

"That's not what I meant. I mean when we're done today. Where are we going? Not back home."

"You speak German," I said. "We could stay here."

"How about England?" she said. "Forge some forms and get student visas."

"If we're going to forge papers anyway, let's just get our citizenship."

John again told us to be quiet. "Kat, talk in German. Pretend to be tourists."

We were only twenty yards from the cop, and he turned to look up at us.

"Geh weg," he said. *"Dies ist ein Tatort."*

"Wir suchen für den Olympic plaza," Kat replied.

"Gehen Sie weg; oder werden Sie verhaftet."

The cop turned his back to us to speak to the paramedics, and John pulled out his gun.

"No!" I cried out, but my voice was covered by the sound of three gunshots. One for each paramedic and one for the cop.

"What are you doing?" Kat screamed.

"I'm finishing Endgame," he said, walking up to the bodies. The Sumerian watched us through droopy eyes. John took the cop's gun—a Sig Sauer—and held it out to me.

"Where are the others?" John asked the Sumerian.

"Fighting," he said. "I have lost."

I noticed now that he had a new injury—there was a half-bandaged wound on his torso.

"Where did they go?" John insisted.

The Sumerian shook his head, coughing up blood. He raised his hand slowly and pointed. "That way. They will be close. Neither is wounded, and they want to fight. Are you the pacifists?"

John stood up, shaking his head. He walked to the end of the narrow street.

"What do you mean?" Kat asked.

"Three Americans visited me this morning. They told me to stop fighting. They said all I had to do was walk away and never Play."

Kat nodded emphatically. "Yes. That's us."

"I will walk away."

Kat stretched the bandage around his side. "It's deep," she said. "I think you've got a punctured lung."

"Move," John said, returning. "I think they're just a few blocks away. You can hear a crowd to the west."

Kat stood up and reached into the ambulance for a box of bandages. I helped her, since she couldn't use her right hand.

BANG!

I spun around to see John pointing a smoking gun at the Sumerian. There was a bullet hole in the kid's forehead, and he began slumping over onto his side.

"What the hell was that for?" I shouted.

John looked back toward the cross street. "We're killing all the Players. No mistakes."

Kat threw the box onto the road. "He said he was going to walk away. He said he was going to stop."

I pointed my gun—the cop's gun—at John. "What happened to all of our rules? What happened to trying to talk to the Players?"

"Of course he would say he was going to stop. We had him defenseless and injured. He was saying what he needed to say to survive."

"You've made me a murderer, John," I said. "I was just a college kid. I just wanted to make a difference. I wanted to protest the war. I wanted to get out from under my dad's thumb. And this is where we end up? Shooting a wounded teenager in the street?"

"You've known what we were about since day one," he said, tucking his gun into the back of his pants. "You just pretended that we could do this without killing."

"I pretended? *I* pretended? You asked me to write the dialogues. You had me train the others on how to sell, how to build a relationship of trust with the Players. You told me to do that, and now you're saying *I* was pretending?"

"We have to stop them all," John said, looking back over his shoulder. "They've killed enough of us. They killed Mary—didn't you see that? And now we outnumber them again. Three on two, and soon it may be three on one, if the Harappan and the Nabataean are really trying to kill each other."

"We don't know what they're trying to do," Kat said. "We don't know where they are."

"Follow the sirens. Speaking of which, we need to get out of here."

I was fuming. "Yeah, because of *your* gunshot."

"Yes," he said, turning back to face me. "Yes, because of my gunshot. We're killing them all. Every Player. And if you don't like that, then you should have damn well said it three months ago. When you killed that sheriff, you knew what you were in for. Every time you sighted down your gun at the range, you knew that you were preparing for war. You could have left at any time, but you didn't. You stayed, and you trained right along with the rest of us. You delivered the invitations, and you killed the Minoan. You're a part of this, Mike, whether you like it or not, so don't act like you're morally superior. Do what you need to do to get your head straight, but do it now, because we're going to end this game."

I kept my gun on him for a long ten seconds.

"It's okay," Kat said, putting her hand gently on my back. "Let's get it over with. When we're done, we won't have to see John ever again. We won't have to think about this ever again. For all we know, the Players are killing each other right now anyway. We can do this, and get it over with, and leave. You and me. Together."

I let out a long breath and then lowered the gun.

"Come on, then," John said. "I think they went this way."

We ran to the left down the cross street. I was getting lost, not knowing which way was north or south, east or west. I just followed John and held Kat's hand.

How were we supposed to stay in this country? We'd spoken easily about forging papers, but it was Barbara and Douglas who had done all of that, and they hadn't come back from their mission to kill the Olmec Player.

As we walked behind John, I pulled the walkie-talkie out of my backpack. I sent a call out on our channel.

"Anyone listening, this is Mike. Does anyone copy?"

There was static.

"This is Mike," I said again. "Anyone listening?"

Nothing.

"Maybe their walkie-talkie is turned off," Kat said. "Or in a backpack, like ours was. We need to get back to the safe house."

We walked on, hearing sirens here and there but not seeing anything. These streets were so narrow that I wondered if John was actually following a real sound or just echoes.

"Do we know who that sniper was working for?" I asked John.

"I couldn't tell. His face was dark, but I don't know if that was because of his skin color or because of camouflage paint. He was doing a really good job of hiding on that roof."

"So he could be either Nabataean or Harappan, right?"

"Or none of the above," Kat said. "Besides, he's dead. Or she's dead. I thought she looked like a girl when she fell."

"But if she was, say, Nabataean, that would mean that the Nabataeans are cheating by bringing along extra combatants. There could be another up here somewhere, ready to take us down."

"Could be," John said, and then he held up his hand and made a fist—the sign to stop.

Kat and I froze, watching and waiting while John moved forward to look around the end of a building. He stopped, and his hand went to his gun. I grabbed mine, and Kat awkwardly took hers in her left hand. We slowly moved around the edge of the building, following John's lead.

I could hear the fight now, the scrape of metal on wood, the heavy breathing and grunting of exhausted combatants.

And then I saw them.

It was a wide avenue, with a wide island in the middle of the street. Among the trees, benches, and flowers, the Nabataean and Harappan were locked in an epic battle.

CHAPTER EIGHT

We weren't the only ones watching the fight. I could see faces in the windows up and down the street. And outside, there were onlookers watching from what they must have considered was a safe distance—but as soon as they saw our guns, they began to clear out. There was a siren coming from somewhere down the road, out of sight behind buildings and trees.

The Harappan was whirling, a blur with his curved sword. The Nabataean was standing mostly still, parrying each strike with his spear—about two inches in diameter, and made of some very hard wood, it was hardly getting nicked by the sword. But the Nabataean was on the defensive, backing up as the Harappan was advancing. John fired, hitting the Harappan in the chest—he fell back onto the stone. The Nabataean turned back to see us, and he ran for the cover of a newsstand. John and I fired at him as he ran, but he was fast and out of view almost immediately. A motorcycle cop appeared at the end of the road—John took a couple of shots in his direction, and the bike slid out from underneath him. The cop crawled for the cover of a parked car.

I couldn't see anyone from where I was—the Harappan had disappeared under the shrubbery, and the Nabataean was well hidden.

"Both of you," John said, "go to the far side and work your way up."

"The Nabataean's the last," I said, and nodded. That side was where the newsstand was.

"I don't know," John said. "Did you hear the ping? The Harappan's

248

wearing a barrier vest. Bulletproof, I think."

"What does that mean?" I asked. We'd never practiced shooting at targets with bulletproof vests.

"It means I wish I still had my Kalashnikov. Pistols at this range won't penetrate. Either get closer, or shoot for the head."

"Okay," I said.

"What about the cop?" Kat asked.

"Will you just get going?"

Kat glanced at my face, and our eyes met for a moment; then we crossed the street, running in a low crouch. The road was lined with shops with large front windows. I kept my shoulder against the glass as I moved up, looking for a sign of either Player.

The cop shouted something in German that I didn't understand.

"Do I have to know what that was?" I asked Kat without turning to look at her.

"'Stop' and 'surrender,' I think. High school German didn't cover this kind of vocabulary."

John was opposite us, on the other side of the street, moving cautiously, his gun in a solid two-hand grip. He moved with confidence. He looked like a soldier. I imagined I looked like an idiot. I looked like a target.

Suddenly the Harappan was on his feet again, throwing something at John. John fired back at him, and glass on our side of the street exploded into a million little pieces. I ducked and scrambled to take cover by a lamppost. I lined up my sights on the Harappan—John was downrange, but not in my sight line, and I decided to take the shot. Without a noise I was smashed to the ground.

The Nabataean had swung his heavy spear like a seven-foot-long baseball bat, and it had knocked me to the sidewalk.

Dazed, I saw Kat fire wildly with her pistol—her left hand shook despite trying to hold it steady with her wounded arm. But as I lay on the ground, I saw the big man pause and reach for his chest. Blood was dribbling down from his sternum, soaking his shirt.

He raised the spear one last time, threw it, and fell to his knees. He said something in a foreign language and then collapsed to the street. The cop was up, gun out, yelling at the Harappan and John.

I turned back to Kat.

CHAPTER NINE

The spear had buried itself deep into Kat's chest, exiting through her back so that she was halfway sitting up. Blood was everywhere. So fast, it was pouring from her body. So much blood.

"Kat," I called, and scrambled through the broken glass to get to her. "Kat, no."

She was gone. There was no life in her eyes, and I grabbed her throat to feel for a pulse, but there was nothing. The spear had gone straight through her heart, piercing her like she was a piece of paper.

No last words. No good-byes.

She had killed him and he had killed her.

And there was nothing left of me.

CHAPTER TEN

I could hear shooting, distant and unimportant.

I touched Kat's face. She was so pale, all color rushing out of her as she bled.

"Kat," I said again, wanting to put my arms around her, but blocked by the mammoth spear. She shouldn't have come. When her arm got cut, she should have stayed in the hospital. She should have stayed at the safe house. She shouldn't have been here, backing me up.

Somehow I had lost track of the Nabataean. Stupid. I'd been so stupid. I'd known where he'd gone, where he was hiding, but I'd focused on the Harappan. Shooting at the Player who was threatening John, not the one who was only a few yards from me. It had been stupid, and Kat had paid for my stupidity. She'd killed him, her last act on Earth, but it hadn't been enough. If I'd kept my eyes on the edge of the newsstand, I could have shot as soon as he'd come out of hiding. But I hadn't. I'd kept my eyes on everything but that.

I looked back at John, but he was gone. The Harappan was gone. The policeman lay dead in the bushes. I wondered who had killed him. It didn't matter, I guessed. Someone had done it, and John and the Harappan were continuing their battle elsewhere. I wasn't going to chase them down and find out. John was a Green Beret. He could handle the Harappan. We'd have won: all the Players were dead.

I looked at Kat. Her eyes were open, and I reached out to close them, but I couldn't bring myself to touch her again. I turned away and tried to think of my other memories of her—of her smile, of her laughter, of her kisses.

But all I saw was her contorted face. Her dead eyes. Her blood on the sidewalk.

More sirens.

I dropped my gun on the ground and stood up. I half expected to see John's body lying across the way, but there was only the cop's.

The windows were filled with faces, and as I turned around, searching for a sign of John, they all just focused on me, perhaps unafraid, maybe foolish. Maybe they'd seen me drop my gun. Maybe they could see into my heart and know that I wasn't going to fight again. That I was done. That my part in the Endgame legends was coming to an end.

I started to jog away, then broke into a full sprint. I didn't know where I was, so I couldn't know where I was going, but I tried to pick the least-busy streets and alleys. I tried to run in the opposite direction of the sirens, but there were sirens everywhere. It sounded like it was going to be an impossible task to avoid them, but I would do what I could.

I was going for the safe house. Maybe there would be someone there. I didn't really care. I was going for the money we had stashed in a communal fund. I was going to take what was left and get on a train and get out of Munich—out of Germany altogether. Maybe, I thought, I'd go back to Turkey. We hadn't encountered any notable security while we were there, and the cost of living was low—the money at the safe house could easily support me for a year, maybe more. I didn't even try to think of anything further away than a year. In the last hour I'd just seen people I cared about die in horrible ways. I didn't need anyone new in my life right now. I'd be a hermit. Maybe I'd get a job on a fishing boat, or in a café. I'd learn more of the language. I'd fade into the background.

Seven blocks away from the street where I'd left Kat, I stopped running, and I walked until I found a gift shop. I bought a white Olympics T-shirt—one with the sunburst logo on the chest—and pulled it on over my blood-spattered shirt. I also bought a map, and

I asked the cashier, who spoke a little English, where we were. He pointed the intersection out to me, and I was able to figure out a path to get back to the safe house. I could have hailed a cab, but I wanted to walk. There was too much going on in my head, and, to tell the truth, I wasn't in a hurry to get back to the house. I wanted to freeze time. I didn't want to get on with my life. I wanted to go back in time, not forward.

I couldn't believe that I had left Kat there on the road. Was there something I could have done for her?

What about Mary? I had just left her too. They were dead, and I'd just moved on, leaving them on the street for the birds.

I got sick to my stomach, remembering their wounds. Both had been brutal, hateful injuries. Both had devastated their bodies, killing them instantly. If there was a good thing, that was it. There'd been no suffering.

I put my hand to my face. I'd started sweating heavily. I still had Kat's blood on my shirt.

I bent at the waist and puked in the gutter. And as I did, I thought about what had become of this entire mission. John was the only hope now—he had to kill the Harappan. If he did that, we would have won. Zero line would have killed all the Players. The Makers—the Annunaki, the Sky Gods, whatever they were called—had no more game to play. They had no more Players. No more Endgame.

Or did they? Was Raakel right? Would the next generation of Players take their place? Would it continue, forever?

That was the thing that hurt the worst—that all of this might have been for nothing.

Were the Makers watching all of this from above? Some kind of alien satellite that monitored the Players?

Would they punish humanity for ruining their fun? I wouldn't bet against it. Maybe they were on their way right now. Maybe they'd punish me and John for trying to stop Endgame.

I walked the final blocks to the safe house. I continued to hear sirens, but they never came close to me. I never saw flashing lights or police cars or motorcycles.

The safe house was just as I'd left it. I'd hoped I'd find John there, but I didn't. No one was there. I went into the dining room, where all our gear had been laid out—all the pistols were gone, but there were a dozen long guns there. Shotguns, AK-47s, an M21 sniper rifle, two HK33s, and several guns I couldn't name. They'd all been smuggled into town by Lee and Lin, both of whom were dead now.

I picked up an Uzi, testing its weight in my hand. I should have taken that to the plaza, not a lousy revolver.

My fingerprints were on it now. They were on everything in this house. Should I bother trying to wipe the place down? Now that Eugene had talked, I was connected to all of this.

I set the Uzi back in its place and moved to the bag with all the forged papers. My Frank Finn passport was in there, along with everyone else's fake IDs. I took mine and put it in my back pocket, then emptied the rest of the bag into the fireplace. I found a bottle of vodka on an end table and splashed it on the passports. I struck a match and the whole pile went up in blue flame.

I put a few logs on top of the IDs and then sat down in a leather high-backed chair. I took a sip of the vodka straight from the bottle and got too much, and my eyes started to water.

"Who are you?" a voice behind me asked.

I was too despondent to bother turning around. Or answering. I took another swig and rolled it around my mouth for a minute.

"Who are you?" the male voice repeated. The accent was Indian.

"Frank," I said. "Finn."

"That's not what I mean," he said, moving into my view. He was holding a small pistol I didn't recognize. It looked Russian, maybe.

"I am Pravheet."

"I'm walking away," I said.

"You are La Tène?" he asked, sitting down in the chair opposite me. Aside from his pistol pointing at me, we looked like two old friends sitting by a fire.

"Me? No."

"Your friend," he said calmly. "The one I just killed. He was not a Player."

"No," I said. "Neither am I."

"Then who was? The girl killed by the Nabataean?"

"No."

"Fine," he said. "Don't tell me. She died, and he died, and now you will die."

"You don't have to do this," I said. "I'm not a Player."

"You're American, aren't you? I know the Cahokian Player by sight, but I don't know La Tène. I assume it's you. Or are you something else? Minoan?"

"Something like that," I said, taking another hit off the bottle. I wasn't a drinker, and the vodka burned.

"When there is a Calling, only the Player is supposed to come. The Makers will show their displeasure on you and your line."

"It doesn't matter," I said. "We failed."

"You have."

"You don't have to kill anymore," I said. "You can stop Playing."

He smiled. "Surrender? To you?"

"No, I don't mean that. I mean that you don't have to Play. There are no other Players. They're all dead. You can refuse to Play the game."

"There will be a test," he said. "There is more to Endgame than simply defeating the other Players."

I screwed the cap on the bottle and set it on the table next to my chair.

"This wasn't a real Calling," I said. "I'm with a group called Zero line. We are not Players. Our goal was not to kill, but to persuade. Let me guess: your invitation to the Calling was an explosion and the symbol of these Olympics burning."

"Yes," he said, his brow furrowed. "The same as all of the lines. A sign from the Makers."

"It was a couple bricks of C4 and a thermite stencil," I said. "Look around this room—there's clothes and gear for twenty people. In the next room you'll find a table full of guns. We, Zero line, invited you here. Our goal was to try to talk you out of fighting. What would happen if you quit? Walked away?"

"My entire line would be destroyed in flame and ruin."

"No, because all of the lines would walk away."

"Then all of the lines would perish," he said. "The Makers do not tolerate disobedience. We are their servants, and all they ask of us is to prepare for Endgame."

"It doesn't matter now," I said. "You're the only Player left. When there's a real Calling, there will be no one else to Play against. We have won. Humanity—Zero line—has won." But even as I spoke, the words felt hollow. I had no idea anymore if that was true. It didn't feel like we'd won. This didn't feel like any kind of victory I wanted.

He put a finger to his chin. We stared at each other for several seconds. I turned my attention back to the fire. The passports were all destroyed.

"If what you say is true," the Harappan said slowly, "if this was a sham Calling, then you are all fools and have died for nothing. How many of you were killed?"

"I don't know," I said. "There were once twenty of us. Some never made it here."

"Then twenty have died for nothing."

"What do you mean?"

"There will always be Players. If you were to kill me, and it was not during a true Endgame, then someone from my line would immediately take my place as Player. There will always be Players. There could be a true Calling today, and twelve new Players would be brought forward."

I continued to stare at the fire. I couldn't believe it. I wouldn't believe it. Walter had known about Endgame. He'd known it from personal experience. He would have known if all this was worthless.

"But I don't believe that you're so ignorant. You are the La Tène Player. And all of this is a ruse to get me to give up so you can shoot me in the back. You're a poor Player. All of your line was working with you, and you couldn't even kill everyone."

"And that's easier for you to believe than that this is all phony?"

He stood up. "You are a disgrace to the game. I come from a proud lineage. You rely on cheap deceptions and a La Tène army."

"You're wrong," I said. He still had his gun pointed at me, and I had nothing to defend myself with. Except the bottle. I picked it up and opened it. My gun was in the other room, so I couldn't shoot Pravheet, but I could light him on fire. Maybe it would give me time to get in the weapons room.

"I will kill you, and with this kill I will have won Endgame."

With all my strength I threw the bottle at the floor between him and the fireplace. The glass shattered, and the clear liquid sprayed across the room.

At that same instant I felt a searing pain in my chest, and my whole body seized.

Blackness started to close in. All around me was flame, but as the fire spread, it dimmed.

I was wet—my shirt was wet.

Pravheet pulled a blanket from the floor and tamped out the flames on his leg.

I tried to get up, but my body wouldn't respond. I could feel my muscles firing, tightening and releasing, but I wasn't in control of any of it.

"No one can stop Endgame. Endgame will come, and Players will Play. What will be will be," Pravheet said, and I felt the barrel of his gun against the back of my head.

All went to black.

Follow the Players from *Endgame: The Calling*—before they were chosen. Keep reading for a sneak peek at:

ENDGAME
—— THE COMPLETE ——
TRAINING DIARIES

JAMES FREY

MINOAN
MARCUS

When Marcus was a little kid, they called him the Monkey.

This was meant to be a compliment. Which is exactly how Marcus took it.

At seven years old, he monkeyed his way 30 meters up a climbing wall without fear, the only kid to ring the bell at the top. Ever since then he's made sure he always goes higher than the other kids, always gets to the top faster. Always waits at the summit with a cocky grin and a "What took you so long?"

He can climb anything. Trees, mountains, active volcanoes, a 90-degree granite incline or the sheer wall of a Tokyo skyscraper. The Asterousia Mountains of Crete were his childhood playground. He's scrambled up all Seven Summits—the highest mountain on each continent—including Antarctica's Mount Vinson, which meant a hike across the South Pole. He's illegally scaled Dubai's 800-meter-high Burj Khalifa without rope or harness, then BASE jumped from its silver tip. He's the youngest person ever to summit Everest (not that the world is allowed to know it).

If only someone would get around to building a tall enough ladder, he's pretty sure he could climb to the moon.

Climbing is an integral part of his training. Every Minoan child hoping to be named his or her generation's Player learns to scale a peak. They've all logged hours defying gravity; they've all broken through the clouds. But Marcus knows that for the others, climbing is just one more skill to master, one more challenge to stare down.

No different from sharpshooting or deep-sea diving or explosives disposal. For Marcus, it's more.

For Marcus, climbing is everything.

It's a fusion of mind and matter, the perfect way to channel all that frenetic energy that has him bouncing off the walls most of the time. It takes absolute focus, brute force, and a fearless confidence that comes naturally to Marcus, who feels most alive at 1,000 meters, looking down.

He loves it for all those reasons, sure—but mostly he loves it because he's the best.

And because being the best, by definition, means being better than Alexander.

It was clear from day one that Alexander Nicolaides was the kid to beat. It took only one day more to figure out he was also the kid to hate.

Marcus's parents called it camp, when they dropped him off that first day. But he was a smart kid, smart enough to wonder: What kind of parents dump their seven-year-old on Crete and head back to Istanbul without him? What kind of camp lets them do it?

What kind of camp teaches that seven-year-old how to shoot?

And how to arm live explosives?

And how to read Chinese?

It was the kind of camp where little kids were *encouraged* to play with matches.

It was most definitely Marcus's kind of place—and that was even before he found out the part about the alien invasion and how, if he played his cards right, he'd get to save the world.

Best. Camp. Ever.

Or it would have been, were it not for the impossible-to-ignore existence of Alexander Nicolaides. He was everything Marcus wasn't. Marcus could never sit still, always acted without thinking; Alexander was calm and deliberate and even broke the camp's

2

meditation record, sitting silent and motionless and staring into a stupid candle for 28 hours straight. Marcus mastered languages and higher math with brute mental force, thudding his head against the logic problems until they broke; Alexander was fluent in Assyrian, Sumerian, ancient Greek, and, just for fun, medieval Icelandic, and he was capable of visualizing at least six dimensions. Marcus was better at climbing and shooting; Alexander had the edge in navigation and survival skills. They even *looked* like polar opposites: Alexander was a compact ball of tightly coiled energy, his wavy, white-blond hair nearly as pale as his skin, his eyes as blue as the Aegean Sea. Marcus was long-limbed and rangy, with close-cropped black hair. If they'd been ancient gods, Alexander would have had charge over the sky and the sea, all those peaceful stretches of cerulean and aquamarine. Marcus, with his dark green eyes and golden sheen, would have lorded it over the forests and the earth, all leaves and loam and living things. But the gods were long dead—or at least departed for the stars—and instead Marcus and Alexander jockeyed for rule over the same small domain. Marcus was the camp joker and prided himself on making even his sternest teachers laugh; Alexander was terse, serious, rarely speaking unless he had something important to say.

Which was for the best, because his voice was so nails-on-chalkboard annoying that it made Marcus want to punch him in the mouth.

It didn't help that Alexander was a good candidate for Player and an even better suck-up. The other kids definitely preferred Marcus, but Marcus knew that Alexander had a slight edge with the counselors, and it was their opinion that counted. Every seven years, the counselors invited a new crop of kids to the camp, the best and brightest of the Minoan line. The counselors trained them, judged them, pushed them to their limits, pitted them against one another and themselves, and eventually named a single one as the best. The Player. Everyone else got sent back home to their mind-numbingly normal lives.

Maybe that kind of boring life was okay for other kids.

Other kids dreamed of being astronauts, race-car drivers, rock stars—
not Marcus. Since the day he found out about Endgame, Marcus had
only one dream: to win it.

Nothing was going to get in his way.

Especially not Alexander Nicolaides.

Tucked away in a secluded valley on the western edge of Crete, the
Minoan camp was well hidden from prying eyes. The Greek isles
were crowded with architectural ruins, most of them littered with
regulations, tourists, and discarded cigarette butts. Few knew of the
ruins nestled at the heart of the Lefka Ori range, where 50 carefully
chosen Minoan children lived among the remnants of a vanished
civilization. Tilting pillars, crumbling walls, the fading remains of
a holy fresco—everywhere Marcus looked, there was evidence of
a nobler time gone by. This was no museum: it was a living bond
between present and past. The kids were encouraged to press their
palms to crumbling stone, to trace carvings of heroes and bulls, to
dig for artifacts buried thousands of years before. This was the sacred
ground of their ancestors, and as candidates to be the Minoans'
champion, they were entitled to claim it for their own.

The camp imposed a rigorous training schedule on the children, but
none of them complained. They'd been chosen because they were
the kind of kids who thought training was fun. They were kids who
wanted to win. None more than Marcus. And other than the thorn
in his side named Alexander Nicolaides, Marcus had never been so
happy in his life.

He endured Alexander for two years, biding his time, waiting for the
other boy to reveal his weakness or, better yet, to flame out. He waited
for the opportunity to triumph over Alexander so definitively, so
absolutely, that everyone would know, once and for all, that Marcus
was the best. Marcus liked to imagine how that day would go, how the
other kids would carry him around on their shoulders, cheering his
name, while Alexander slunk away in humiliated defeat.

He was nine years old when the moment finally arrived.

A tournament, elimination style, with the champion claiming a large gold trophy, a month's worth of extra dessert, and bonus bragging rights. The Theseus Cup was held every two years as a showcase for campers—and a chance for them to prove their worth. There were rumors that the first to win the Theseus Cup was a shoo-in to be chosen as the Player. No one knew whether or not this was the case— but Marcus didn't intend to risk it. He intended to win.

He swept his opening matches effortlessly, knocking one kid after another senseless, even the ones who were older and bigger. Bronze daggers, double axes, Turkish sabers—whatever the weapon, Marcus wielded it like a champion. Alexander, who'd started off in another bracket, cut a similar swath across the competition. This was as it should be, Marcus thought. It would be no fun to knock him out in an early round. The decisive blow needed to come when it counted, in the championship, with everyone watching.

The two nine-year-old finalists stepped into the ring for a final bout. Personal, hand-to-hand combat. No weapons, no intermediaries. Just the two of them. Finally.

They faced each other and bowed, as they'd been taught.

Bowing before you fought, offering up that token of respect, that was a rule.

After that, there were no rules.

Marcus opened with a karate kick. Alexander blocked it with ease, and they pitted their black belts against each other for a few seconds before Alexander took him in a judo hold and flipped him to the ground. Marcus allowed it—only so he could sweep his leg across Alexander's knees and drop him close enough for a choke hold. Alexander wriggled out and smashed a fist toward Marcus's face. Marcus rolled away just in time, and the punch came down hard against the mat.

The camp was on its feet, cheering, screaming Marcus's and Alexander's names—Marcus tried not to distract himself by trying to figure out whose cheering section was bigger. The fighters moved fluidly through techniques, meeting sanshou with savate, blocking a tae kwon do attack with an onslaught of aikido, their polished choreography disintegrating into the furious desperation of a street brawl. But even spitting and clawing like a pair of animals, they were perfectly matched.

The fight dragged on and on. Dodging punches, blocking kicks, throwing each other to the mat again and again, they fought for one hour, then two. It felt like years. Sweat poured down Marcus's back and blood down his face. He gasped and panted, sucking in air and trying not to double over from the pain. His legs were jelly, his arms lead weights. Alexander looked like he'd been flattened by a steamroller, with both eyes blackened and a wide gap where his front teeth used to be. The kids fell silent, waiting for the referee to step in before the two boys killed each other.

But this was not that kind of camp.

They fought on.

They fought like they lived: Marcus creative and unpredictable, always in motion; Alexander cool, rational, every move a calculated decision.

Which made it even more of a shock when Alexander broke.

Unleashing a scream of pure rage, he reached over the ropes to grab the referee's stool, and smashed it over Marcus's head.

Marcus didn't see it coming.

He only felt the impact.

A thunderbolt of pain reverberating through his bones.

His body dropping to the ground, no longer under his control, his consciousness drifting away.

The last thing he saw, before everything faded to black, was Alexander's face, stunned by his own loss of control. Marcus smiled, then started to laugh. Even in defeat, he'd won—he'd finally made the uptight control freak completely lose it.

The last thing he heard was Alexander laughing too.

* * *

"You always tell that story wrong," Marcus says now. "You leave out the part where I let you win."

Xander only laughs. At 14, he's nearly twice the size he was at that first Theseus Cup, his shoulders broader, his voice several octaves deeper, his blond hair thicker and forested across his chest. But his laugh is still exactly the same as it was on the day of the fight.

Marcus remembers, as he remembers every detail of that day.

You never forget the moment you make your best friend.

"Yeah, that was really generous of you, deciding to get a concussion and pass out," Xander says. "I owe you one."

"You owe me two," Marcus points out. "One for the concussion, one for the cheating."

They are hanging off a sheer rock face, 50 meters off the ground. They will race each other to the top of the cliff, 70 meters above, then rappel back down to the bottom, dropping toward the ground at a stomach-twisting speed.

Marcus has heard that most kids his age fill up their empty hours playing video games. He thinks this is a little more fun.

"I most certainly did not cheat," Xander says, trying to muster some of his habitual dignity. Most people think that's the real him: solemn, uptight, deliberate, slow to smile. Marcus knows better. Over the last five years, he's come to know the real Xander, the one who laughs at his jokes and even, occasionally, makes a few of his own. (Though, of course, they're never any good.) "Not technically, at least," Xander qualifies. He jams his fingers into a small crevice in the rock face and pulls himself up another foot, trying very hard to look like it costs him no effort.

Marcus scrambles up past him, grinning, because for him it actually *is* no effort. "Only because no one ever thought to put 'don't go nutball crazy and smash furniture over people's heads' in the rules before," Marcus says.

"Lucky for both of us," Xander says.

Normally, Marcus would shoot back a joke or an insult, something about how it's not so lucky for him, because Xander's been clinging to him like a barnacle ever since. Or maybe something about how it was luckier for Xander, because now, with Marcus as a wingman, he might someday, if he's lucky, actually get himself a date.

But not today.

Not today, the last day before everything changes. Tomorrow, they will find out who has been selected as this generation's Player. It'll surely be either Marcus or Alexander; everyone knows that. They're the best in the camp at everything; no one else even comes close. It's what brought them together in the first place. After all that time wasted hating each other, they'd realized that where it counted, they were the same. No one else was so determined to win—and no one else was good enough to do so. Only Marcus could melt Xander's cool; only Xander could challenge Marcus's cockiness. In the end, what else could they do but become best friends? They pushed each other to go faster, to get stronger, to be *better*. Competition is all they know. Their friendship is built on the fact that they're so well matched.

Tomorrow, all that changes. Tomorrow, one of them will leave this place as a winner, and embark on his hero's journey. The other will leave a loser, and find some way to endure the rest of his pathetic life. Which means today is not a day for joking. *I couldn't have made it through this place without you,* Marcus would like to say. And *no one knows me like you do.* And maybe even *you make me want to be my best self.*

But he's not that kind of guy.

"Yeah, lucky," he agrees, and Xander knows him well enough to understand the rest.

They climb in silence for a while, battling gravity, scrabbling for purchase on the rock. Marcus's muscles scream as he stretches for a handhold a few inches out of reach, finally getting leverage with his fingertips and dragging the rest of himself up and up.

"It's probably going to be you," Xander says finally, and they both know what he's talking about. Marcus can tell Xander's trying not to breathe heavily, but the strain in his voice is plain.

"No way. Totally you," Marcus says, hoping the lie isn't too obvious.

"It's not like Endgame is even going to happen," Xander says. "Think about it—after all this time, what are the odds?"

"Nil," Marcus agrees, though this too feels like a lie. How could Endgame *not* happen for him? Ever since Marcus found out about the aliens, and the promise they'd made to return—ever since he found out about the Players, and the game—some part of him has known this was his fate. This is another difference between him and Xander, though it's one they never talk about out loud.

Marcus *believes*.

When they were 11 years old, Marcus and Xander spent an afternoon digging for artifacts at the edge of the camp's northern border. It was Xander's favorite hobby, and occasionally he suckered Marcus into joining him. What else were friends for? That day, after several long hours sweating in the sun (Marcus complaining the whole time), Marcus hit gold.

Specifically a golden *labrys*, a double-headed ax. The labrys was one of the holiest symbols of the Minoan civilization, used to slice the throats of sacrificial bulls. Marcus gaped at the dirt-encrusted object. It had to be at least 3,500 years old. Yet it fit in his palm as if it had been designed just for him.

"No one's ever found anything that good," Xander said. "It's got to be a sign. That it's going to be you who gets chosen."

"Whatever." Marcus shrugged it off. But inside, he was glowing. Because Xander was right. It did have to be a sign. The ax had chosen him—had *anointed* him. Ever since then, he's believed he will be chosen as the Player. It is his destiny.

But that's not the kind of thing you say out loud.

"It doesn't even matter which of us gets picked. Without Endgame, being the Player's just a big waste of time," Marcus says now. "Though I bet you'd be a chick magnet."

"But what good would it do you?" Xander points out. "It's not like you'd have time to actually date."

This is a game they play, the two of them. As the selection day draws closer, they've been playing it more often. Pretending they don't care who gets picked, pretending it might be better to lose.

"Imagine getting out of here once and for all," Xander continues. "Going to a real school."

"Joining a football team," Marcus says, trying to imagine himself scoring a winning goal before a stadium of screaming fans.

"Going to a concert," Xander says. He plays the guitar. (Or at least tries to.)

"Meeting a girl whose idea of foreplay isn't krav maga," Marcus says. He's still got an elbow-shaped bruise on his stomach, courtesy of Helena Loris.

"I don't know . . . I'll kind of miss that part," Xander says fondly. He's been fencing regularly with Cassandra Floros, who's promised that if he can draw blood, she'll reward him with a kiss. "But not much else."

"Yeah, me neither," Marcus says. "Bring on normal life."

He's a few meters above Xander, and it's a good thing, because it means Xander can't see his sickly, unconvincing grin. A normal life? To Marcus, that's a fate worse than death.

A fate he'd do anything to avoid.

The counselors try their best to give the kids some approximation of a normal upbringing. In their slivers of free time, campers are allowed to surf the Net, watch TV, and flirt with whomever they want. They even spend two months of every year back home with their families—for Marcus, these are the most excruciating days of all. Of course he loves his parents. He loves Turkey, its smells and tastes, the way the minarets spear the clouds on a stormy day. But it's not his world anymore; it's not his home. He spends his vacations counting the minutes until he can get back to camp, back to training, back to Xander.

Deep down, he knows this is another difference between them. Sure, Xander wants to be chosen. But Marcus wants it more.

Marcus *needs* it.

That has to count for something.

Marcus is happy to pretend that he and Xander are evenly matched, that the choice between them is a coin flip. It's easier that way; it's how friendship works. But surely, he thinks, their instructors can tell that it's an illusion. That Marcus is just a little better, a little more determined. That between the two of them, only Marcus would sacrifice everything for the game, for his people. That only Marcus truly believes he's meant to be the Player—and not just any Player, but the one who saves his people.

They're both pretending not to be nervous, but deep down, Marcus really isn't.

He knows it will be him.

It has to be.

He reaches the top with a whoop of triumph, Xander still several meters behind. Instead of savoring his victory or waiting for his best friend to catch up, he anchors his rappelling line, hooks himself on, and launches himself over the cliff. This moment, this leap of faith, it's the reward that makes all that hard work worth it. There's a pure joy in giving way to the inexorable, letting gravity speed him toward his fate.

Tomorrow, everything changes.

And it can't come fast enough.

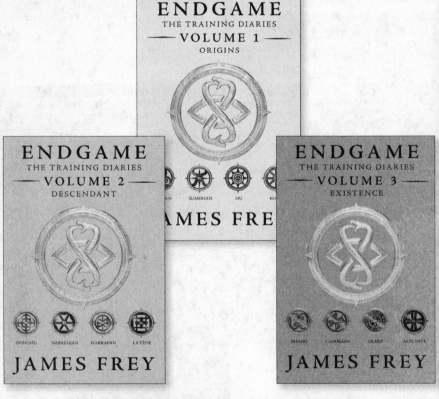

DON'T MISS A SINGLE PAGE
OF THE ACTION-PACKED,
#1 *NEW YORK TIMES* BESTSELLING
I AM NUMBER FOUR SERIES

HARPER
An Imprint of HarperCollinsPublishers